THE UNKNOWN SPY

'Mystery and action to keep you hooked for the second
and third instalments'

Flipside

Books by Eoin McNamee

The Ring of Five

The Unknown Spy

The Navigator

City of Time

The Frost Child

THE UNKNOWN SPY

EOIN McNAMEE

Quercus

First published in Great Britain in 2011 by

Quercus
21 Bloomsbury Square
London
WC1A 2NS

A CIP catalogue reference for this book is available
from the British Library

ISBN 978 0 85738 129 3

10 9 8 7 6 5 4 3 2 1

Typeset by Nigel Hazle

Printed and bound in Great Britain by Clays Ltd, St Ives plc.

For Caitlin and Finbar

The countryside around the old house was dark and silent. The house was very old and might have appeared uninhabited were it not for a single light burning in a window just under the eaves. The night was cloudless, and stars glittered in the icy sky. The previous few days had seen the first snowfalls of the year and the snow lay heavily on the fields and woods. A fox's tracks led towards the frozen lake in the grounds of the house, but otherwise not a living thing was about, all the wild creatures huddled against the cold.

The animals stirred and whimpered in their sleep. Something evil was abroad. On the topmost branches of a tall pine tree overlooking the house there was a sudden flurry and the strong branches bowed down and dumped their load of snow on the ground.

The branches sprang back. But this time, instead of being weighed with snow they carried a different burden. A tall stooped figure with long grey hair and eyes that burned yellow stood in the tree. A man and yet not a man, for from the middle of his back sprouted a pair of long feathered wings. The fierce eyes were fixed on the single light burning under the eaves of the house. The creature had risked much to be here. There was a solemn treaty forbidding him and his kind from crossing the border between the Lower World and the Upper where he now stood, and he could not be sure of the outcome if his presence was revealed.

But the prize was great. The boy was the only one who could unite the two worlds. The creature and his companions had tried once to turn the boy to evil, but he had stubborn values of friendship and loyalty. This time they would succeed.

The creature's name was Conal. Once he had been a winged messenger, an envoy who came and went between the two worlds in time of peace. But he had been corrupted and had become one of the Ring of Five. The Ring were the leaders of the Lower World and its deadly army of Cherbs. Together with his three companions Conal had sought the fifth member of their fellowship, without whom their powers were not complete. They believed they had found him in Danny Caulfield, a boy of unusual appearance – a pixie-like face and different coloured eyes: the marks of the fifth, the one they required to complete their fellowship.

Conal and his companions had failed before, but they would not fail this time. The boy had begun to train to be a spy at Wilsons Academy of the Devious Arts, the school for spies. He had been a natural, discovering in himself almost at once a gift for treachery, a part of him that longed for the thrill of secrets and betrayal. He had resisted it, but that would only make the prize all the greater, the moment so much sweeter, when Danny finally turned his back on friendship and love and embraced the dark world of mistrust.

Conal shifted his weight on the branch and spread his wings. He had found the boy. It was time to consult with his colleagues. The forces of darkness were gathering but the boy's protectors had chosen well. Conal could see the untidy nests in the bare trees around the house. The ravens would be sleeping and he did not dare risk waking them. Conal launched himself gently into the frozen air. The great wings flapped once, the creature wheeled in the air and was gone.

1
PAID AGENTS

Danny lay on the bed in his warm little room, a Nintendo DSi lying forgotten on the bedspread beside him. That was the problem, he thought. Once you had been a spy, out in the world with your life in jeopardy every minute, when one false slip meant betrayal and perhaps death, then a computer game seemed very tame. But that wasn't his main worry.

He had arrived back from Wilsons Academy for the Christmas holidays to find his parents their normal kind but absent selves. He thought that they might appreciate him more since they hadn't seen him for three months, but if anything they were away more often. Even on Christmas day (after a morning of present opening under the tree and a delicious turkey dinner) his father had received a phone call. Ten minutes later his car had swept out of the driveway. His wave to his wife and son was cheery, but Danny could see the fatigue around his eyes.

That night he and his mother had sat by the fire, his

mother reading and eating chocolates while Danny watched a Christmas film. It was almost too good, Danny realised, to have her to himself for a whole evening.

'Goodness,' she said, 'I can't remember the last time I had a chance to just sit and read.'

'I haven't watched a film in ages,' Danny said.

'*It's a Wonderful Life.*' She smiled. 'I was half watching it over your shoulder. It was my favourite when I was your age.'

She stood up.

'Would you like some hot chocolate?' He nodded and watched as she walked towards the kitchen. Even now in a dressing gown, her hair tied up, she was elegant. She paused beside him, her hands resting gently on his hair. There and then he almost blurted out the truth about where he had spend the last three months. His parents thought they had sent him to the boarding school called Heston Oaks. Instead he had been virtually kidnapped and spirited off to Wilsons spy school. While at home, he found that someone – probably the devious Master Brunholm – had constructed an elaborate cover story including fake letters home.

Part of him ached to tell, but he feared that then he would not be allowed back to Wilsons, and he could not bear the thought of not seeing his new friends again. That's what he told himself anyway, although he wondered if the part of him that loved secrets and shadows enjoyed hiding the truth.

'Have your hot chocolate, then clean your teeth and bed,' his mother said, moving off. Danny grinned inwardly. Imagine telling someone who could be a member of the Ring of Five, the most terrifying group of spies ever seen, to brush his teeth!

While his mother heated the milk in the kitchen he looked at the photographs on the fireplace. His mother and father were tall and blond. He was short and dark. Were they his parents at all?

'Here you go.' His mother handed him a steaming mug of hot chocolate.

It made him feel what he had missed in the past, and what he was going to miss in the future when she started to go out every evening again.

Besides, he thought, as he pulled the bedclothes around him, perhaps she wasn't even his mother after all. His adventures at Wilsons had made him question whether his unusual features and different-coloured eyes could ever have come from these two blond people who purported to be his parents.

But his most immediate worry was that it was three days after Christmas and he had not seen either of them for forty-eight hours. His mother had left abruptly on St Stephen's day and he had not seen her since. She had stayed away overnight once or twice before, but she had always phoned to let him know. He had tried both their mobiles but they had been turned off. There was plenty of food in the house, and he was used to being on his own, but he was lonely and worried.

They might not be my real parents, he thought, but they're all I've got.

For the tenth time that evening he went to the window and stared out at the snow, unbroken for miles around. This time he knelt down and squinted into the distance. He could see a far-off light on the road – a car! Small at first, but growing rapidly. He blinked and looked again. There was another set of lights behind the first, moving just as quickly. How could the drivers keep up the pace on the icy road? Don't think *how*, he said to himself, think *why*. There could be only one reason for the speed. He opened the window a little and his heart dropped. From the lead car he could hear the throaty growl of his father's Mercedes. The car dropped a gear and he heard the second car do the same. His father was being chased!

He pressed his head against the windowsill, trying to remember something he had learned in his spying classes that would help. The two cars would be at the house in minutes. He had to think. Concealment! That was it! His father's car would need to be hidden.

Taking the stairs two at a time he ran down, grabbing a broom from the closet as he went. He turned off the hallway light before opening the front door so that he wouldn't be seen. The cold air made him gasp. The car engines were clearly audible now, the roar of the Mercedes and the smooth powerful hum of the car behind. Danny ran around the side of the house, feet skidding on the hard-frozen snow. He flung open the doors of the garage and ran back to the front, brush at the ready. It would be a close thing.

The Mercedes was first, coming round the last corner flat out, fishtailing, and flattening a small sapling. His mother was behind the wheel, her face pale. His father was in the passenger seat, his head flung back. Danny didn't have time to absorb the information. He gestured frantically with the brush. His mother looked at him in shock, then instantly understood. Spinning the wheel frantically she threw the car into a long, graceful slide, then straightened the wheel. The car sped through the back yard and into the garage. Danny slammed the big doors as the Mercedes engine was killed. As fast as he could he brushed away the tyre tracks, running to the front of the house to finish off just as the second car rounded the corner. If it hadn't been for the fallen sapling he

8

would have been caught in the headlights, but the beams pointed momentarily across the frozen fields. Danny looked around wildly. There was no cover near, except for the shadow of the steps to the front door.

The car slowed then stopped. A door opened. Feet crunched in the snow. Danny crouched in the small pool of shadow. He knew from concealment classes at Wilsons that you could hide almost in plain view if you didn't move a muscle. Movement drew the hunter's eye. Danny didn't dare look up. The whites of eyes seen in darkness would also give you away. The feet stopped moving, then a harsh female voice spoke.

'They are still in front of us! Fly, Sasha, fly like the wind!' The engine note rose as the car door slammed shut. The tyres spun then gripped, sending an arc of frozen snow high into the air. As the car picked up speed Danny risked a glance up. There were four men and one woman in the car, all of them tough-looking, and Danny found himself shrinking back into the shadows.

He gave the car a full minute to clear the house, then he leapt to his feet and raced around the side of the house. The garage door was open and he saw light from the kitchen. As he went towards the light he looked down. The virgin snow at his feet was spotted with deep-red blood. When he reached for the door handle he found it smeared with blood. The door swung slowly open. His father was slumped against the kitchen table. His mother was bent over him, but as the door creaked she spun round. To his shock Danny found himself looking up the barrel of a large and deadly-looking revolver. Her hair had fallen down over her face and there were streaks of oil and blood on her cheek, but her steady brown eyes did not falter. Slowly the gun was lowered.

'Are they gone?' Her voice was brisk and commanding. Danny stared back at her before nodding dumbly. Where was the elegant, remote woman who had sat by the fire beside him a few days previously? This new mother was wearing no make-up. Her black jeans and top were streaked with mud.

'Don't stand there gaping,' she snapped. 'Help me. Quick. Get him under the arms.'

He moved to do as she said, questions flooding his mind. As he reached her side he opened his mouth to speak, but a glance stilled him. He looked down at his father for the first time. The man's face was pale and his breathing was quick and shallow. The shoulder of his shirt was sodden with blood.

'Heave,' his mother ordered. Together they got him on to the kitchen table.

'The bullet's gone into his shoulder and taken some of the fabric from his shirt into the wound,' she said. 'We have to get it out. Now.'

Danny looked at her blankly. 'We need to get a doctor . . . hospital—' he stammered.

'No time,' she said. 'Besides, they'll be watching the hospitals. There's a box in the top drawer of the writing desk. Get it.'

Danny ran for the box. It was a steel case that he had never seen before. He handed it to his mother. She flipped it open. There were surgical instruments inside and several phials of liquid. His mother opened one of the phials and poured some on to a cloth. She held it over his father's mouth. 'Breath deeply, Agent Stone,' she said. 'We need to put you out.'

Danny watched as the cloth covered the man's nose and mouth. Agent Stone? But there was no time to quiz her. The man was out cold now, his breathing shallow. She took a scapel from the case and what looked like a pair of pliers. With one swift stroke she cut through the flesh around the bullet wound.

'I'll hold the wound open,' she said. 'You reach in for the bullet and the material.'

Danny gulped as she pressed the pliers into his hand. He wasn't particularly squeamish, but he'd never

11

carried out kitchen-table surgery before, particularly when the patient was supposed to be his father. But as he hesitated the man groaned again.

'We have to do this, Danny,' his mother (or whoever she was) said. 'Please.' She met his eyes and this time there was something of the person he remembered in them.

He gulped and nodded.

Swiftly she ripped open the shirt, exposing the wound. Danny closed his eyes. When he opened them again he was looking down into an opened wound, blood everywhere, muscle and sinew exposed.

'Quickly!' Even though the kitchen was cold Danny could feel a trickle of sweat run down his back. He lowered the tip of the pliers towards the open flesh. The matted scrap of shirt fabric was clearly visible. He focused on it, ignoring what was around it.

'Now!' He plunged the pliers downward and grasped the cloth. In one quick movement he removed it and dropped it on the table. Now for the bullet, the small grey slug deep in the wound . . .

'You'll have to dig for it.' As if in a nightmare, Danny reached into the wound. He had to dig and twist to extract the bullet. It seemed to take hours. When he was done he slumped back into a chair. He stared numbly as his mother efficiently bandaged the wound.

'Go into the drawing room,' she said, her voice gentler now. 'I'll finish here.'

It was almost an hour before she joined him. She had made hot chocolate and handed him a mug. She had showered and was wearing a dressing gown. She sat down beside him and looked into the fire.

'He's sleeping now,' she said. 'He should be okay.'

'You called him Agent Stone,' Danny said, 'Dad.'

'Did I?' She looked thoughtful and a little sad. 'Funny the things that give you away.'

'You're not my real . . . ?' The word stuck in Danny's throat.

'Mother? No, though sometimes I feel like I am. A lot of the time, in fact.'

'Well, if I'm not your son, then who am I?' His voice sounded harsh to his own ears.

'That is a little complicated,' she said.

'Is it?' Danny said sarcastically. He was trying to be tough, but his heart was hammering in his chest.

'I'm afraid so.' She sighed and hugged her knees. 'He said it was time to tell you. Past time.'

'Tell me?' Danny said, his voice cracking.

'You were given to us as a mission, your . . . Agent Stone and me.'

'A mission?'

'To protect you and . . . well, watch you.'

'In case of what?'

'This is very difficult,' she said. 'We don't really know why. We were just given a mission. Your father—'

'Agent Stone,' Danny interrupted.

'Don't be too hard on us, Danny. We were given this mission and we have worked night and day for many years. To guard you, but also now to find out why! Wise hands gave us this mission, but they have long been replaced and there is no one in the service to which we belong to help us. There is much danger – you saw what happened tonight . . .'

'Who are they – the attackers?'

'I don't know, Danny. We were recruited by the security services, but now we can't get in touch with the ones who hired us. Their phones are cut off. The offices we went to are deserted. All we have now is you . . .'

Danny held up his hand. He didn't want to talk any more. There was too much to take in. This woman looking at him seemed a stranger. What right did she have to ask him to understand?

He got to his feet. 'I'm going to bed.'

'All right,' she said. 'We can talk again in the morning.'

'Perhaps,' he said. 'Goodnight.'

She watched him as he walked away. It was too much for a boy of his age to bear, she thought, and he should not have found out like this. Still, she could talk to him in the morning, explain things in more detail so that he might begin to understand.

'Goodnight,' she called after him, then under her breath, her lips barely moving, she formed the word 'son'.

Danny tossed and turned, words racing through his head. *Agent Stone. A mission!* He had long suspected that the people he lived with were not his real parents, but now he was faced with it his mind was in turmoil. After several hours he fell into an uneasy sleep in which he dreamed he was back at Wilsons school for spies, sitting in Ravensdale, the strange village canteen, with his friends, and then lying in bed in the Roosts – the dormitory – trying to ignore the voice of Blackpitts. Blackpitts was the school announcer, whose voice organised the students' day via a hundred speakers. *Cadet Caulfield, Cadet Caulfield!* the voice in his head said. *Go away*, Danny moaned in his sleep, but the voice did not go away. *Cadet Caulfield!* Danny sat bolt upright in the bed. It really was the voice of Blackpitts! It was coming from behind the bed. Of course, he thought, the Radio of Last Resort!

The Radio of Last Resort had been given to him

on leaving Wilsons so that the school could contact him if needed. And now here was Blackpitts's voice coming through the speakers.

'Awake at last,' Blackpitts said through the little transistor radio, sounding faintly amused. 'Please hold for Master Devoy.'

Sleep fell away. Devoy was the head of Wilsons, a master spy. Why was he calling? Danny threw back the bedclothes and sat up.

'Cadet Caulfield . . .' Devoy's tones were smooth and untroubled, but Danny knew that he had trained himself to show no emotion. 'I am sorry to disturb you at this hour of the night, but it is urgent that you return to Wilsons immediately. Fairman will pick you up in twenty minutes. I don't like to interrupt your holiday but this will not wait.' The Radio of Last Resort crackled and went silent. Twenty minutes! Danny grabbed a bag and started to stuff clothes into it. He half smiled before taking a battered-looking overcoat from the back of the door. It smelt musty and looked old-fashioned, but it had many hidden secrets.

Ten minutes later he was in the hallway. He peered into the living room. The woman who had masqueraded as his mother had fallen asleep on the chair beside the fire. He tiptoed down the hall to the downstairs bedroom, where the man who wasn't his father was also asleep, his face grey. He looked terribly unwell, and Danny had to resist the temptation to go over to him, perhaps whisper something in his ear. But it was better this way. Better that he leave without saying goodbye.

He opened the front door and closed it gently behind him. He walked down the road between the long rows of bare lime trees. The night was starlit but there was a faint gleam of dawn to the east. His feet crunched in the snow and the cold nipped at his ears and nose, but the battered old coat kept him warm. He heard an engine in the distance, a noisy rattling cab engine. It grew closer and closer. Danny put down his bag and leaned back against one of the lime trees. The car drew up and the cabbie leaned out. He had deep-set eyes and big yellow teeth. 'Get in,' he growled. Danny climbed into the back. As the cab jolted forward he leaned his head against the headrest. He was on his way back to Wilsons, the only place he now belonged.

Danny had been the subject of fierce debate between Master Devoy and his deputy, Master Brunholm. Now Devoy stood at the window of his office in Wilsons Academy of the Devious Arts, looking out, while Brunholm once more pressed his case.

'You agreed with me, my dear Devoy, that the

best course of action would be to bring Danny back to Wilsons immediately. His location in the Upper World is no longer safe.'

'Yes, of course I agree,' Devoy said. 'So why send him back into danger again?'

'Because we have no choice! Who else can we send?'

'If he is caught, it will be seen as treaty-breaking. It will bring war. Our job is to guard the Upper World, not unleash mayhem on it.'

'And what if the Ring of Five find the Treaty Stone first, Devoy? If they find it and break it, then there is no treaty. There are risks. Can the boy be relied upon? He is a true spy. He has the smell of treachery on him.'

'I won't allow it,' Devoy said.

'You will allow it,' Brunholm said, getting up and approaching Devoy, looking into his face, so close that his luxuriant moustache almost brushed Devoy's skin. 'You will permit it, because you have no choice.'

'What about his parents?'

'Parents?' Brunholm shrugged. 'You mean the paid agents hired to guard him? They know nothing of his relationship with Wilsons. I made sure of that. They are expendable. Let Conal and the Ring have them. They can torture them until their eyeballs pop out of their skulls; they'll learn nothing.'

2
THE UNKNOWN SPY'S WIFE

Danny had tried to stay awake in the cab as the snowy fields lightened, illuminated but not warmed by the rising sun. But the heater was on and the air was warm and fuggy and before long he had fallen asleep. He slept as the cab hurtled along, Fairman guiding it through the barren lands that lay between the Upper and Lower Worlds. Few people knew the routes, and Fairman was the only one permitted by treaty to use them. Once there had been coming and going between the two worlds – the angels in old paintings were in fact messengers of the Lower World – but war had broken out. A harsh treaty had ended the war, a treaty that promised death to those who broke it. One term of the Treaty was that there should be no more movement between the worlds. The Upper World was too vulnerable to attack from the Lower, with its deadly army of Cherbs.

Danny didn't wake until they were on the road leading to Wilsons. Fairman would have wanted it this way. The routes through the barren lands were his, and he didn't want some little spy nosing them out and recording them for future use.

Danny stared up at Wilsons as they drove up the driveway. The huge rambling building towered above the cab. There were turrets and buttresses and blind windows and complicated angles, all done in a mixture of styles. Statues of Greek nymphs stood in niches and there were gargoyles on the roof line. There was snow on the ground here too, and great icicles hung from the eaves. He looked across the gardens to the Roosts, the tree-level dormitories where the pupils slept. A thin thread of smoke rose from the girls' Roosts. He wondered how many of his friends were there – all of them, he hoped. Most of them were orphans and had nowhere else to go.

Fairman stood on the brakes, making Danny lurch forward.

'Ouch.'

'We're here,' Fairman said. 'Get out.'

'What do you do when someone's paying?' Danny muttered, getting his gear together. 'Do they ever get a please and thank-you?'

'Folks pay a high price to ride this cab,' Fairman said, baring his teeth in an unpleasant grin. 'Please and thank-you don't mean nothing to them.'

Danny shivered. He didn't want to think what price they paid. He got out and watched the cab speed off before turning to look at the school, thinking himself to be alone. But in fact several pairs of eyes were studying him. Brunholm watched with satisfaction from the third landing, his plans unfolding nicely. Above his head, in a niche once reserved for the statue of the goddess Diana, stood the siren Vicky, mischief bubbling in her pretty eyes.

So the Fifth is back, she thought. I wonder who would pay for that information.

And high above the siren's head, perched on a crumbling gable, the black eyes of a rook gazed steadily down.

Danny thought about going over to the Roosts to see his friends, but he wanted to know why Devoy had got him back early. It wouldn't be for anything good, he thought sourly, particularly if Brunholm was involved. He went into the entrance hall. Unusually there was no one behind the desk. Danny was uneasy. He didn't know how he did it or when he slept, but the porter Valant was always there. He went to the desk and rang the bell, but there was no response. He was about to turn away when he heard a groan. He quickly lifted the wooden flap and went behind the counter. Valant was lying on the floor, his eyes fluttering, a hand to his head where a large bump was starting to rise.

'What happened?' Danny said.

'Hit from behind,' Valant groaned. 'Took me for an amateur. I just heard a movement behind me then lights out.' He sat up, fingering his head. 'I must be getting old.'

'Why . . . I mean what . . . ?' Danny asked but the man's eyes had already gone to the great board above their heads.

'Keys,' he said grimly. 'He was after keys and he got them.'

Danny looked up. The board held every kind of key under the sun, from Yales to great ornate iron dungeon keys. It was said that only Valant knew what they were all for. The porter got to his feet and set off down one of the corridors, Danny following.

'He knew what he wanted and he got it,' he said over his shoulder.

'What key did he take?'

'The key to the Unknown Spy's room. His wife was staying with him. If she's abroad in Wilsons . . .'

He didn't have to finish the sentence. The Unknown Spy and his wife had been undercover for so long that their minds had given way under the pressure. They could not remember who they had been, or what lost mission they'd been on. Everyone they met was a potential enemy. You could reason with the Unknown Spy to some extent, but his wife shot first and asked questions later. Last time she'd been on the loose there had been several serious injuries.

They hurried down the corridor. The wooden door to the Unknown Spy's room stood open. Danny made for it, but Valant stopped him. He took an old-fashioned flintlock pistol from his inside pocket and cocked it, then, beckoning to Danny, crept slowly forward.

The room was in darkness, the way the Unknown Spy normally kept it, but Danny dug in the pocket of his trenchcoat – he was sure there'd been one . . . and there it was: a battered metal flashlight. He flicked it on. The beam showed that the room had been ransacked – drawers emptied, furniture slashed open and the stuffing strewn across the floor. There was a body lying on the carpet in front of the empty fireplace.

'Here,' Valant said, thrusting the gun into Danny's hand. 'Keep your eyes peeled. Whoever did this can't be far away.'

He went down on one knee beside the body. It was a woman. Her face was lined and her grey hair tumbled over her shoulders, but Danny could tell that she had once been beautiful.

As if reading his thoughts, Valant sighed. 'Ah, that such a beauty should end like this. She's dead.'

'Who is she?'

'No one knows her real name. She's the wife of the Unknown Spy. When they came here many years ago she was like a queen, regal and haughty and quite, quite mad. Look.'

A knife protruded from her back, a knife with a strange metal handle, twisted in the shape of a raven.

'The ravens have a part to play in everything. In death as in life,' Valant said, straightening up. There was a flutter in the roof space and a dark shape glided out of the door. 'Nothing happens here that they don't know about,' he went on.

'Could they not tell us who did it?' Danny asked. 'Spell a name out in twigs or fly to the place where they live?'

Valant shook his head. 'The ravens do things for their own reasons, not for ours,' he said. 'And a dead human means no more to them than a dead bird lying at the side of the road does to us. No, the urgent thing now is to find the Unknown Spy.'

They found him five minutes later. He was sitting on a bench in the shrubbery, muttering to himself. He did not look up as they approached.

'She was dead when I found her, stiff and cold,' he said. 'She was dead when I found her.'

'Did you see anyone?' Danny asked.

The spy glanced up, then leapt to his feet. 'You!' he exclaimed. 'They told me . . . they said . . . What did they say . . . ?' His voice tailed off. Despite all their questions he would not say anything else.

Valant shook his head. 'We had better wake Master Devoy and give him the news,' he said.

Half an hour later they stood in the Unknown Spy's room with Devoy and Brunholm. Devoy was wearing a suit, but Brunholm had on an extremely loud floral dressing gown, which looked incongruous beside the cold dead body.

'Call McGuinness,' Devoy said. 'It seems we have a murderer in our midst.'

'I've already done it,' Valant said.

'And I wasn't far away.' They turned to see the figure of the Wilsons detective standing in the doorway behind them.

McGuinness was wearing a raincoat. His grey hair was cropped tight and he had the air of having seen everything bad that people could do to each other so that nothing surprised him. He took in the scene with an expert eye, then knelt to examine the body.

'Well?' Brunholm growled.

Danny resisted the temptation to tell the man that even McGuinness couldn't solve a crime in two minutes, but McGuinness merely fixed him with a thoughtful expression and said, 'There are two main possibilities – first, that someone wanted to murder her; second, that she stumbled across someone who was searching the Unknown Spy's room.'

'Looking for what?' Brunholm demanded.

'Yes, indeed, looking for what?' Devoy said in a musing voice.

'For that I'm afraid you'd have to ask the Unknown Spy,' McGuinness said.

'Or find out who he really is,' Danny heard himself say. The others turned to look at him.

'Well – if we find out who he is, maybe we can find out what the killer was after.'

'Makes sense to me,' McGuinness said.

'Yes, well,' Brunholm said, 'you can get on with working through the normal channels – full resources of the college available to you, no stone left unturned, etcetera, etcetera.'

Danny eyed him. The slippery Brunholm didn't seem at all enthusiastic about finding out the Unknown Spy's real identity.

Devoy turned to Danny as if seeing him for the first time.

'Ah, yes, of course, young Caulfield. Well, at least you have arrived safely. I must speak to you later. It's breakfast time now however, and I'm sure you're hungry. Most of the pupils have gone home for the holidays, but there are still a few here with whom you will be acquainted. Skip along to Ravensdale and have something to eat. I'm sorry that your first hours back have been so distressing.'

In spite of the shocking sight of the dead woman, Danny was in fact very hungry, and he was delighted to take himself off to the strange little village called Ravensdale, some of whose houses had been converted into canteens for the pupils. He made his way along a maze of corridors, remembering to look out for signs such as the painted ravens on the floor pointing in the direction to go. When he reached the curtained entrance to Ravensdale he took a deep breath before entering.

He found himself on an ancient village street with old houses on either side. Above his head a raven cawed. Otherwise nothing moved. He glanced at the names on the house doors as he walked. The Jedburghs. The Kamirilla Amarillos. He knew that if you walked to the top of the deserted street you would find a gallows. But he wasn't going that far. He saw a door with CONSIGLIO DE DEICE on it and gratefully plunged in. The Consiglio was his assigned dining place.

The first thing to greet him was a smell of frying bacon. The second thing was squabbling voices.

'You'd eat it if it was a blood sausage,' a thin raggedy-looking boy with wings was saying to a pale-faced girl with prominent incisors which made her look like a vampire.

'Leave Vandra alone, Les,' a blonde girl with a slightly absent look on her face said, while a dark-haired boy with sallow skin studied a piece of bacon suspiciously.

'Er, I'm back,' Danny said. The reaction was instant. The blonde girl threw her arms around his neck, covering him in crumbs and butter. Les, the winged boy, leapt up with a huge grin on his face, while Vandra the Physick bared her incisors in a smile which, if you didn't know her, would be truly terrifying. (Although if anyone had been looking, they would have seen a hint of colour creep into her cheeks at the sight of Danny). Even Toxique, the trainee assassin, shook hands vigorously with Danny.

Dixie, the blonde girl, disappeared, reappearing at the other side of the table beside the Physick, who glared at her crossly.

'Do cut that out, Dixie.'

'I can't help it,' Dixie said. 'I'm excited. We didn't know if you were going to come back or not.'

'I wasn't sure myself,' Danny said. 'Devoy sent for me to come early. I still don't know why.'

'I see blood,' Toxique said suddenly, 'blood and death.'

'Give it a break, Toxique,' Les said.

'Honestly!' Vandra said. 'I thought you'd got over all that blood-and-death stuff.'

Toxique looked abashed, but Danny grasped his arm. 'You're right,' he said quietly. 'There *is* blood and death in the air.' He told them about the Unknown Spy's wife.

'Blimey!' Dixie said. 'Things have a habit of happening around you – did you ever notice that?'

'Least it makes life interesting,' Les said. 'It's been pretty boring around here since the holidays started and everyone went home.'

'Boring, boring, boring,' Dixie said, rolling her eyes.

'Christmas was nice,' Vandra said. 'Devoy got us all presents as usual and we had a good meal.'

'Except the meal was in Brunholm's rooms,' Les said. 'Toxique was convinced he was going to poison the lot of us. We had to listen to Brunholm singing "Good King Wenceslas" – not for the faint-hearted.'

'The lady was murdered,' Toxique said quietly. 'We need to find out by who, and why. Could be one of us next.'

'He's right,' Vandra said. 'If Devoy brought you here early, then something's up, and the murder could be connected. At the very least we should put our heads together and think about it.'

'Perhaps not solve the murder,' Danny said, 'McGuinness is working on that, but if we could find out about the Unknown Spy and his wife, who they really were . . .'

'Good idea,' Dixie said brightly. 'How?'

'We need to get a look around the Unknown Spy's room,' Les said. 'Stands to reason there's got to be answers there.'

'Danny isn't doing that today,' Vandra said. 'Look at him – he's dead on his feet.'

'Here,' Les said, sliding a dish of bacon, sausage and fried egg towards him. 'That'll set you up.'

'Whoops,' Dixie said. 'How was your Christmas? Never thought to ask.'

Danny stuck a fork into a sausage and took a great bite, as much to avoid answering Dixie as from hunger. He was aware however of Les watching him with concern, and, when finally he had finished eating and washing the food down with hot sweet tea and they were all walking together down the Ravensdale street, he found Les beside him.

'Are you okay?' Les asked. 'Did something happen at home?'

'No, nothing,' Danny said. Then, seeing Les's sceptically arched eyebrows, 'Nothing much anyhow.

I don't want to talk now. I'll tell you when I've had a chance to think about it.'

'You can't say fairer than that,' Les said. 'In the meantime we'll get you back to the Roosts and let you have a bit of a nap. Things could get a little busy around here. If Devoy sends for you, I'll hold him off.'

They emerged from Ravensdale into the main building and took a side exit into the gardens. The snow lay thick and undisturbed on the lawns and shrubberies. The air was cold and stung Danny's lungs, but it felt fresh on his tired eyes. A robin alighted on a snowy twig near them, then followed their progress across the gardens. When Danny saw the treetop dormitories in front of him he had a sense of belonging, which increased when they climbed up the stairs and the warm, familiar odour of the place (including, it has to be said, a faint aroma of boys' socks) hit his nostrils. The iron stove in the centre of the dormitory glowed dull red. Danny sank down in his bed gratefully.

'See you later,' Les said with a grin.

Danny took his shoes off and pulled the blankets up around him. He knew he should undress, but the bed was soft and the room was warm. A picture of the woman who had pretended to be his mother drifted into his head, but he pushed it away bitterly. She had no claim on him now. This was his home, and his friends were his family. Within minutes he was fast asleep, the room around him quiet and peaceful.

A long way away, in the house Danny had left, it was also quiet, but it could not be said to be peaceful. All morning the woman Danny had known as his mother had felt a sense of dread that she could not account for. There was no sign of the car that had chased them the night before. The surrounding countryside was dead silent, the cold lying on it like a weight. The ravens had left that morning, as they always did, to scavenge what food they could find in the winter landscape.

Her partner, Agent Stone, was sleeping peacefully. She had given him antibiotics and some morphine against the pain. She sat down at the fire, her eyes grainy with fatigue, her heart heavy. She could not remember a time when she had not been on duty, all to do with Danny. She was Agent Pearl now, but once upon a time she had had a real name – she had been Alison, a young woman with a life and ambition. The ambition had led her to this job – a vital job, she had been told. But for many years now they had had little contact with the mysterious section of the security services who had employed her, apart from a cheque in her bank account every month and an email with terse instructions every so often.

Danny, she thought tiredly, remembering the look of utter betrayal on his face that morning. At the start it had been a job, although Danny had been an easy child to look after. But it had become more than a job. Tucking him in at night, cooking for him, worrying about him when he was out of her sight . . . sometimes she had started to think of Danny and Agent Stone as her real family. She felt a pang of guilt. If that was the case, then she hadn't been a very good or attentive mother.

She sighed. She had been told in an anonymous email that Danny would be going away to 'school' and she was not to ask any questions. But she couldn't help wondering where he had gone. He had seemed changed when he came home the last time, more confident, and yet unsure, like someone who had been handed a great responsibility but didn't know what to do about it. What were they doing to him? Where was he now? A fierce protective feeling swept over her.

A sudden fall of soot in the chimney made her jump. She frowned. There was no reason for the soot fall. She went to the window. The countryside was empty, the snow untracked, yet the ominous feeling had grown.

She went to the kitchen and took the revolver from her handbag, checking that it was loaded. She went to Agent Stone's bedroom. He was sitting up in bed looking haggard, a gun in his hand.

'You feel it too,' she whispered. He nodded. Of the two of them, he was the brains, the one who had worked for years on Danny's case, trying to draw together the boy's history, putting himself in many dark and dangerous places.

'Check outside,' he whispered.

Carefully she unlocked the back door and stepped out, the gun in her hand. The crunch of her feet in the snow was too loud, her grip on the revolver too fierce, the hairs on the back of her neck too tight. Yet nothing stirred, there was no sign of danger. Forcing herself on she did a full circuit of the property, peering into the garage and the outhouse. When there was nothing more to search, she let herself back into the house and went to Agent Stone's bedroom.

'Nothing,' she said. 'I can't see anything.'

But she had not looked up when she was outside. It was probably just as well that she didn't, that she had not been caught in the open, for she would have been cut to shreds. They were waiting for her, and if she had glanced over her shoulder there would not have been time to scream. For lined up on the roof of the house, like a flock of loathsome vultures, their wings folded behind them, were Conal's Seraphim, their eyes cold, bright metal blades by their sides.

Agent Pearl locked the front and back doors and closed and bolted the wooden shutters upstairs and downstairs. She stood in the hallway looking around for other possible entry points as she had been trained to do. Her eyes were drawn to the huge window at the stair return, a beautiful stained-glass portrayal of the Eve of Saint Agnes, the cold light setting its colours afire. And yet as she looked the colours appeared to darken, to dim and go out. With a huge crash the window was splintered into a thousand pieces, and there, in place of a window, stood a man – or was it a man? Tall, very tall, with lank grey hair and burning yellow eyes. She felt her insides turn to water as she saw that on his back, spread wide, were two huge wings.

She recoiled, and as she did so the Seraphim Conal threw his head back and emitted a terrible shriek of triumph. He launched himself and glided forward, others taking his place in the window.

Before she had a chance to raise the gun Conal had her pinned against the wall. She could feel his weight against her chest. His eyes were burning and his breath was cold and foul.

'Where is he?' Conal said. 'Where is the boy?'

She heard a shot then, and over Conal's shoulder saw one of the Seraphim falter in the air, then plunge to the ground. Conal spun round. Stone was standing in the bedroom doorway, pale and bloody, the gun in his hand. She ducked under Conal's wing and ran to him. The air of the hallway was full of wings, great swooping blades that would stun her if she collided with them. She reached Stone. Together they backed into the doorway. Despite his wound, Stone's eyes were bright with excitement.

'What are they?' Pearl gasped.

'Seraphim!' he said. 'The old books talk about them, but I never thought they really existed. This changes everything.'

The Seraphim had landed and were standing in a semicircle facing them. Pearl flinched at the air of menace.

'Where is the boy?' Conal growled. 'Where is the Fifth?'

'He's not here,' Stone said, 'and you won't find him.'

Conal gave a signal. Half of the Seraphim took to the air and sped up the staircase. Others made towards ground-floor rooms. There was a great crashing and rending as doors were burst open, rooms ransacked.

'He isn't here,' Pearl said. 'We won't give him up to you.'

'You think not?' Conal sneered, and took a step closer.

Pearl raised her revolver, but as she did so the

shutters in the bedroom behind them burst into a hundred pieces and a tall female Seraphim stood behind them. She flung her spear. It struck Stone a glancing blow on the forehead. He cried out and fell to the ground.

'How many bullets do you have in that gun?' Conal mocked. 'Six? Do you think you can kill all of us? Throw down the weapon and give yourself another few hours of miserable life. Others have survived the Ordeal of Memory!'

The female Seraphim had a ghastly grin on her face. Another spear thudded into the wood of the door. Pearl whirled round, and in a second the female was on her, the wings flapping about her face, hands like talons gripping her arms and a rancid smell overwhelming her. She felt consciousness start to swim away, but as it faded she heard a fearful cry from one of the Seraphim: 'The ravens! The ravens are coming!'

As Agent Pearl sank away, she wondered why the Seraphim should be so afraid of the ravens.

3
THE BUTTS

Danny woke at lunchtime feeling ravenous. He went out on to the balcony outside the Roosts and looked down to where his friends were using a battered old sleigh on the slope behind the shrubbery. A door to the side of the building opened and a group of what at first looked like pensioners came out, pensioners dressed in woolly hats and ancient-looking tracksuits. They looked around anxiously as if afraid of being watched, then a small figure emerged from the door.

'All right, ladies and gents,' she cried out in a shrill voice, 'you know what to do. Remember, it's Wing Hygiene Week!'

Grumbling, the others unfolded rather dusty wings and begin flicking snow into the feathers and rubbing them together. Danny grinned. These were the messengers who lived in Wilsons. They were elderly and very self-conscious about their wings.

'They would die of embarrassment if they knew they were being watched,' a quiet voice said. Danny turned. Master Devoy, the head of Wilsons, had been standing quietly against the wall of the Roosts.

'Master Devoy!' Danny was taken aback.

'I thought I'd let you sleep,' Devoy said, 'but there is an urgent matter we must discuss. First of all, was anything different during your stay in the Upper World? Were there any untoward happenings?'

Untoward? Danny felt a stab of pain as he remembered his mother's face. But he put the thought away.

He quickly told the head about how his father and mother had been pursued home under fire and how his father had been wounded.

Devoy nodded. 'The fabric of things is starting to come apart. I hope your parents are safe.'

Danny looked at him, startled. It hadn't occurred to him that they would still be under threat.

'I'll see you at five in my study. Some things should not be talked about in public.'

Danny watched Devoy descend from the Roosts and cross the snowy lawn. A sudden gust of wind blew across the surface snow, and Devoy disappeared into the mini-snowstorm as if he had never been.

The four cadets played in the snow all afternoon, using the sleigh, building a snow effigy of Brunholm and throwing snowballs at the siren when she appeared on the lawn. The siren climbed out of reach and bestowed a small cold smile on them. Danny wondered if it was altogether wise to provoke her. Vicky was very beautiful but also very malicious, and she had a long memory.

But that afternoon they didn't care. There was a sense among them that soon there would be little time for being silly and playing games and they were determined to make the most of it. There was a great freedom in having the school to themselves, with no teachers or other pupils about, and this too would not last. It took Vandra to point out to Danny that it was almost five. He threw a few last snowballs as if in defiance, but in the end he put his head down and trudged off as the others headed towards Ravensdale for muffins and hot tea.

Brunholm was waiting in the hallway to take him to Devoy's office. He took off at speed with Danny running to keep up. They crossed the silent Gallery of Whispers and went through a maze of corridors, up the stairway to the third landing and on to the treacherous stairs to Devoy's office (Danny keeping an eye out for piano wire strung at neck height on the way).

Master Devoy's office was an old-fashioned place decorated with spy paraphernalia from across the ages – miniature cameras, poison-tipped umbrellas and the like – and Devoy looked completely at home in it, a spymaster of the old school. Danny sensed the tension in the room the moment he entered. Although Devoy had trained his face to remain absolutely motionless no matter what the circumstances, the manner in which he turned round from the table was a little too swift, his greeting a little too warm. Devoy regarded Danny for a moment, then shook his head.

'You learn too quickly, young man. You sensed my anxiety. And yes, you are right. I am anxious, and for good reason. More than anxious. I believe the Ring are moving with speed and aggression. Everything we have worked for is in jeopardy.'

Devoy lifted a deadly stiletto from the mantelpiece, testing the point with his finger.

'They intend to break the Treaty and take over the Upper World,' Brunholm said, smashing a fist into his palm a little too vehemently, Danny thought. Was he acting?

Devoy whirled around, the stiletto pointed at Danny.

'The Treaty Stone itself is discovered! The whole foundation of the two worlds is at risk.'

Brunholm had found his way to Danny's side, so close that Danny could feel hot breath on the side of his face.

'There is a kingdom,' he said, his voice low and

intense, 'a kingdom called Morne. It is a part of the Lower World that exists in the Upper. The Stone is kept there for safety. But it is safe no longer. The Ring have discovered it.'

'We must have it, Danny,' Devoy said. 'We must!'

Danny stared at him, his eyes fixed on the deadly stiletto in his hand. 'Why me?' he stammered. 'I mean, you have experienced spies.'

'Yes,' Brunholm said, 'but none who have lived in both the Upper World and the Lower. You must travel to the kingdom through the Upper World. Your experience in the Upper World is vital to get through. Believe me, boy, if there was anyone else I could send, an adult, you would be drinking cocoa at home.'

'The kingdom is placed in the Upper World to protect it,' Devoy said, 'to keep the enemy out. Once you are there it will require all your skills as a spy to get to the Treaty Stone before the enemy does.'

'I don't understand why the Ring want the Stone. Either there is a treaty or there's not,' Danny said. 'What's to stop them attacking the Upper World anyway if they want to?'

'The Treaty written on the Stone is binding under pain of death enforced by the dead. You remember your oath in front of the dead, Danny?'

Danny shivered. He remembered taking his oath as a spy, the cold voices whispering around him. He had no doubt that they would enforce the Treaty.

'The only way to break the Treaty is to smash the Stone. That's what the Ring want to do, and we must stop them,' Brunholm said. 'If the Stone is broken, all rules are gone.'

Then Devoy spoke. His voice had become something cold and remote, majestic in a brittle way, like thinking about the stars at night.

Here is the Treaty writ in stone. Here is the bargain sealed in blood. Death to the faithless. Death to the oathbreaker.'

'The words written on the Stone,' Brunholm said.

Danny shivered. Who did they think he was to send him to steal such a deadly thing?

'You will not go alone,' Devoy said. Danny realised that the master had read his thoughts, and resolved not to let him do it again.

'You will have a team of companions with you,' Brunholm said. 'All your band of pals, except that little tyke Knutt.'

Seeing Danny's mouth open in protest, Devoy interjected. 'It's the wings, Danny. How can he go openly in the Upper World with wings?'

'We don't have time to argue over trivialities,' Brunholm said gruffly. 'Too much is at stake.'

'And yet we cannot rush into things without careful preparation, as much as time permits,' Devoy said. 'Go back to your friends. Say nothing!' He looked resolute, ready to face danger, but Danny noticed a bead of blood on his finger where the stiletto had accidentally pricked it.

Danny went down the stairs, avoiding the treacherous gaps by instinct. The mission itself was enough to take in, but the thought that he would have to leave Les behind worried him.

When he got to the hallway his friends were waiting for him.

'Well,' Dixie said eagerly, 'are we going on another mission?'

'I think so . . .' he said.

'I understand,' Vandra said. 'Leave him alone – he's been told not to say anything.'

'I bet it's a tough one,' Les said. 'Here. I thought you'd be hungry after meeting with Devoy and Brunholm.' The winged boy pressed a large hunk of chocolate cake into Danny's hand. 'I don't mind what the mission is,' he went on, 'long as we do it together – isn't that right, Danny?'

'As long as we're together,' Danny said, the words out of his mouth before he'd considered them, the realisation accompanied by a dark little thrill at telling the lie. Danny groaned inwardly. No matter how much he fought it, betrayal was in his blood.

'One thing at a time,' he said, making his voice brisk and workmanlike. 'Vandra's right – I can't discuss the mission. But we have our own mission tonight to find out who the Unknown Spy is.'

In daylight the idea of solving the murder of the Unknown Spy's wife by finding out the true identity of the pair had felt like a straightforward matter. Now that they were safely tucked up in the Roosts with a cold wind stirring the trees and the promise of further snow in the air, it didn't seem such a good idea.

'Maybe we should leave the crime-busting to our ace detective Mr McGuinness,' Dixie said, suppressing a yawn, when they met on the balcony.

'No,' Danny said. 'It's important.'

'He's right,' Vandra agreed. 'We can't let a murderer just prowl Wilsons. Any one of us could be next.'

By common consent Toxique had not come along. He was hypersensitive to any hint of death or danger in the vicinity, which was useful on a mission, but he couldn't help calling out – moaning on about death and blood, as Dixie put it – which made them all nervous and jumpy.

'Who's on point of entry?' Danny asked, the term coming to him from a class that he thought he had forgotten.

'I am,' Les said. 'There's a cellar door under the Unknown Spy's corridor. I've already picked the lock. We're ready to go.'

They set off down the stairs of the Roosts, moving silently in single file. Despite Dixie's misgivings, Danny looked round his small team with approval. They were all dressed as spies: dark clothes, high collars or hats pulled down over their eyes so that they could not be seen or easily identified; they carried a variety of equipment, torches and lock picks hanging from belts. A term ago they would never have been so well prepared. Danny was surprised and impressed that he had absorbed so much of what they had covered in spying class.

They kept close to walls or other shelter, moving warily and stopping frequently to check their surroundings. When they got to the cellar door Les quickly whipped off the padlock, the others forming a watchful semicircle around him. Then they all moved swiftly and silently into the cellar as if a part of the night had detached itself and flowed darkly through the small door.

Inside the cellar Danny lit a small torch and shaded it with his hand. Les indicated the direction they should go with a nod, and they all followed.

The cellar opened on to a dank narrow corridor, dripping with water, little ferns growing from the walls.

'You sure you've been here before?' Vandra whispered.

'Yes,' Les said, 'but you know what Wilsons is like.'

It was always hard to find your way reliably in the school. The corridors and staircases had a way of seeming to change direction, of not leading to the same place from one day to another. You had to look out for clues as to what direction you were going in, but in this damp corridor there were no clues. They walked on for five minutes, an uneasy feeling growing in all of them that they weren't getting any nearer to the room of the Unknown Spy.

'It was dead easy today,' Les said. 'I saw the cellar door under the spy's window, I popped the lock and a manhole came out on the corridor outside his room.'

Danny shrugged. 'It doesn't matter, Les. We'll follow this for a while and see where we end up. Sometimes I think the building itself is like an old spy, full of secrets and tricks and dead ends. Maybe we're being led towards something else.'

'Yuck,' Dixie said, trying to brush a spiderweb from her hair. 'Maybe it's leading us towards the biggest spider's nest in the world. Feels like it anyway.'

On they trudged, the tunnel getting older and older. Here and there were carvings on the walls, figures in relief or etched into the stone, but the carvings were too old to make out the faces of the people depicted, although there appeared to be a cruel turn to some of the features, making Danny secretly glad that they weren't clear.

They were just about to head back when it happened. A sudden gust of cold air struck them, air that got colder and colder, growing from a gust into a howling gale. Danny felt ice sting his flesh like needles and hoar frost forming on his lips. Vandra cried out in pain and Les cursed. The cold was so intense that the bulb of the torch dimmed and went out, and the torch fell from his hand. In the howling of the wind around their ears they heard whisperings, dread voices speaking words that they did not understand but sensed were full of fear and loathing. Danny was aware of shapes around him, haggard white faces with empty sockets where their eyes should have been. At first they appeared without bodies, but then the bodies formed, frost bodies but hideously mutilated, gaping empty spaces where their hearts should have been, their bellies rent open. He was surrounded by them and he could feel cold hands clutching at his old raincoat, plucking at the fabric. Then with sudden terrifying force the hands were inside his coat. He gasped and sheer naked fear gripped him. The hands were strong and sinewy and freezing and he felt that they would grab his own heart from his chest and leave him lifeless and mutilated while they gorged on his warmth and life. He fell back on to the ground, consciousness fading.

In the distance a light flared and he heard a voice cry out, 'Ware old ghouls! Ware . . . .'

Then blackness came over him and he knew no more.

He woke up in a warm room, lying on a neatly made bed. There was a smell of hot chocolate in the air, and when Danny raised his head he saw his companions sitting round a fire with blankets over their shoulders, sipping from steaming mugs.

The room was plain and neat, everything in its place, shirts folded perfectly on a shelf, a single polished silver trophy on the mantelpiece over the fire, some military decorations in a frame on the wall. There was a movement near the door and he looked up to see Valant looking at him with concern on his face.

'If you're wondering where you are, you're in my

quarters,' the porter said, 'and if you ask me you're damned lucky to be alive, wandering down in the Butts on your own.'

'Sorry,' Les said with a a weak grin. 'That was my idea actually. Thought it was a bit of a short cut.'

'Thought you would avoid my beady eye in the hallway more like,' Valant said. 'However, no harm done.'

'Who . . . or what . . . were they?' Vandra asked.

'They were ancient spies and traitors – the dead of Wilsons. The Unquiet, they are called. You met them before, when you took your oath.'

'They were horrible,' Dixie said. 'Full of holes and all.'

'I suppose some of them were horrible,' Valant said. 'The fact is that in medieval times spies were hanged, drawn and quartered. They had their entrails and sometimes their hearts cut out and held up for all to see.'

'You'd be a bit shook up after that,' Dixie said.

'They wandered the earth, haunted by their own cries of agony, unable to rest,' Valant went on.

Les looked impressed.

'But they found their way to Wilsons,' Danny said slowly, 'the only place in the two worlds where their treachery does not render them outcasts, where they can have peace from their own screams.'

'Very cunning,' Dixie said.

'I could hear it,' Danny said, 'in their voices.'

'They gathered around Danny,' Vandra said. 'We thought they were going to kill him.'

'Really?' Valant said. 'I thought you had just stumbled across them by accident – they are inclined to roam the Butts a bit. They seem to like it there. Has that dungeon feel, I suppose.'

'What are the Butts?' Danny asked.

'The secret passages that connect all the different parts of Wilsons – if you know what you're doing, of course, which obviously you four didn't. I wonder why the Unquiet took a fancy to Danny here.'

'I don't know,' Danny said. 'All I remember is that they were cold, very cold.'

Danny remembered the chill sinewy hand that had reached under his coat. He tucked his hand in to the place where it had touched him, and to his shock found a small parcel wrapped in what felt like oilcloth.

'Is everything all right, Mr Caulfield?' Valant was looking at him curiously.

'Yes. Yes, fine,' he said hastily. 'I just thought for a moment they'd taken off with my heart.'

As his friends laughed, Danny hastily slid the package into a more secure place. Was it underhand not to tell his friends that the ghost spy had given him something, or was he merely being cautious? He told himself that it was good sense, but a part of him felt sneaky. It was one of the things he hated about the spy side of himself, the way he always had to distrust his own motives.

'Are you going to tell Devoy about this?' Les said nervously. 'It'll be a Regulation Three offence at least.'

'It depends. What were you doing in the Butts?' Valant said sternly. 'Tell the truth now!'

'We thought we could help find the killer of the Unknown Spy's wife,' Vandra said.

Valant looked at her sternly. 'If I had smelt a lie you would have been in Master Devoy's study before your feet could touch the ground,' he said, 'but I believe you, and I think that the Master has more on his mind than a bunch of amateur detectives. Now, if you're feeling a little less chilly, I suggest we get you lot back to the Roosts before you are missed.'

'Er, how do we get back?' Les asked.

'Here,' Valant said. 'I think I can entrust this to . . .' His eyes swept over the four, barely pausing at Dixie and Les, dwelling for a while on Danny, before with a thoughtful look turning to Vandra.

'. . . our Physick here, who has a trustworthy if rather melancholy look.'

He handed her what looked like a glass ball.

'What is it?'

'A precious thing,' Valant said firmly, 'so I'll expect you to take care of it. You want to find your way back through the Butts, so tell it so.'

Vandra gave him a dubious look and turned to the glass.

'The Butts,' she said shortly, as if it was a trick. But the glass started to cloud over immediately. It turned a murky brown, then a drippy grey, and a network of paths appeared in it.

'Where are we?' Dixie said, poking her head over Vandra's shoulder. Straightaway five tiny figures appeared in the top left-hand portion of the globe, enclosed by the walls of a room. The lines on the map shimmered and moved as they watched, sometimes merging with each other, sometimes turning back on themselves.

'No wonder we got lost,' Les said. Dixie said nothing. There was something eerily beautiful about the map and the tiny silvery paths. She stared at it, the light reflecting in her blue eyes until they shone like amethysts.

'Just follow your progress on it,' Valant said. 'You'll find your way back.'

'What is it?' Dixie breathed.

'It is a Globe of Instant Postitioning In Ephemeral Places,' Valant said.

'A Globe of Instant . . . G . . . I . . . a GIPIEP!' Dixie said brightly.

'If you must,' Valant said, a little wearily, 'but if you have to shorten it, I'd be more inclined just to refer to it as a Globe. Now . . . off you go.'

'It's a very precious thing,' Danny said, 'so how come you're giving it to us?' The words sounded more suspicious than he had intended.

Valant looked at him a little oddly, but he answered reasonably enough.

'Because you might need it in the future. Now go!'

'Aren't you coming with us?' Vandra said.

'You were resourceful enough to get into the Butts in the first place. I believe you can get out without my assistance. The Unquiet will not trouble you when you have the Globe. I am surprised that they approached you at all. Normally they are very shy. Perhaps they sensed your uncertainty.'

Danny fingered the package and wondered if there was another reason.

Despite a few false turns they found their way back, Vandra guiding them through the dripping tunnels of the Butts, which appeared to be made of solid stone yet in the Globe twisted and writhed in the most disconcerting manner. Twenty minutes later they were out in the gardens, the wind whipping the snow into their faces. Walking in single file and holding on to each other, they made it back to the Roosts.

They split up on the balcony, the boys going one way, the girls the other. Bone weary, Danny and Les sprawled in front of the stove and told Toxique what had happened. Toxique's nostrils flared at the mention of the Unquiet, and Les groaned.

'Please don't start going on about blood and death and all,' he said.

Toxique gave him a dark look.

'You must be roasted, sitting there with your coat on,' Les said to Danny.

'I'm fine, the Unquiet touch left me really cold,' he said. Another lie. In fact he was afraid the parcel might fall out.

As soon as they went to bed he took out the package and unwrapped it. The material was old and appeared to be bloodstained. It was a piece of canvas, folded in two then folded again and again. In the middle of it was a ring. It was made of gold, and etched on its surface were two letters intertwined: S and G.

4

THE BEETLES OF TRANSMISSION

Devoy and Brunholm left them alone for the next two days and they spent their time in the Roosts, by common consent ignoring the main building. For some reason the danger they had faced from the dead looked even more terrifying by the cold light of day. Although the friends spent a lot of time together, in many ways they were separate. Danny was struggling with the fact that Les would have to be told he was not going on the mission. And behind everything was the thought of the parents he did not have.

On the third morning they were awoken by a familiar voice.

'That's right, campers,' the voice said, 'term starts again tomorrow, so let's see a little enthusiasm. Breakfast in ten minutes, and a First Regulation Offence for stragglers.'

'Put a sock in it,' Danny muttered.

'I heard that, Cadet Caulfield, but your ungracious

remark cannot dim my renewed enthusiasm for life at Wilsons Academy of the Devious Arts.'

All that day the other pupils drifted back, full of stories about their holidays, trips taken, parties thrown. But there were also tales of worried parents gathered together in groups, talking intently, and some pupils said that their parents had employed security guards.

It was in this atmosphere that the first summonses arrived. First Danny was called to Devoy's office. He returned silent and downcast, and when Dixie asked him what had happened he snapped at her.

'No need to bite my head off,' she said, but then her summons came. She also was silent and unapproachable when she came back. Next it was Vandra's turn. Les greeted her when she came in, but she walked straight past him, her face set.

'What's up with you lot?' he said., 'You'd think somebody had died or something.'

But no matter how much he asked, none of them would tell him what had taken place. He went off on his own, muttering. Danny watched him go. There was an old summerhouse in the woods where Les went when he needed to think, and Danny reckoned that was where he had gone.

Les didn't come back until teatime, when he sat

on his own at the far end of the table in their house in Ravensdale, trying to look unconcerned.

Danny walked back to the Roosts on his own, his thoughts troubled. He wished that Devoy would move ahead with the mission. He needed action. As he approached the stairway to the Roosts a figure detached itself from the shadows. Danny's hand went to the pocket of his raincoat, but there was no need. It was McGuinness.

'Glad to see you're wearing the coat,' the detective said approvingly. The coat had once belonged to the master spy Steff Pilkington and, although shabby, had many strange and wonderful qualities. It wasn't exactly fashionable, and Danny wouldn't have been seen dead in it in the Upper World, but slipping it on every morning had become one of the few reassuring elements of life in the unreliable world of Wilsons.

'Did you find out anything about the Unknown Spy's wife?' Danny asked.

'My investigations are making some progress,' McGuinness said, 'despite the presence of some freelance investigators muddying the waters.' Danny felt his face turn red.

'However,' McGuinness continued, 'there is something you might be interested in. Come with me.'

He led the way back into Wilsons, and down the corridor to the Unknown Spy's room.

'He has taken temporary lodgings with Master Devoy,' McGuinness said. 'The killer left no clues, but as to your idea about finding out the Spy's identity . . . Look.'

He handed Danny a calendar. There was nothing unusual about it that Danny could see until he noticed that the 5th was ringed. He flicked through the calendar. The fifth of every month was ringed!

'And there are many calendars, decades of them,' McGuinness said. 'Look at this. He held up a copy of *Spy News* (Incorporating *Covert Times*). Every time the number five was printed on the page it had been circled or underlined or had a question mark beside it.

'Everything's the same,' the detective went on, holding up a shirt on which the size five was circled.

'My guess is that he's trying to remember something, and that something is to do with the Fifth.'

The detective's wife, Starling, was also a spy and had helped Danny escape the Ring. Danny realised that McGuinness knew about his being the Fifth. 'Me?' he said.

'Yes. He has no memory of his life before Wilsons, but something appears to be gnawing at him. Every time he sees the number five a thought is stirred, but he can't quite grasp it. It's not much to go on, but until we find what the killer was looking for . . .'

Danny walked back across the lawn to the Roosts. Before he had reached the ladders he saw Dixie and Vandra, determined expressions on their faces. They were obviously waiting for him.

'What is it?' he said.

They drew him aside into the shrubbery.

Dixie spoke first. 'What did Devoy tell you today?'

'I'll tell you what he told us,' Vandra said furiously before he could answer. 'We're to pretend that we've fallen out with Les, that we're not friends with him any more.'

'It's for his own good – and for yours, he says,' Dixie said bitterly.

'I said that we're friends, and Brunholm puts this sneery face on him and says it's about time we learned that spies don't have any friends. That it would be a valuble lesson for us.'

'We're going on a mission and leaving Les behind,' Vandra said miserably.

'I know,' Danny said, having had the same brusque lecture at his meeting with Brunholm and Devoy. One part of him was relieved that the secret about leaving Les behind was in the open. Another part of him was irritated that he was no longer the only one who knew the secret.

'Well, what are we going to do about it?' Dixie said.

'I don't know,' Danny said. 'There's something wrong about the way they're going about it. They're saying that it's best that Les doesn't get too attached to us, because we're going away.'

'But when did Brunholm start caring about hurt feelings?' Vandra said.

'Exactly,' Danny said. 'So what is he up to?'

'I don't care what he's up to,' Dixie said crossly. 'I'm not going around pretending that Les isn't my friend. I'm going to tell him everything.'

And without waiting for the others she started up the staircase to the Roosts. Vandra and Danny looked at each other, then scrambled after her. Dixie looked at them as if challenging them to stop her, before she disappeared and reappeared at the top of the stairs.

'It's really irritating when she does that,' Vandra said, breaking into a run. Dixie waited for them to reach her, then charged through the door to the boys' Roosts. Les was standing just inside, and Dixie took a step back in surprise.

Les looked from face to face, then burst out laughing.

'What's so funny?' Dixie demanded.

'Your faces,' Les said. 'I was going to let you say your bit, but I couldn't keep a straight face.

'We were just going to say . . .' Vandra started.

'I know what you were going to say,' Les said. 'I've been listening to you for the last ten minutes.'

'How . . . ?' Danny said.

'Put your hand in the left-hand pocket of your skirt,' Les said.

Vandra did so with a suspicious look on her face. She withdrew her hand, looked at it, shrieked loudly and jumped back. A black object fell to the floor, an object that started to move slowly away from them.

'Don't stand on it!' Les said, stepping forward rapidly and scooping it up.

'What *is* it?' Vandra asked. 'Ugh!'

Les grinned. 'It's a Beetle of Transmission.'

'What on earth is that?'

'You need two of them. The hearer has one and the listener has the other. Look. The hairs on their bellies vibrate in time to our voices. When one beetle vibrates the other picks it up and it comes out as sound.'

Half fascinated and half repelled, they stared at the beetle which he held upturned in his hand. As he spoke the dense hairs on its underside rippled in time to his voice.

'You put it to your ear and you can hear what is being said near the other one, as long as it's not too far away. Here.'

He took an identical fist-sized black beetle out of his own pocket and handed it to Danny. Danny took it gingerly, feeling the hard shell cold against his hand, the tiny legs moving against his palm. He turned it over and saw the little hairs rippling on the underside.

'Put it to your ear,' Les said, holding his beetle to his mouth. Trying to quell the feeling of revulsion Danny put the creature to his ear, shuddering as the little hairs touched him. Les whispered into the beetle's belly and Danny jumped as he heard Les's voice as clear as day.

'I know what you're up to . . .'

His surprise was followed by annoyance. What did Les mean? He couldn't know all of Danny's secrets . . .

But when he lowered the beetle from his ear and saw his friend's cheerful, open grin he felt ashamed of his suspicions.

'I could hear what you were talking about down below. You're going on a mission and they don't want me to go with you.'

'You don't sound annoyed . . .' Vandra said, puzzled.

'You don't have wings, otherwise you'd know,' Les said. 'There's always stuff you can't do. I reckon this must be a mission in the Upper World, so stands to reason you can't have a boy with wings. The whole point of being a spy is that you don't stand out – ain't that right?'

'We reckon there's more to it than that,' Vandra said. 'Brunholm is up to something.'

'He's always up to something,' said Les with a shrug.

'The Upper World!' Dixie said. 'Super, absolutely super!'

'Can't be many Physicks up there either,' Vandra said, touching one of her prominent incisors self-consciously.

'Its all right, Vandra,' Danny said. 'You'll look perfectly normal, or as good as. I mean, there's lots of variety in people, . . .'

'When you're in a hole, stop digging,' advised Dixie.

Danny noticed tears in Vandra's eyes.

'But none of them are as beautiful as the Wilsons girls,' he said.

'Yeuch!!' Dixie said. She pulled a face but Vandra was beaming.

'We'll make a deal,' Danny said. 'When Brunholm's around we'll ignore Les. It'll keep Brunholm onside, and maybe we'll be able to find out what he's up to.'

Behind them the door opened and Toxique came in. There was no point in involving Toxique in any of it. His doom-laden pronouncements were completely beyond his control, and he was likely to talk out of turn at any moment.

'Girls shouldn't be in here,' Toxique said shortly, and went over to sit heavily on his bed.

'Girls don't want to be here,' Dixie said, turning with a flounce. 'Smells of boy!'

She walked out, followed by Vandra.

Danny sat down beside Toxique. 'What's wrong?' he asked gently. Toxique was the only pupil who stayed in the school even though both his parents were alive. His father thought it would 'harden him up'. Toxique's family were professional assassins going back many generations, and the heavy burden of following in their footsteps had fallen on his shoulders. Toxique's father believed that his son lacked the necessary ruthlessness and didn't hesitate to tell him so in frequent letters.

'Another letter,' Toxique said glumly. He pulled it from his pocket and read.

'For generations this family have been the assassins of choice when the termination of a king or prime minister has been called for, though we are not too proud to stoop to

the ending of a peasant's existence if required. Our service has always been discreet and efficient. Our calling is as necessary to the smooth functioning of society as that of a lawyer or an architect . . .'

'I get the idea,' Danny said, 'but it's just the normal stuff, surely?'

'Well, that part is, but listen to this: *No member of our family has ever reached their third term at Wilsons without carrying out at least one termination. This happy tradition is in danger of being broken, and I am sure that even you do not want the burden of being the one to break it. Please choose your subject and carry out all necessary steps to maintain the family's honour by the end of term . . .*

'He wants me to bump somebody off,' Toxique said in despair. 'What am I going to do?'

'When did this come?' Danny asked.

'Four days ago. I haven't been able to concentrate on anything since.'

'Let me think about it,' Danny said. 'We'll sort it out, I promise.'

'You mean that?'

'I do,' Danny said, wondering what he had let himself in for.

'The door is going to open in a few seconds,' Toxique said absently, 'and some faces you won't want to see are going to walk in.'

Toxique had the Gift of Anticipation and could

frequently tell what was just about to happen, a gift which Danny thought was much greater than just being a simple assassin. He was never wrong and this time, unfortunately, was no exception. The door opened and Smyck and Exspectre walked in, one tall and thin, the other small with large dark-rimmed eyes that made him look, as Dixie said, like a bushbaby.

'We're back. What's wrong with Toxique?' Exspectre said.

'Probably assassinated that freak Dixie by mistake,' Smyck said with a laugh. But the laughter did not touch his cold eyes.

'Leave it out, Smyck,' Les said.

'If you picked him for your subject,' Danny said, 'I think I'd side with your dad. Sometimes family tradition is a good thing.'

Toxique gave a wan little smile but his gaze rested thoughtfully on Smyck, long enough for the tall boy to look uncomfortable and hurry off.

'I was only joking,' Danny said. 'You do know that, don't you, Toxique?'

Twenty miles away, on the other side of the channel of water that separated Wilsons from its enemies, Conal the Seraphim stood in front of three others. On the left was Rufus Ness, the leader of the Cherbs, a powerful, brutal character with a cunning look, his eyes, like Danny's, brown and blue. On the right stood Nurse Flanagan, a glamorous-looking woman in a red dress. She was smiling, but the smile had no warmth. In the middle stood a man of medium height with a gentle, almost chiding smile on his face, as if he was a teacher who had found a child doing something bold but was waiting patiently for a reasonable explanation. Ambrose Longford, the leader of the ring.

'You fled because of a flock of birds?' Ness said incredulously.

'Not because of a flock of birds,' Conal said, his yellow eyes glittering dangerously. 'Ravens!'

'They *are* dangerous,' Longford said. 'More dangerous than you know.'

'Surely not so perilous that they send our Seraphim fleeing with their tails between their legs,' the woman said with a little laugh.

'They make a poison with the filth from the bottom of their nests and coat their beaks with it,' Conal said. 'The poison is deadly . . .'

'And particularly to Seraphim,' the leader said smoothly. 'The bird part of their genetic make-up is very susceptible to the poison. No, you did the right thing, Conal. Imagine what it would have meant for the Treaty if the countryside of the Upper World had been littered with the corpses of Seraphim! Would you be casting doubts on the courage of the Seraphim then, or would you be running for your life with the whispers of the dead in your ears, Rufus?'

'Perhaps it was the intention of the ravens to undermine the Treaty,' Nurse Flanagan suggested, again with that little laugh which had no trace of real amusement, 'to portray us as treaty-breakers and leave us at the mercy of the dead.'

'Perhaps. Were they there to guard Danny, or were they using him as bait to lure us into an attack? We will probably never know. All I can say is that the ravens will have to be watched in this matter.'

'The real matter is that we did not capture the boy,' Ness said impatiently.

'Yes, Rufus, but I have been thinking – there's more than one way to skin a cat.'

'What do you mean?'

'Wilsons will have worked out by now that we are seeking the Treaty Stone.'

'Why would they think that?' Nurse Flanagan said, examining a highly polished nail.

'Because it is the only way we can destroy the Treaty and invade the Upper World. If the Treaty Stone is found and broken, then there is no Treaty.'

'The Upper World will be ours for the taking,' Rufus Ness said with a satisfied grunt.

'But the Treaty Stone is held in the Upper World. We are not permitted there,' Conal said.

'And you failed in your first secret mission to the Upper World anyway, so there's no point in trying that again,' Nurse Flanagan said smoothly, drawing an angry glare from Conal.

'Enough,' said Longford. 'Squabbling will not bring us the Treaty Stone.'

'But what will?' Conal said.

'Not what, who,' the leader said. 'I know how Devoy's mind works. He will want to find the Treaty Stone and hide it from us. But the Stone is in the Upper World. So he must send someone who is permitted in the Upper World and is used to its ways.'

'The boy?!' Ness said. 'Devoy wouldn't dare send the Fifth.'

'He might not, but Brunholm will persuade him that the Fifth is the only person for the job. Doubtless he will send that ragtag group he surrounds himself with – the Physick and the girl and that miserable messenger boy.'

'Are they not barred by the Treaty?' asked Nurse Flanagan.

'There is a loophole. Those who drew up the Treaty did not think that anyone under the age of sixteen was a threat, and at the time there were children to be moved from the Lower to the Upper World, so they are exempt. Another reason why Danny is the obvious choice.'

'I see,' Nurse Flanagan said. 'So what is your plan?'

'If Danny succeeds in stealing the Treaty Stone, then we must get it from him. We have planted the seed of treachery in him. With the right persuasion he will join us and bring the Stone with him.'

'You sound very sure about that, considering that his friendship with the others won out over us the last time. He did not betray them,' Conal said sourly.

'We went about it the wrong way before. We must make sure that his friends abandon him. Then he will join the four of us and the Ring of Five will be intact.'

'And with the Treaty Stone destroyed, the Upper World will be ours,' Ness said, rubbing his hands together and cracking his knuckles with a very unpleasant sound.

5

A POISON DART

Danny, Vandra and Dixie stood in Devoy's office, each of them intent on the Master's words, each heart beating fast. Brunholm turned to the blank wall behind him, swept away a cloth that had been covering a map and pointed. The cadets moved closer. It was a living map. Even though the map was pinned to the wall, the rivers flowed with threads of real water, clouds scudded across the skies and smog hung over the towns and cities.

Brunholm's finger was pointing to a mountain range, the peaks white with snow, and as they looked, a blizzard swept across the range from north to south, coating pine forests at the base of the mountains with more snow.

'The mountain kingdom of Morne,' Brunholm said, whipping out a giant magnifying glass from under his cloak and holding it up to the map. Through the lens they saw large stone buildings perched on a crag on the western flank of the mountain. Snow-covered gardens and terraces ran down the sides of the crag until they reached forbidding cliffs on three sides.

'To the outside world it is hidden so it isn't interfered with. By the Treaty it is allowed to accept scholars from the Lower World, so you will travel there as students. Danny, you will go as a student of the history of the Lower World. Our young Physick can go as a student of medicine, and you . . .' He turned to Dixie, who was watching him with an expression that managed to be eager and vacant at the same time, '. . . you can go as a student of . . . something or other.'

'How do we find it?' Danny asked.

'It is a kingdom of unreliable location,' Devoy said, 'and therefore moves from mountain range to mountain range. At the minute it is in a mountain range called the Carpathians, but we expect it to move soon. We'll keep you informed. Now, that is enough briefing for the time being. We will have more detailed instructions for you in the following days. In the meantime I do not have to tell you not to speak of this to anyone.'

Danny said nothing, staring at the dark stone buildings of Morne, half turned inwards, it seemed, full of mystery and secrets. Part of him feared its stone walls and high narrow windows, part of him longed for it. Vandra had to grasp him by the arm to pull him away.

The Unknown Spy had been allowed back into his room for the first time that day. Valant had cleaned it thoroughly, but it wasn't the same. He sat behind his desk in the darkness. He had forgotten many things, but he had not forgotten his wife's face. He sat on until darkness fell, his eyes unseeing. He had often sat like this, feeling that there was a great secret just out of his grasp, if he could only reach back into his memory. Now there was nothing but his sorrow.

He heard a careful click. He had not forgotten the sound of a lock being picked and stealthy feet entering a room. He reached for the drawer where he kept his revolver, but when it slid silently open he felt in vain in the empty space. Valant had removed the weapon.

A voice spoke in the darkness, a high-pitched hissing voice. He could not tell whether it was male or female.

'You do not need your pistol. I do not intend to harm you.'

'Who are you?' the Unknown Spy said. His voice was calm. He had been in a thousand dangerous situations in his career as a spy.

'That is of no consequence. I have information for you, about the death of your wife.'

'What information?' The Unknown Spy's voice

was cold. Was the creature in the dark responsible for his wife's murder?

'I did not kill her, but I can identify the killer for you.'

'Why would you do that?' There was a curious high-pitched sound in the darkness. His companion was laughing.

'A belief in justice, perhaps?'

'I don't think so.'

'No. You are right. A belief in revenge then.' The wheezing laugh had stopped.

'Then let me have my revenge,' the Unknown Spy cried, 'and then leave me to it!'

'Very well,' the voice said. 'The boy with the wings, the Messenger Les Knutt, killed your wife.'

There was a shuffling sound in the unlit room. The door clicked again. The Unknown Spy was alone in the darkness with his revenge.

'Whoa,' Vandra said. 'Easy!'

'Yes,' Danny agreed. 'Get into a kingdom which moves about the place, steal the Treaty Stone while pretending to be students and get out, presumably chased by the kingdom's army – dead easy.'

'Lay off the narky tone,' Dixie said.

'Sorry,' Danny said, looking contrite. 'Every time I meet Brunholm he puts my teeth on edge.'

'I can't wait to see the Upper World,' Dixie said excitedly, disappearing and reappearing in the corridor ten feet ahead of them. Then she pointed out of the window. 'Look,' she said.

They could see into a hidden inner courtyard which was rarely used and only visible from that window. There were four elderly Messengers in the the courtyard. In the old days, before war had riven the Lower World, the winged Messengers had flown between the two worlds carrying information. Once the Treaty had been signed and the worlds divided, they were no longer needed. Some had gone over to the enemy and had become the Seraphim. The others had fled to Wilsons and faded away, becoming ashamed of their former life – so much so that, unless absolutely necessary, flying was regarded as vulgar and unnecessary and their wings as a burden.

Now four of them stood in the square, led by Gabriel, once an aerial ace but now earthbound like the rest of his kind. Or was he? The three friends crouched to watch as Gabriel rose into the air, flew around the courtyard once at a leisurely pace, then casually performed a loop the loop before landing in front of the others. With varying degrees of success the three others, two respectable-looking lady Messengers and an absent-minded looking male, imitated him.

'Let's go down there,' Dixie suggested.

'No,' Danny said. 'They'd be too embarrassed.'

But Dixie wasn't listening. She smiled at Danny, before disappearing and reappearing in the courtyard right beside Gabriel, who leapt so far into the air he had to use his wings to give himself a soft landing.

'Quick,' Vandra said. 'There's a door here. Maybe we can smooth things over.'

When they reached the courtyard one of the female Messengers was complaining bitterly to Gabriel. None of them noticed the new arrivals.

'You promised all this would be highly confidential. "Oh no, Gertie, no one will ever see us!" Now we'll be the laughing stock of Wilsons!'

'Steady on, Gertie old girl,' the male Messenger said.

'It's all very well for you to talk, Waldron,' Gertie said.

'Yes, Gertie,' the other female said sternly. 'You have to remember what all of this is about.'

'The last time the Cherbs attacked we were caught unprepared,' Waldron said. 'We only escaped by the skin of our teeth. We must have at least one attack squadron if they come again.'

'Even if the others don't agree,' Gabriel added.

'We won't tell anyone, honest,' Danny said.

'Oh no!' Gertie exclaimed. 'More of them!'

'Isn't that the boy they said was the Fifth?' Waldron exclaimed.

'Really?' Gertie said, peering at him. 'He's not very impressive, is he?'

The other female Messenger, a small careworn-looking creature in a frayed cardigan, appeared to be lost in thought, moving her wings in little circles and talking to herself. Dixie watched her as she took two small jumps from the ground before gliding back to land. Dixie applauded.

'Not quite as good as the old days, my dear.' The lady Messenger smiled and did a little curtsy.

'I thought the Messengers were a little . . . embarrassed about flying,' Dixie said.

'Most of them are blithering idiots!' the Messenger snorted. 'They'd rather sit around and knit or something.'

'What would you prefer?' Dixie said.

'To get stuck into them, attack from out of the sun so they don't see you coming and knock tar out of their filthy Cherb hides.'

Dixie looked suitably impressed by the bloodthirstiness of the outburst. She stuck out her hand.

'Dixie Cole.' The lady Messenger took her hand and wrung it with unexpected strength.

'Daisy McEachen – absolutely charmed to make

your acquaintance. If I ever need a tail gunner I'll give you a shout. Always nice to have a human crew member on board. You can sit on my back when I'm flying and cover my tail.'

Dixie looked delighted at the prospect, but Danny was distracted. A small piece of stone had dislodged from the parapet far above their heads and fallen at his feet. There was a flicker of something black on the rooftop . . . Why was someone sneaking around up there? Danny grabbed the people nearest him – Vandra and Gertie – and drew them into the shelter of the wall. Before he could shout out to the others something flew through the air. Daisy, who had lifted absent-mindedly into the air, gave a little gasp, cartwheeled and fell to earth. Gertie screamed. Vandra and Dixie reacted quickly, moving swiftly to positions where they could observe the attacker.

Danny ran to Daisy. Her eyes were closed and she was breathing shallowly. A dart, its feathers black and red and sinister-looking, was buried in her arm.

'Vandra!' Danny called out. The small Physick hurried to his side. Gabriel had recovered a little and was rising cautiously into the air, his eyes alert. Vandra examined the dart, then knelt and smelt Daisy's breath.

'Smells of marzipan,' she said grimly.

'Is that bad?' Danny said.

'Means the dart was tipped with cyanide,' Vandra explained. Her face, pale at the best of times, had turned deathly white and her hand shook a little.

'Vandra,' Danny said, 'if it's too dangerous, you don't have to . . .'

'I do,' Vandra said. 'I am a Physick.'

Danny knew what she meant. A Physick was a healer who healed by drawing the patient's illness or poison upon themselves. Vandra would have to take the cyanide out of Daisy. Her body was strong – Physicks had Physickal gifts that enabled them to deal with disease and toxins – but there were no guarantees, and there was no protection against pain.

Vandra bent her head, her prominent incisors protruding. She extracted the dart from Daisy's arm and plunged her teeth into the shoulder just above the wound. She stiffened, spasms running through her muscles. Danny looked on helplessly. Behind him he heard a shout. A figure dressed in black was running across the rooftops, passing one of the huge crumbling chimneys.

'Gabriel,' Danny said, 'can you get me up there?'

'Put your arms around my neck,' Gabriel said. Danny did so, wondering if the Messenger's frail-looking neck and body would manage his weight. Danny had once flown on the back of Conal the Seraphim, who had borne him easily, but the Seraphim had grown strong in their vanity and cruelty, whereas the Messengers had declined.

Gabriel's back seemed to bend as Danny climbed on. There was a strong whiff of mothballs from his jacket, but his wings were surprisingly powerful, lifting them upwards with great beats. When they got to the level of the rooftop Danny could feel Gabriel tiring. As they cleared the parapet a gust of snowy wind drove them away from the chimneys, Gabriel desperately trying to fight against it. The swirling wind carried them out over the edge of the roofline. Gabriel faltered and Danny lost his grip. For a sickening moment he clung by one hand to the collar of Gabriel's flimsy coat, his legs dangling over a drop of a hundred feet.

With an enormous effort the Messenger was able to get Danny on to his back again, but the wind forced them across the rooftops, blowing snow from the slates in great whirling clouds around them.

'Can you land?' Danny shouted over the howl of the wind.

'Too much . . . turbulence . . . can't see landing spot . . .' Gabriel gasped. Neither did he see the great red-brick chimney rearing up in front of them. With an impact that drove the breath from their lungs, they struck and started to fall. Danny braced himself for a hard landing, but instead they dropped softly into a pile of snow that the wind had blown against the chimney breast.

Gabriel groaned and tried to shake snow from his feathers. Danny leapt to his feet.

'Are you all right?' he said. Gabriel nodded.

'Stay here then.' Danny looked around to get his bearings. The rooftops of Wilsons were vast, full of great peaks and troughs. There were chimneys and buttresses with windows in them, doors that looked as if they had been locked and sealed forever. Here and there were clusters of aerials and dishes hinting at mysterious purposes. The chimney they had hit was the very one where he had seen the attacker. Casting around on the snowy roof for footprints, he found small neat tracks leading away. He began to follow.

The attacker had been able to run lightly over the roof, but Danny found himself blundering, slipping into gulleys and catching his shins on objects hidden under the snow. He tripped over a roof peak and slithered down the other side on his belly, landing chin first on a patch of ice. He rolled over, to find himself looking down the barrel of an ancient blunderbuss. The gun was held by a small red-bearded man wearing a parka. There was rope looped over his shoulder and climbers' crampons on his belt.

'Very busy on the rooftops this morning. Unauthorised entry all over the place.'

Danny got to his feet, eyeing the blunderbuss warily. 'I'm a pupil at Wilsons,' he said. 'We were in the courtyard down there and someone attacked us with a dart. I was chasing him.'

'One of these?' the bearded man said, holding up a red and black dart.

'Yes.'

'He threw one at me too.'

'Good thing it didn't hit you,' Danny said. 'It's poisoned.'

'Is it?' The man raised an eyebrow. 'So what makes you think you can come up here willy-nilly? These rooftops is highly organised places,' he said. 'You can't just be running about.'

'Sorry,' Danny said.

'There's lead flashing is hard to fix, and there's expensive copper sheeting and slates and tiles, not to mention the aerials. Looking after the roofs is a full-time job.'

'I'm sure it's hard,' Danny said, guessing correctly that the little man was responsible for the roofs, 'but they look like very well cared-for roofs.'

'Do they?'

'I've never seen better-looking roofs. Look at the way they're keeping out the snow,' Danny said.

'Snow is difficult,' the man said. 'Causes expanding, and we all know what expanding leads to . . .'

'Yes, of course,' Danny agreed. 'Expanding leads to . . . leads to . . .'

'Leaks!' the little man said. 'The Roof Man's mortal enemy! Leaks and drips.'

'Shocking,' Danny said, as the man lowered the gun. 'And, er, the attacker . . .'

'Gone,' the Roof Man said shortly. 'Must have had a key to one of the roof doors. It's the only way you can get up and down.' There was a clattering clanking noise from behind him. They both turned to see Gabriel. The Messenger had tried to take off, but the wind had blown him into one of the clusters of antennae, where he had become completely entangled. The little man lifted his blunderbuss to his shoulder. Danny dived forward desperately and knocked the barrel aside just as the Roof Man fired. The shot went harmlessly upward.

'What are you doing?' Danny cried.

'Look at my good aerial!' the Roof Man cried. 'I haven't seen such a mess since the great storms of 'thirty-nine. Pesky birds!'

'It's not a bird, it's a Messenger,' Danny gasped as the Roof Man struggled to reload.

'I don't care what it is. I want it out of my aerials,' the Roof Man grunted. With a supreme effort Gabriel wriggled free of the antenna and dropped to the roof in a tangle of wings and limbs. The Roof Man lowered his gun and clambered up among the aerials, straightening and redirecting them with care.

'Come on, Gabriel,' Danny said. 'We'd better get out of here. Sorry about your aerials, Mr Roof Man.'

'Come up here with nothing to do but make trouble,' muttered the Roof Man. 'Why can't they stay on the ground?'

'You didn't happen to see what the attacker looked like, by any chance?' Danny asked as he clambered on to Gabriel's back.

'Small and fast-moving was all I seen,' the Roof Man said. 'Too busy watching out for his darts to get a right look. Well rid of the like of that off the roof.'

Still grumbling, he did not look round as Gabriel half stumbled, half launched himself from the roof and glided unsteadily towards the ground, lost for a moment in a snow flurry blown from a ledge. Danny could see the three Messengers and Dixie below. Daisy sat up, supported by Gertie, but Vandra now lay pale and still on the ground.

The Roof Man moved to the edge and looked down at the small group. The irritable old workman had vanished. The face that looked down was cold and cunning, the eyes glittering with malice. He scratched at the ginger beard and part of it came away. He took one of the red-and-black darts from his pocket. The

Physick had saved the Messenger from his poison, but if it had cost her her own life then it would have been a good day's work. Besides, he had plenty more darts. 'Plenty more darts,' he said to himself in a voice that the Unknown Spy would have recognised, before he turned and skipped off lightly across the snow-covered roofs.

6
AN OATH

Danny knelt beside Vandra. She looked dreadful, her pale face positively grey, her chest barely rising and falling and spasms racking her muscles every few minutes while she grimaced with pain.

Dixie had gone to get Valant. They returned with two wheeled stretchers and lifted Vandra on to one. Daisy was able to get up on to the other by herself.

'The poor dear,' Daisy said quietly. 'She saved my life. I will not forget that.'

They wheeled the stretchers quickly along the quiet corridors of Wilsons, then stopped in front of an ancient cage lift. There was only room for two of them with the stretchers.

'Gabriel and I will take them to the Apothecary,' Valant said. ' You may visit the Physick in the morning, not before. She needs rest and what assistance the Jamshid can give her.'

*

Danny and the others watched the lift clank upwards into the gloom. He didn't say anything to the others, but he was determined to find the person who had hurt his friend.

They met Les coming across the lawn.

'What happened?' he demanded. They explained.

'Probably the same person that attacked the Unknown Spy's wife,' said a quiet voice. McGuinness was leaning against a tree beside them, his coat blending into the colour of the trunk so that he was virtually invisible.

'What makes you think that?' Danny said.

'These kind of incidents are rare in Wilsons, and both require a close knowledge of the layout of the college which, as you know, is complex. Speed and cunning have characterised both attacks. And they have both been successful, or would have been, except for the Physick. This is a professional at work – make no mistake about it. The question is why. The why of a crime almost always leads you to the culprit.'

'Lead me to him,' Les said angrily, 'and he'll not bother anyone ever again.'

'She'll get better, Les,' Dixie said, putting a hand on his arm.

'You have to keep your eyes peeled,' McGuinness said, lowering his voice confidentially. 'Until we know what motivates this person, everyone is in danger.'

'Time for tea,' Blackpitts announced from a speaker hidden in the tree, making them jump. 'It really is a wonderful day,' he went on.

'What's he so cheerful about?' Les growled.

They went off to tea in a gloomy mood, not helped by the sniggering at the other end of the table from Smyck and his friends, accompanied by warnings to each other to 'watch the game pie' in case it was poisoned and the like.

After tea Danny found himself wandering on his own. Without thinking about it he made his way towards the summerhouse in the woods. The place had not been used for many years – its curtains hung in tatters – but its old planks seemed to retain a sense of sunwarmed days and summer evenings, and it always lifted his spirits to sit there.

He'd brought a slice of cake from Ravensdale and he wrapped himself in a blanket and sat on the window seat watching the sun sink in the west, the bare black limbs of the trees silhouetted against it.

He wondered about his parents. He hated to admit it to himself but he missed them. They had always been there, and now there was nobody. They were agents, but who were they working for? Why did he have to be guarded? He already knew that he was the Fifth, the link between the Cherbs and ordinary people, and that the Ring of Five sought him as their missing member. Was that the reason? Did he have to be kept from joining the Ring?

He sat in the summerhouse for an hour, his mind swirling. When he finally stood up, stiff and cold, it was dark. He felt in the pockets of his coat. It had many pockets that weren't immediately apparent, and he found lock picks, a comb, a pen with a secret compartment, a broken spy camera and a foldable grappling iron before he put his hand on the old-fashioned but reliable electric torch.

As he pulled the torch out something clinked against it – the S and G ring. He studied it in the torchlight. Who were S and G, and why had the dead hand given it to him?

Returning the ring to his pocket, he started to walk back towards Wilsons, keeping the torch shaded with his hand so that he wouldn't be too visible – not so much because there was a killer at large, but because he had started to acquire a spy habit of secrecy, of not being seen when you didn't want to. There were noises in the darkness – night creatures starting to move about – but they didn't disturb him. Then he heard something different – not a badger scuffling in the leaves, but a struggling noise. As he got nearer he could make out groans and panting. It was coming from somewhere away from the path to his left. He switched off the torch and listened. A voice in his head told him to leave it, walk back to Wilsons, that it was none of his business.

'I can't leave it if they're in trouble,' he said to himself. And a quiet cold voice he barely acknowledged said, 'Go to whoever it is. Anybody about at this time of night is up to no good. They might be useful to you!'

He put the torch on, shielding it again, then picked his way through the undergrowth, pausing every few steps to listen. Whoever or whatever he had heard was growing tired – the struggling had become feeble, but there was no sign that Danny had been detected. The groaning noises stopped altogether. Instead he heard someone sobbing. Whoever it was didn't sound dangerous any more. Danny straightened up and took his hand away from the torch.

He had found Vicky the siren. She had been caught in a trap and was hanging in a net from a tree branch. Under the net, sharpened spikes had sprung from the earth. Whoever had set the trap had clearly taken no chances. Vicky's dress was torn and her hair was full of leaves, but when she saw the torchlight without knowing who was holding it, she cried out in a breathy girlish voice, 'Oh, thank goodness, kind stranger. I have been caught in this dreadful trap. I was just getting some medicine for my poor sick mother and some evil person left this awful thing here. If you could help me I would be so grateful . . .'

'It's all right, Vicky, I know who you are.' Danny angled the torch so it showed his face.

'Oh,' she said, her voice becoming bad-tempered and sulky. 'It's you. I suppose you lot helped Brunholm build these traps. My dress is *ruined*.'

'No,' Danny said, 'I wouldn't help Brunholm build something like that. Course I wouldn't.'

'You wouldn't?' She sounded surprised. 'Well, maybe if you could just step over here for a second and cut one or two strands of this net . . .'

'Why would I do that?' Danny said, feeling the cunning part of his brain taking over, the part whose nature was to manipulate and betray. And now seemed its chance, deep in the forest at night with a trapped creature.

'I could do things for you,' Vicky said with a coy smile. 'I could help you.'

'I don't think there's anything you can do for me,' Danny said, pretending to turn away.

'Wait, wait, don't go, there must be something I can do. If Brunholm gets his hands on me . . .'

Danny waited. He knew that Brunholm had been setting traps for Vicky for months, ever since Danny and Les had been fooled into releasing her from her cell in Wilsons.

'You're probably better under lock and key,' Danny said. 'All you do is make ships run aground on rocks by beguiling sailors.'

'I've given up beguiling, honestly I have,' Vicky said. 'I've put all that behind me. I'm a very respectable siren now.' She put on a respectable face, which Danny didn't believe for a moment.

'Besides,' Danny said, 'you'd promise me anything to get free, and then you'd try to double-cross me.'

'I swear I wouldn't. I'll make the siren's oath. The dead come for you if you don't keep it.' Vicky shivered at the mention of the dead, and something made Danny feel she was telling the truth. As far as he could see, nobody around Wilsons joked about the dead.

'Okay then – let's hear the oath.'

'You have to tell me what you want me to do.'

'I want you to be my eyes and ears when I want you to, to find out any bit of information I ask.'

'Is that all?' Vicky said. 'You sure you don't want more? I could throw in some theft and informing if you like. A little assault could be in the deal as well,' she went on helpfully.

'No, thanks,' Danny said quickly. 'The eyes and ears will do very well. Now, what about this oath?'

'Oh, the oath.' The siren closed her eyes, put her

93

head back like a child in school about to say a poem, and began to recite in a high-pitched voice:

'This is the oath as siren I make
This is the oath I cannot break
The dead await the liar
The faithless burn in their cold fire.
State your wish . . .'

'I want you to be a spy in the school for me when I ask you,' Danny said.

The siren listened gravely then replied:

'Your wish for me you have said
I obey or will be dead.'

She opened her eyes. 'That do?'

'That'll do.'

'Well then,' she said impatiently, 'cut me loose!'

It was difficult to get Vicky out without dropping her on to the spikes below. Finally Danny realised that he still had the knife of Implacable Intention, a blade that did exactly what its owner wanted of it. The siren watched him intently as he weighed the knife in his hand.

'What are you going to do?' She eyed him nervously.

For answer Danny threw the knife. It ripped a swathe through the netting on its way out. The siren shrieked as she tumbled sideways out of the net, the tips of the spikes glinting in the torchlight beneath her. Describing a deadly arc in the air the knife swung back towards her. She went silent as the blade plunged through the shoulder of her dress, pinning her to the trunk of the tree behind her.

Dangling from the tree, the siren examined the place the knife had struck. She fingered the ruined fabric and gave Danny a dangerous look.

'If you swing round to that branch on your left,' Danny said, 'you should be able to get down.'

She did as he said, and just as she reached the branch the knife fell from the tree trunk into Danny's waiting hand. 'Don't forget,' he told her.

She looked at him through narrowed eyes, then dropped from the tree and disappeared into the undergrowth.

As he walked back Danny didn't feel very good about himself. He had recruited a valuble ally and bound her to him but the way he had gone about it felt dishonest and sneaky. He should have just released her. He had got an advantage from her, but he had the worrying feeling that it might be turned on him somewhere down the line.

The forest path opened out into the lawns of

Wilsons, and the buildings sprang up in front of him. For all the danger lurking here – the assassin, the dead roaming the Butts, the devious games of Brunholm – the main building, its many lights blazing, looked welcoming and his heart leapt. This was where he belonged, he thought as he hurried towards it.

In another world the woman he had once known as his mother fed another piece of broken furniture into the fire. She was afraid to go outside to get fuel in case the winged creatures returned. They had terrified her, no matter how delighted Agent Stone was to confirm his theory that there really was a Lower World. All she could remember was the burning eyes and the foul stench of them. During the attack she had fallen unconscious, but she had seen the ravens coming and the Seraphim fleeing before them. She felt a little bit safer when she looked out of the window and saw the ravens in their raggedy nests in the bare trees. Even when most of them flew off to find food during the day, some remained behind.

Agent Stone was getting better, but since seeing the Seraphim he had spent most of his time in the library, barely pausing even to eat. She was on her own during the day, and she spent hours in Danny's room, sitting on his bed. She had pretended that they were a family and now she felt that she was being punished for it. She prayed that Danny was safe and that the Seraphim had not caught up with him, for surely they had been looking for him. And she hoped that, wherever he was, he would be able to forgive her.

7
PECULIAR GEOGRAPHY

The following morning the friends went up to the Apothecary straight after breakfast. Vandra was sitting up in bed. She looked ill and her voice was faint, but, as Dixie said, 'At least she had her eyes open'. They stayed for only a short while. The Physick was always gloomy while recovering from poison, and barely responded to their questions. They knew she would get better as the days went on, and that was enough for them.

Classes had started and the halls and corridors had been filled with pupils when they went up to the Apothecary, but now they were deserted. Dixie looked at her timetable.

'Oh dear,' she said. 'We're late for geography!' Les and Danny exchanged a glance and they all broke into a run. They tried to slip in quietly at the back, Dixie disappearing and reappearing at her desk, but it was no good. The wooden-backed blackboard duster whistled through the air, glancing off Les's head with a dull sound. Dixie nervously disappeared from her desk but mistakenly reappeared beside the teacher's desk, where a flung textbook of *Bottomless Lakes of the Lower World* just missed her. Spitfire, the geography teacher, was brilliant at her job, and the pupils liked her, but she had a hot temper and didn't suffer fools gladly. Danny got a raised eyebrow, which meant that she would talk to him later.

'Now, class,' she said, 'back to the exam topic of this term: the geography and history of the Upper World.'

It was odd sitting there listening to his world being described in the same way that someone from a foreign place would describe a country that they had studied but never been to. It was clear for a start that Spitfire had no idea what religion was. She said that people could only guess at what the strange buildings that dominated so many towns and cities were for, but that in some of them there were paintings and statues of Messengers, which meant that they might have been communication centres between the Upper and Lower Worlds before the Treaty.

She turned the lights out and began to project some photographs and paintings of Danny's world on to a screen.

'Our limited contacts with the Upper World have

enabled us to get some idea of what modern life is like there,' she said.

The trouble with Spitfire's photographs was that there was no way of telling what era they were from, so that a picture of a modern building was followed by one of a steam train.

'The steam engine appears to be the only mode of transport,' Spitfire said. 'Unlike us, they do not appear to have any automobiles.'

Danny opened his mouth to say something, then closed it again. Strangely there were no cars in any of Spitfire's images, so she had made the assumption that there weren't any in the Upper World. Then Spitfire moved on to people. An old photograph of a man in a top hat and tail coat was described as an example of 'everyday work clothing', whereas a girl in a bikini was wearing 'normal leisure clothing'.

'What are you laughing about?' Les whispered as Danny snorted. A 'typical schoolchild' wore a cap and shorts and carried a catapult in his pocket. An aeroplane on the ground bemused Spitfire, and Danny realised that there were no aircraft in the Lower World.

'We believe that this is some kind of futuristic train,' Spitfire explained. She went on to describe the landscape. 'The terrain would appear to be similar to our own with cold winters and temperate summers,' she said, seemingly unaware of the existence of deserts and ice caps or all the variations in between.

'Must be kind of funny where you live,' Les whispered, 'what with no cars and wearing shorts to school and all.'

Danny wanted to speak, but Spitfire's eye fell on him and he realised that it wasn't the time or the place to put her right. So he sat meekly listening to signs of food shortages (skinny models on a catwalk) and indications that people were constantly spying on each other's communications (satellite dishes on houses). Spitfire obviously thought this last point very important.

'It's one of the reasons that Wilsons is vital to the Lower World. Spying is obviously regarded as central to the interests of the Upper World, and we must be ready if by any chance they should cross our borders.'

Danny realised that there were no mobile phones or televisions in the Lower World, never mind computers. He had never thought of the two places as being so different. He put up his hand.

'Please, do you know what a television is in the Lower World?'

'A tele-vision?' Spitfire said. 'No, please do enlighten us.'

'It's like . . . a box, and moving pictures are beamed

on to it. There's programmes like, I don't know, the news and cartoons and drama in the corner of the room.'

'Really Mr Caulfield, such a vivid imagination,' Spitfire said. 'Actors being transferred into a box in the corner of the room? I don't think so.'

'Pull the other one, Caulfield,' Smyck sniggered.

'Does sound a bit odd, Danny,' Les muttered, looking a bit embarrassed for his friend.

'Sounds a bit odd?' Danny looked at Les incredulously, not wanting to point out that having wings was more than a bit odd, never mind being in a spy school with dead people running about in the basement.

'Now that we've all been most wonderfully entertained by Mr Caulfield, perhaps we should get back to work,' Spitfire said firmly.

After some more peculiar notions about the geography of the Upper World Blackpitts announced the end of the class, giggling to himself as if he was enjoying some private joke.

'What is wrong with that man?' Les said. As the pupils filed out of the class Spitfire told Danny and Dixie to stay behind. Les looked back a little wistfully as he left the classroom.

'Now,' Spitfire said, unlocking a drawer in her desk, 'this is top secret. Mr Brunholm requested that you be given it for your upcoming mission.' She took out a map case and produced a large document from it, unrolling it carefully on to her desk. 'There!' she said triumphantly. 'The Upper World!'

Danny stared. There was a great splodge of land, and here and there were flashes of blue. Mountains with snow-capped peaks were dotted about and there were beautifully drawn groups of buildings labelled 'Unknown city'.

'Er, did you do this?' Danny asked.

'Yes,' Spitfire said, beaming with pride. 'It took many hours' work, using all our available knowledge. What do you think?'

'If you don't mind my asking,' Danny said, 'when was the last time someone from here went to the Upper World?'

'Well, I can't speak for the other side – the Ring and the Cherbs,' Spitfire said with a sniff, 'but it's been generations since anyone from here has *admitted* to going over to the other side. Fairman brings back bits and pieces and I believe he's had a few illegal fares. Where does this stuff come from, after all? People find photographs and things in old houses. Someone must have crossed the border, but no one admits it.'

'I see,' said Danny, thinking that it must have been a very long time since anyone either crossed or took a good look around them when they did.

'Take the map and study it well,' Spitfire said, rolling it up. 'Keep it safe. It could be deadly in the wrong hands.'

Deadly in any hands, Danny thought. But he tucked it under his arm anyway.

Classes continued as normal for the rest of the day. Poisons. Maths. Disguise. Danny and his friends were tired when they'd finished, but he knew he had to talk to them. He arranged to meet them in the Infirmary after tea. He included Les even though he wasn't going on the mission.

Vandra looked a lot better, and she sat up in bed when Dixie said they had been given a map of the Upper World.

'Give me a look!' she said. 'I've always wanted to see it.'

'But the thing is, that map isn't anything like the Upper World,' Danny said. 'That's what I want to tell you!'

However, nothing would satisfy them but to open the map out on the bed and pore over the strange cities and snowy mountains, trying to guess how many people lived in such and such a place and what they were like.

'It's . . . it's . . . completely different,' Danny said. 'There are planes and mobile phones and things

104

like that.' They looked at him as if he was talking nonsense and went back to the map. It was hard to discuss mobile phones with people who used a beetle as a listening device.

They'll just have to see when they get there, he thought.

Vandra moved in the bed and grimaced with pain.

'Are you okay?' Dixie asked.

'Kind of,' Vandra said. 'I will be. It was a very strong dose. I was only just able to deal with it. If it hadn't been pure, I wouldn't have been able to cope.'

'What do you mean?' Les asked.

'If there had been any impurities, my system couldn't have taken it. That was pure, professionally made. We're not dealing with an amateur here.'

'No, we're not,' Toxique said quietly. Danny had forgotten that he had come with them.

'You said the feathers on the dart were red and black?'

Danny nodded.

'Red and black are the colours of the house of Toxique. We use them when we want people to know who the assassin is. I'm not surprised that the poison was pure. The Toxiques make the purest poisons in our own workshops. It's a matter of family pride.'

Danny was the first to see the implications of this. 'Does anyone else know about this?'

Toxique nodded. 'Brunholm and Devoy would both know. Toxiques have been coming to Wilsons for generations.'

'Does anyone else know that you're supposed to assassinate someone this term?' Les asked carefully.

'And did anybody see you, to provide an alibi for when the dart was fired?' Dixie said.

'Dixie!' said Danny.

'I'm only trying to keep him out of trouble,' Dixie protested.

'Shes right, you know,' Toxique said. 'I went for a walk in the woods yesterday afternoon. No one would have known where I was. And yes, my father wrote a letter to Devoy saying that there was no point in my training to be an assassin unless I got to actually kill someone and show off my skills. And now,' he said, using his Gift of Anticipation, 'I'm in trouble.'

The door burst open and Brunholm strode in. 'I heard about this dart, young man,' Brunholm said, 'the colours of Toxique. I demand an explanation.'

Toxique stood up. 'I am aware of that,' he said with great dignity, 'and I am also aware that the poison was probably manufactured by a Toxique, such was its purity.'

'So what's your defence then? I know you are

supposed to kill someone this term. Thought you'd try your hand at a poor defenceless Messenger, is that it?'

'My defence is this: the lady is still alive,' Toxique said.

'Meaning?' Brunholm said.

'Meaning that if the assassin had been a Toxique, she would be dead. A true Toxique never fails to kill.'

'That's the point,' Brunholm cried. 'A true Toxique! But are you a true Toxique or a reluctant one? That's the question!'

'Leave him alone,' Dixie said. 'Toxique doesn't tell lies.'

Brunholm's eyes glittered dangerously. 'I believe that punishment is called for in the family Toxique for failed assassinations?'

'Yes,' Toxique said unhappily.

'And if your family feels that this was a failed attempt, then it is their duty to carry out such a punishment?'

'You know a lot about my family,' Toxique said.

'The Wilsons library is full of books about the glorious history of the Toxique family,' Brunholm said. 'It is one of the most eminent names in the history of spies and assassins. They have never lowered their standards.'

'Then you know the punishment,' Toxique said heavily.

'Yes, and I know that in the past it has been carried out on the mere suspicion of a botched assassination.'

'That's true.'

'What is the punishment?' Les asked.

'Death,' Brunholm said.

'Slow and agonising death by poison,' Toxique said.

'No!' Dixie said. 'Specially when you didn't try to kill the Messenger in the first place!'

'When it comes to the family name,' Toxique said, 'fairness doesn't come into it.'

'You'd better hope that they don't get wind of this,' Brunholm said. 'Either that, or that we catch someone for throwing the darts.'

He glared at the cadets, then turned on his heel and stalked out of the infirmary.

'Phew,' Danny said. 'He wasn't too happy.'

'He'd better find out who did it,' Vandra said. 'I'm not going to be up to sucking any more poison for a while.'

Danny said nothing. He had seen Vandra's shudder at the words 'slow and agonising'.

Toxique lifted his head. 'Devoy's coming this way,' he said quietly.

A few seconds later the door opened and Devoy came in. He went straight to Vandra. 'The Apothecary has informed me of your condition,' he said, 'and has said that you are not yet well enough to leave your bed, so I will be carrying out your preparation for the mission in the infirmary. Mr Toxique and Mr Knutt, you will be good enough to excuse us?'

Toxique nodded and walked towards the door. Dixie squeezed his arm, and Danny winked at Les, who gave him a thumbs-up as he followed the dejected-looking Toxique.

8

A Crossbow of Exquisite Sensitivity

'Now,' Devoy said, 'we have received news of an incursion by Seraphim into the Upper World.'

Danny didn't notice the quick look that the Master cast in his direction before going on.

'This is evidence of their intentions with regard to the Upper World, and I think we can expect more of these types of raids, stretching the boundaries of the Treaty to the limit. The Treaty Stone is no longer safe in Morne and must be removed. The matter is now urgent.

'The last report I have of the kingdom of Morne is that it is located in a place called Tibet. Is that familiar to you, Danny?'

'Well . . . from books, yes . . .'

'Splendid. Then it shouldn't be too hard to find.' Danny shook his head. Was there any point in saying that Tibet was at the other end of the earth from where he lived? Or that it was a vast mountainous place where they spoke a different language and where strangers might not be all that welcome? But before Danny could voice his doubts, Devoy strode to the door and wrenched it open. Danny's heart sank. Les and Toxique were on their knees listening at the door. Devoy's voice was icy.

'Mr Knutt, Mr Toxique, eavesdroppping on a conference of this nature is a Tenth Regulation offence, verging on the Eleventh. These are matters of state!'

'What's an Eleventh Regulation offence?' Danny whispered.

'I don't know,' Dixie said. 'It must be terrible!'

'It's my fault, Master Devoy,' Toxique said, hanging his head.

'As if you were not in enough trouble, Mr Toxique.'

'It's his Gift of Anticipation!' Les said.

'Meaning what?' Devoy demanded.

'I was just leaving the room, when the gift told me that an untrue thing was about to be spoken.'

'An untrue thing?'

'I didn't know what it was at the start,' Toxique said miserably, 'so I listened in.'

'He only wanted to help,' Les said.

'Silence!' Devoy snapped. 'What was this untrue thing?'

'That the . . . the . . . kingdom of Morne was in Tibet.'

'What do you know about Morne?' Devoy said.

'N-nothing. I never even heard of it before now. It's the gift. Things just come into my head.'

'And what came into your head?'

'That the kingdom of Morne has moved to Ireland within the last few days.'

'Ireland!' Danny said. 'I know where that is as well, and it's a lot closer than Tibet.'

'I see,' Devoy said. 'And is your gift ever wrong?'

'Never,' Toxique whispered.

'Then,' Devoy said, 'I have to thank you, Mr Toxique, and I will exempt Mr Knutt from punishment as well, although I doubt whether his motives were as pure as yours. Please leave us now. I will know if you breathe a word about what you have heard here. And if it reaches my ears that you have broken your promise . . .'

'No, sir, we promise, never!' Les said, grabbing Toxique. 'Cross my heart and hope to die. Come on, Toxique . . .'

Les half dragged the trainee assassin away from the room. The door slammed.

'Please, Master Devoy,' Dixie said, 'what is an Eleventh Regulation offence? I thought they only went up to ten.'

Devoy gave her a long considering look, then clapped his hands briskly together. 'Now. Back to our mission. You know where this Ireland is, Danny?'

'Yes, sir. It's where I'm from. It's an island.'

'An island?' Devoy frowned. 'Do they have bridges or boats?'

'There's no bridge to Ireland, sir, but there are boats and . . .' He was going to mention aeroplanes, but he remembered how the Wilsons people had reacted to the idea of television.

'Wonderful,' Devoy said. 'I imagine it will be possible to steal one of these boats, or to bribe the ferryman.'

'You could do that,' Danny said, 'but you could always just pay the fare.'

'Pay the fare?' Devoy said suspiciously. 'You mean they would demand a terrible forfeit, perhaps a hold over your very soul?'

'Er, no,' Danny said. 'Usually a few coins, well, banknotes really.'

'It's almost too easy,' Devoy said. 'It might be a trap.'

'I don't think so,' Danny said, thinking of the huge ships that crossed the Irish Sea every day, carrying cars and trucks.

'We'll see,' Devoy said. 'It is a good thing that Morne has moved – it usually covers its movements by creating snowy conditions – look for snowstorms, or snow lying where it's normally rare.'

Danny suppressed a grin. The Wilsons people made fun of him when he tried to describe a television set, yet they talked without batting an eyelid about a secret kingdom that moved around the world.

'You will have to have local currency,' Devoy said. 'I gave Fairman some gold and asked him to change it for money from the Upper World.'

A suitcase stood unnoticed by the door. Devoy brought it over and opened it. Danny gulped. It was full of bundles of banknotes in different currencies – euro, dollars, pounds. There must have been tens of thousands of each.

'Is there a problem? Perhaps there isn't enough,' Devoy said. 'Fairman could always get some more.'

'No, no,' Danny said quickly. 'I think it'll be just enough.'

'Good,' Devoy said. 'Now, we have to talk about infiltration. You will be travelling in with Fairman. The problem is, where to take you to?'

'If we go as far as my house,' Danny heard himself saying, 'we can use that as a base and operate from there.'

'That sounds reasonable,' Devoy said, 'but what about your parents?'

Does he know that the people I live with are agents? Danny thought. Perhaps not. 'We'll say we're going on a study tour,' he said. 'They'll swallow that.'

'If you're sure,' Devoy said. 'Right, for the next few days we'll be working on your new identities. In the meantime, are there any questions?'

'What does the Treaty Stone look like?' Vandra asked.

'And how do we find it?' Dixie said.

'And steal it and carry it off? Danny said.

'Your questions are reasonable, and I wish I could answer them, but the truth is I can't. The Stone is held in Morne – we know that for sure – and will be protected. As to the rest, you'll have to find out for yourselves. Mr Brunholm will give you all the information we have on Morne itself. Now go back to the Roosts and get a good night's sleep. From now on you are on alert for the crossing into the Upper World. The crossing is difficult at the moment after the Seraphim incursion, and Fairman will not give us much notice when he decides it's time to go.'

They were tired when they left the infirmary, but there was to be no rest. They got back to the Roosts at ten o'clock to find Toxique sitting on his bed moaning about blood and death and, down the far end of the the boys' Roosts, Smyck and Exspectre with satisfied grins on their faces.

'What happened?' Danny asked.

'Smyck,' Les said with a moan. 'He found out about Toxique and the family punishment and everything. He's threatening to tell Toxique's dad about the failed assassination attempt and blame it on Toxique. And to make it worse, Toxique's dad is coming to Wilsons tomorrow!'

'How did he find out?' Dixie said.

'It was my fault,' Les said. 'I left the beetles in my locker and forgot to lock it. Smyck took them and hid one under my bed. I was trying to make Toxique feel better about everything, and Smyck heard it all!'

Danny swung round and looked at Smyck, who grinned and gave him a sarcastic thumbs-up. Danny strode towards him.

'Listen, Smyck,' he said, 'this is no joke. If Toxique's dad thinks that Toxique tried to assassinate someone and failed, then Toxique is in serious danger.'

'Yeah, sure,' Smyck said with a sneer. 'Toxique's always going on about blood and death and stuff like that. I bet nothing will happen to him. Whoever heard of a family killing their own son?'

'Whoever heard of a family of assassins either?' Danny said. 'You don't know what they might do.'

'In that case,' Smyck said, putting his face close to

Danny's, 'you'd better mind your manners, Caulfield, because the least squeak from any of you and I'm straight up to Toxique's old man to tell him how useless his son is.'

'If you do that . . .' Danny said, his fists clenched.

'You'll do what?' Smyck laughed, but he jumped back when Dixie appeared beside Danny.

'He'll get you,' she said calmly. 'After all, he always does, doesn't he, Smyck?'

Smyck threw his head back and laughed. 'He would have to be watched very carefully the following day.'

After Danny got into bed he whispered across to Les, 'Les, we've got preparation tomorrow for this mission. Can you trail Smyck?'

'Course I can.

The following morning both Roosts were late for class. Blackpitts must have slept in, for he didn't wake them until half an hour after their usual time. There was a chorus of displeasure directed at the unseen announcer and he was quite snappish back, saying that it was their own responsibility to get themselves up and he was only doing them a favour by calling them at all.

They rushed off to Ravensdale for breakfast, snatching up cold toast and dried-out pieces of bacon, and realising with dread that their first class that

117

morning was illegal entry with Exshaw, who had been known to use extreme force against latecomers.

As the other students darted off to class, Blackpitts directed the 'mission team' to Brunholm's quarters. There were startled and suspicious looks from the other students, who hadn't known about a mission. Les whispered a quick 'Good luck', and took off at a run, dragging Toxique behind him by the hand.

Danny and Dixie climbed the stairs towards Brunholm's quarters. They were in one of the oldest parts of the building. None of the dimly lit corridors were straight, mysterious doors and passages led off to all sides, disappearing into darkess. There were portraits of solemn men and women in black cloaks on the walls, some wearing a mask or holding the edge of their cloak across their face to conceal their identity. As they approached Brunholm's office Danny started to notice certificates on the wall, all belonging to Brunholm. A place known as the Institute of Advanced Surveillance was 'pleased to note' that Brunholm had acquired a 'distinction in miniature cameraship.' There were certificates and awards for 'Advanced Concealment of Weapons' and 'Intermediate Poisoncraft'.

'Nice bunch of awards,' Dixie said with a sniff as the passage grew darker, lit now only by flickering candles at great distances from each other. Finally they came to a door quilted in green leather. Above the door was a brass nameplate reading 'Marcus Brunholm, BRACS. TENS'. Danny raised his hand to knock, but the door swung open before he touched it.

'Very impressive,' Dixie said. 'It even creaked. I suppose we're meant to be spooked out.'

But Danny knew that Brunholm's parlour was spooky enough without ghostly creaky doors. He had sneaked into it with Les once before, and he recognised with a shiver the little jail cell where the siren Vicky had been held as part of one of Brunholm's schemes. The blowpipe and poison darts were still on the wall, though now in a locked glass case.

'Kind of feels like Brunholm in here,' Dixie said.

'I know what you mean,' Danny agreed. The furnishings were dark and ornate with lots of velvets and dark leather. There were paintings of sickly-looking flowers and a strong smell of cologne.

'It's the kind of room that if it was a person you wouldn't trust it, if you know what I'm saying,' Dixie said. Danny often couldn't follow Dixie's thought processes, but this time he nodded.

''Scuse me,' Dixie said, patting her stomach. 'That's what comes of bolting breakfast.'

Danny didn't hear it the first time, but it came again – a low moan.

'That wasn't me this time.' Dixie looked around. 'Where is Brunholm anyway?'

'It wasn't you the first time either,' Danny said, as the sound came again. 'Let's go.'

He led the way to the corridor which housed the teachers' bedrooms. Each shabby brown door bore a nameplate.

'They all sleep here?' Dixie said.

'So's they can keep an eye on each other, I expect,' Danny said. 'Here it is . . .' From behind a door with 'Master Marcus Brunholm' written on it in ornate swirling lettering they heard the moan again. Danny knocked tentatively, then harder. The moaning got louder.

'We'd better go in,' Danny said.

'Be careful . . .' Dixie warned as he opened the door and put his head into the room.

'Master Brun . . .' he began. In a tenth of a second his mind took in the scene. The floral wallpaper on the wall, the pink bedspread and the fluffy pillows plumped up on the bed. The cushioned bedhead with a terrified Brunholm spreadeagled against it, frozen to the spot, his eyes fixed on something on the dressing table, the moaning coming from a mouth that he seemed unable or unwilling to open. Danny's gaze took in the dressing table and the device that sat there, a silver machine about the size of a man's head with a bow resting horizontally across the top, two silvery antennae springing from it. As his gaze reached the device the antennae twitched and the whole apparatus swung towards him. Instinctively Danny pulled his head back and slammed the door just as something struck it with terrible power.

Danny gasped, his heart racing. 'What was that?'

Dixie was absently fingering what looked like the point of an arrow which had pierced the door from the other side. 'By the look of this,' she said, 'it's a Crossbow of Exquisite Sensitivity.' Danny stared at her. 'It's a what?'

'An automatic crossbow with a hair trigger. Once you set it up and activate it it's sensitive to any movement. If it detects the slightest twitch, it fires a crossbow bolt at the source.'

'That's why Brunholm was moaning,' Danny said. 'He didn't even dare open his mouth to call out.'

'He's a dead man,' Dixie said, with an air of finality (and not much in the way of regret).

'We can't let him be killed by that thing,' Danny said. 'We need him for the mission.'

'Is that all you need him for, Danny?' Dixie said, giving him a level look.

Danny didn't meet her eyes. Brunholm was completely without scruples, sly and selfish. All the attributes needed to be a truly successful spy. Part of

Danny, the part he didn't like to acknowledge, had a sneaking admiration for Brunholm, and his friends knew it. And every time Brunholm betrayed somebody or let them down, Danny learned something.

'How many arrows does it have?' Danny asked.

'Lots,' Dixie said. 'Lots and lots.'

'And how quick does it move?'

'No,' Dixie said firmly. 'Maybe for you or for Les, but not for Brunholm.'

'We need him, Dixie, whether you like it or not,' Danny said. 'And he will be grateful.'

'Sure,' Dixie said sarcastically. 'He's always grateful and really nice about things.'

Five minutes later Dixie pushed the door open and stood stock still in the doorway. The crossbow's antennae twitched as though suspicious. Dixie winked at it. Almost faster than the eye could see, the crossbow spun and fired an arrow straight at her. Dixie disappeared and reappeared beside a leopard-skin dressing gown on a stand at the other side of the room just as the arrow struck and stood quivering in the door frame.

'Every time she moves you move,' Danny shouted to the quivering Brunholm. Danny could see the interior of the room by looking at its reflection in the dressing-table mirror.

This time Dixie moved her hand and disappeared. The crossbow turned and fired as Brunholm threw himself to the floor and edged a few desperate inches forward. Dixie's next move got him to the shelter of the bed where he was able to crawl six feet without being seen by the crossbow. But in the meantime the machine appeared to have worked out what Dixie was doing. As she shuffled again and Brunholm gained a few more feet the crossbow moved with incredible speed, so fast that Danny had to wait for Dixie to reappear by the dressing table to see if she had escaped. The next time she disappeared without moving at all, yet the crossbow was able to discharge a shot as though it had read her mind. Brunholm was almost at the door. Dixie and Danny had agreed that for her last disappearance and appearance she would appear at the wardrobe close to the door.

'Okay,' Danny said to Brunholm. 'One . . . two . . .' As he completed his countdown a thought flashed through his head: *As if the crossbow could read her mind* . . . As the word 'three' left his mouth Danny grabbed a chair from the corridor and flung it into the air directly between the wardrobe and the crossbow. Three things happened very quickly: Dixie disappeared, Brunholm flung himself across the threshold and the crossbow swung round and fired an arrow straight at the wardrobe where Dixie was about to appear!

Danny saw as though in slow motion – Dixie appearing at the wardrobe, the arrow cleaving the air, its tip glittering. For a moment he thought all was lost, that the chair would fall too quickly! Just as Dixie's mouth made an O shape as she grasped what was happening, the arrow struck one chair leg, carrying it away and slamming the whole chair against the wall. In a flash Dixie disappeared and reappeared beside Danny, her breathing fast and shallow.

'It read my mind,' she gasped. 'It knew where I was going to reappear and it aimed for there.'

'Look at my chair,' Brunholm growled 'Best Chinese lacquerwork in that chair.'

'Don't say it,' Danny murmered to Dixie. 'Just don't say it!'

Without a backwards glance Brunholm strode towards the parlour, where he threw himself down in an armchair and, despite its being early, poured himself a large brandy from a decanter.

'Did you see anyone in the corridor when you came up?' he demanded. They shook their heads. 'Must have sneaked up on me when I was asleep,' he said. 'Damned cunning individual. I haven't seen a Crossbow of Exquisite Sensitivity in years. Blackpitts!' he shouted.

'Yes, Master Brunholm,' the announcer said sweetly. 'You called?'

'Get McGuinness up here at once,' he said, 'and inform Master Devoy that there's been another assassination attempt.'

'Another one?' Blackpitts said. 'How exciting!' Blackpitts loved gossip, and an attempted assassination was as juicy as it got.

'It's probably too late,' Brunholm said to the cadets. 'I can't imagine this character leaving any clues behind.'

They waited while Brunholm fetched some clothes from a closet marked Laundry. He went off up the corridor and emerged several minutes later fully dressed.

'Look!' Dixie said. She was by the window, pointing out. Danny went over and looked down. They were much higher up than he had expected, but Wilsons could deceive you like that. Down at the front door was a sleek black car. Beside the car stood Devoy and another man.

'Wait,' Danny said, digging in the pockets of his coat and producing a battered pair of binoculars. He focused on the man beside Devoy. He was wearing a suit and a black overcoat, and his hair was swept back. If you saw him in the street you wouldn't look twice, but Danny recognised the sallow skin and dark, deep-set eyes.

'Toxique's dad,' he said. 'We have to keep Smyck away from him!'

'Why would that be?' a quiet voice said behind them. They turned to see McGuinness.

Brunholm spoke before Danny could answer. 'Detective, I am glad to see you, though if you were doing your job I wouldn't have been put through this ordeal.'

'Ordeal?' McGuinness said.

'A Crossbow of Exquisite Sensitivity! In my bedroom!'

'Wait here,' McGuinness said, striding off down the corridor. A few minutes later he was back, the now silent crossbow in his hands.

'How did you do that?' Danny asked.

McGuinness looked bleakly at the device. 'Its secrets are not easily yielded. Many's the good man died learning all there is to know about the Crossbow of Exquisite Sensitivity.'

He placed the crossbow on a low coffee table. Danny stepped forward to look at it. It was beautifully made in silvery metal, with intricate springs and other mechanisms. When he touched it he could almost feel the coiled power of it.

'Who made it?' he asked.

'It is very old,' McGuinness said. 'It was made by the Cherbs, who were great craftsmen . . .'

That's enough of that foul object,' Brunholm broke in. 'Have you seen what it did to my bedroom? I can't think where I will find silk wallpaper to match what it ruined, not to mention my Chinese chair.'

Here he turned and gave Dixie a dirty look. McGuinness moved swiftly to Dixie's side.

'You're hurt,' he said. Blood was oozing from her blonde hair just above her left ear.

'It's nothing,' Dixie said. 'It nearly got me with the second-last arrow. It was almost like it could hear me thinking!'

McGuinness parted her hair and examined the wound.

'Inside pocket, just above the left breast,' he said to Danny without looking round. Danny fished in his pocket and brought out a battered tin with 'field dressings' written on it in felt-tip pen. He opened it and handed it to McGuinness, who took out a tube of foul-smelling paste and smeared a little on Dixie's wound.

'Arrow was probably poisoned,' Brunholm said. 'Cherb weapons usually are.'

'There was no poison used when that arrow was made,' McGuinness said, finishing off with a plaster. 'There now, but I wouldn't recommend any schoolwork for the rest of the day, and it would be better if Danny here kept her company, just in case of any adverse reaction.' McGuinness didn't exactly wink at Danny, but there was the suspicion of a twinkle in his eye.

'Of course, of course,' Brunholm said irritably, waving his hand at them before pouring himself another large brandy. 'I couldn't possibly teach them anything today.'

'Let's go,' Danny whispered, 'before he changes his mind.' He turned to thank McGuinness, but the detective was already on his hands and knees in the corridor, examining the floor through a large magnifying glass.

'This way,' Danny said quickly. 'I want to show you something.'

He led Dixie towards the front of the building. He intended to show her the room that he and Les had found when they had first come up to the masters' quarters, just as a curiosity, the way you would look at something gruesome in an old castle or museum, but as he stood before the nondescript door he felt a sudden reluctance.

'What is it?' Dixie asked.

'Nothing,' Danny said. 'We should go back.'

'Don't be silly,' Dixie said. 'Let's have a look.'

She took hold of the door handle and pushed. The door swung silently inward. Danny followed her in.

'What is . . . all this stuff?' Dixie whispered. The room was full of instruments of torture. There were racks and thumbscrews and devices for making you think you were drowning. There were whips and manacles and strange, cruelly shaped metal devices. And in one corner an iron maiden, a metal coffin in the shape of a human body, lined with iron spikes.

'It's a torture chamber,' Danny said, unable to hide his own horror. Last time he had been here the equipment had been dusty and covered with sheets. Now the sheets were gone and the instruments of torture were oiled and gleaming.

'I don't think I like the look of this,' Dixie said.

'Neither do I. Who would be preparing torture instruments? And why?'

9
A LOOPHOLE IN THE LAW

The following morning Danny and Dixie were summoned to Miss Duddy's room. Duddy taught camouflage, concealment and deception, and she was breathless with excitement at the idea of preparing them for the Upper World.

'I have consulted widely with my colleagues as to what might be appropriate,' she said, 'and I have selected some classic disguises for you. Now, Danny, please try this on.'

She produced a long blond wig, a kaftan, a pair of bell-bottoms and a string of beads.

'I believe the look is known as "the hippy", Duddy said, looking pleased with herself. Danny groaned inwardly.

'You will be almost invisible,' Duddy went on. 'You'll blend into any crowd.'

Duddy handed Dixie a long afghan coat, a flowery skirt and a headband. Dixie slipped on the coat and did a twirl.

'Vandra isn't here,' Duddy said, 'but I think I've picked out a look that will make her totally inconspicuous. Danny shook his head as Duddy took out a pink Mohican wig, a torn T-shirt and a biker jacket.

'This is the "punk" look, which I believe is common in the Upper World,' Duddy said. 'I have some make-up to go with it. Her teeth will be part of the look.'

Dixie grabbed the pink mohican wig and stuck it on her head.

'Ye-ess . . .' Duddy said, 'I do believe you can mix the two looks.' Danny despaired silently. How would they stay undercover in the Upper World?

'These are only a sample of the garments I have prepared,' Duddy said, 'but you can look at the others later.'

'We'll look at them now,' Danny said firmly, picking out jeans and T-shirts for them all.

To be fair to Duddy, Danny thought afterwards, she did provide useful aids to their mission. She gave them a selection of voice dyes – sprays that would change your voice to make it unrecognisable – as well as a small packet of warts and boils. Dixie turned up her nose at them but Duddy looked serious.

'A wart or a boil on your face draws attention away

from their other characteristics,' she said. 'Often a witness can only remember the gross feature.'

There were hair dyes, artificial eyebrows and various items of make-up for the girls.

'Now, Danny,' Duddy said at the end, 'there is one important thing remaining: your eyes. Everyone will recognise and remember you unless we do something about them.'

'I could wear dark glasses,' Danny suggested.

'Not at night,' Duddy said. 'No, that would not be very satisfactory. There are semi-permanent eyeball inks. They involve first removing the eyeball and rolling it in the ink—'

'No!' Danny gasped.

'No,' Duddy said. 'It takes a good deal of time for the inflammation and swelling to go down. No, we'll have to go with a simple membrane.'

'You mean like a contact lens?' Danny said, relieved.

'I don't know what you're talking about, but if it's anything like a coloured organic membrane placed over the lens of the eye, then you are right.'

Duddy brought them into the empty classroom and sat them down. Her face was serious.

'This is a deadly mission you are embarking on,' she said, 'and I wish I was going with you to share my skills. But obviously I can't. So you must remember the important principles: don't draw attention to yourself; remember that things or people hidden in plain view are often the last to be discovered; think stealth, think concealment. The greatest spies did not need disguises. They knew how to direct attention away from themselves. The great Steff Pilkington himself could move undiscovered among a group of his closest colleagues, avoiding their attention by studying how they reacted to others. "Keep it simple, keep it safe" is my motto. Good luck!' Duddy shot to her feet, saluted smartly, then turned away, took a large handkerchief from her pocket and blew her nose loudly.

Dixie and Danny looked at each other. Dixie made a face, but Danny was touched by their teacher's heartfelt emotion.

'Steady on, miss,' Dixie said. 'We won't be setting out for a while.'

'You never know,' Duddy murmured. 'Things happen quickly in the spy business.'

Things did indeed happen quickly in the spy business. Ten miles away, on the road leading to Wilsons from Tarnstone, a small black car took a bend at top speed, the rear of the car sliding out before the driver regained control. Behind it came a black Jeep, swaying as it rounded the same corner, its powerful engine roaring as it gained on the smaller car.

The Jeep was full of men, roughnecks and renegades from the port. They had been sent to intercept the driver of the car at the docks as she disembarked from a ship arrived from Grist, the great fortress of the Cherbs. She had given them the slip there, but they were gaining on her. She was taking risks with the small underpowered car, and had almost crashed several times. But she had news that would not wait. She knew she must get through.

As the Jeep closed on her she cursed her luck. For many years she had posed as a man and used the identity of John Starling, a trader, to get in and out of Grist. She had suspected that that identity had been compromised, but she had used it one last time. But one of the agents of the Ring had recognised her on board ship. It had been a close thing to get out of the town, but would she reach Wilsons?

Behind her the front of the Jeep loomed over the back of the small car. The Jeep engine roared. She realised it was going to ram. She spun the wheel to the left. The front of the Jeep dealt a glancing blow to her rear bumper and she fought the wheel to stay on the road. A piece of bodywork fell off and clattered on the tarmac. At the same time there was a bang, and she heard a thud as a bullet embedded itself somewhere in her car. Frantically she looked around for help. There was nothing . . . except for a small figure making its way nonchalantly along the side of the road. As she got closer she recognised Vicky the siren, who was watching the events with interest.

Starling leaned out of the open window as she drew level with the siren. 'Vicky,' she shouted, 'anything you want if you get rid of them!'

'Anything?' Vicky shouted back.

'Anything!'

The rear windscreen shattered as another shot struck it, and bullets churned up the tarmac beside her as a machine gun chattered. Through the broken rear glass she saw the Jeep lining itself up. Steam started to stream from her car's engine. But as the noise of the Jeep's engine became almost unbearably loud, another sound crept in, a voice, almost unbearably sweet and sad, speaking, it seemed, of a heart broken by terrible sorrow, yet capable of infinite love. Starling scrumpled some tissues and rammed one in each ear. She knew a siren's song when she heard it, its endlessly seductive tones, and she had already lifted her foot from the floor, the song drawing her back towards its source.

Behind her the Jeep had slowed and had started to veer towards the side of the road. As she watched it slowed almost to a halt, before coming to rest with both of its front wheels in a ditch. The men got out, moving as if in a dream, happy smiles on their ugly faces as they turned towards the unbearably sweet song coming from the little siren who stood in the middle of the road. She was beckoning to them with her hands but her eyes were on Starling, reminding her that a promise made to a siren was not easily broken. Starling shrugged. There would be time to deal with Vicky later. For the moment she had to get her intellignce to Wilsons.

Two hours later she stood in Devoy's study, watching the Master digest what she had told him.

'You are absolutely sure,' Devoy said, 'that it's not some information that has been fed to you for their own purposes.'

'I have been spying on the enemy for many years,' Starling said stiffly. 'I am aware of their ruses.' She did not have to say that she had put her life on the line many times. Devoy acknowledged this with a graceful nod. There was the sound of feet on the stairs outside and Brunholm burst in.

'I have to presume you have heard of the disgraceful attempt on my life . . .' he burst out before seeing Starling.

'Ah yes, the Crossbow of Exquisite Sensitivity,'

Devoy said. 'I am glad to see you hale and hearty, Marcus.'

Brunholm's desire to tell Devoy in great detail about his own courage and grace under pressure that morning struggled with his curiosity as to why a pale-looking Starling was standing in the Master's study.

'We really need to devise a strategy to protect key staff members from attack,' he said, flinging himself down in an armchair, before adding churlishly, 'What's she doing here?'

'She has travelled in great peril from the fortress of Grist,' Devoy said, 'to bring us some alarming news.'

'What?' Brunholm said, his eyes narrowing. He didn't like others having information that had not first come through him.

'I'm afraid the Ring of Five have happened on the loophole in the law.'

'They have picked a team of cadets, under-sixteens, to travel to the kingdom of Morne,' Starling said. 'Apparently to study, but of course their real aim is to steal and break the Treaty Stone.'

'According to Starling,' Devoy said, 'they have already departed. There is not a moment to lose.'

'Do we know who these agents are?' Brunholm asked.

'No,' Starling said wearily. 'I barely escaped with my life with the information that I got.'

'And grateful for that they are, aren't you, gentlemen?' A quiet voice spoke from the doorway. It was the detective McGuinness. He strode forward and took hold of Starling's arm, for the detective and the spy were husband and wife.

'She will come with me now,' McGuinness said, pulling her to him. 'She is exhausted.'

'And has earned whatever poor reward we can give her,' Devoy said. 'The information she has brought is priceless, and we are indeed grateful.' He bowed graciously as McGuinness and Starling withdrew. But the moment the door had closed behind them Brunholm whirled round in a fury.

'How did they know that under-sixteens were exempt from the death sentence?'

'Longford is clever, more clever and more ruthless than I,' Devoy said. 'There is a logic to it. Even in the bitterest of times there was always a door left open for education, that the young might learn from the mistakes of the past and make a better future.'

'He seems to know everything that goes on in Wilsons,' Brunholm snarled.

'He is a spy,' Devoy said. 'That's his job. In the meantime we must send out our team straightaway. Tonight if possible.'

'They're not ready!' Brunholm cried. 'Besides, the Physick is still recovering.'

'Then Danny and the girl must go,' Devoy said. 'Longford's team have a head start. Have you sent word to Morne to expect them?'

'Yes, of course,' Brunholm said, 'but what about Fairman? Can he take them across?'

'Certainly,' Devoy said. 'Do you not think I know about your smuggling runs, and how you pay Fairman to do your dirty work? At this very moment he is waiting at the back of the building ready to embark on some mission that I am not supposed to know about!'

Brunholm looked abashed. According to the terms of the Treaty, Fairman's taxi was the only vehicle allowed to cross the border. Brunholm had his spies in the Upper World, and he often used the taxi to carry messages and other things for him.

'The Treaty forbids the living from crossing the border,' Fairman had said to him once. 'It says nothing about the dead.'

'Now that we have established that we have the transport,' Devoy said, 'we should assemble our team.'

Danny and Dixie were both awoken by the announcer Blackpitts hissing at them in a stage whisper.

'Cadet Caulfield! Cadet Cole! Library of the third landing in five minutes!'

Danny rolled out of bed and looked over the top of the partition that divided his sleeping quarters from Les's. Despite Blackpitts, his winged friend was still asleep. Danny pulled on his trousers, jumper and battered overcoat. He crept steadily towards the door. Les would be wounded if he knew that Danny had not at least woken him to tell him about the midnight call. Danny groaned inwardly. Would the impulse to betray never leave him?

In actual fact he needn't have worried. Les had been woken by Blackpitts's voice and had pretended to be asleep while Danny had crept out. Then he slid out of bed, shoving his pillows under his blankets in case Exspectre or one of the others looked in the room. Only one event would have led Devoy to summon Danny and Dixie in the middle of the night. The mission was on.

Thirty minutes later a very sleepy Danny and an overexcited Dixie were standing in the library of the third landing while Devoy briefed them on Starling's information. Danny shivered. For some reason it was less frightening to take on adults than it was people his own age.

'Can you tell us anything about the enemy team?' he asked Devoy.

'Nothing,' the Master said, 'except that if they were chosen by Longford they will be resourceful and dangerous.'

'That's nice to know,' Dixie said.

'Hurry,' Brunholm broke in. 'Fairman tells me that he brought students across the border from Grist twenty-four hours ago. There were two of them, a girl and a boy.'

A flustered-looking Duddy burst into the room. She was wearing pink flannelette pyjamas and fluffy slippers.

'This is most unusual,' she said. '*Most* unusual!'

'You must work on Danny's eyes at once,' Devoy said.

'But my lovely disguises!' Duddy cried.

'There is no time.' Devoy's voice was like a pistol shot. 'The fate of Wilsons hangs in the balance.'

The detective McGuinness made a meal for Starling and waited until she had gone to bed before he left. She had told him what she had learned, and he knew that there would be activity in Wilsons until late at night. He crossed the gardens quietly and found a favourite vantage point in the shrubbery from which he could watch.

It was cold, but he hadn't long to wait before a stealthy figure crept across the front of the building.

McGuinness reached into his pocket for a long-barrelled revolver and set out in pursuit.

Five minutes later he found himself at the back of the Wilsons building, outside a disused kitchen annex. It was a half-collapsed wooden hut, with old crates, junk and scaffolding piled around. Hidden among the debris stood an old black taxi, the engine rumbling. The stealthy form made straight for the taxi, and McGuinness set a course to head it off. The figure reached the boot of the cab. There was a flash of tools, then the boot opened silently. The person lifted a leg as if to climb in. McGuinness, who had approached equally stealthily, put the gun to the figure's head.

'Move a muscle and you won't see tomorrow,' he said. A frightened face turned towards him. It was Les.

'Do you have any idea what Fairman would have done to you, if and when he found a stowaway?' McGuinness said. They were sitting on two old oil drums at a safe distance from the taxi.

'I wanted to go on the mission,' Les said sulkily. 'I pretended I didn't care but I did.'

'Stop that,' McGuinness said sharply. 'You're not a child, and the fate of Wilsons and possibly the two worlds hangs in the balance.

'But I could have helped!' Les said.

'You can help more here,' McGuinness said. 'Do you know that your friend Toxique is in danger? His father thinks that it was he who tried to kill the Messenger and failed. Who will help clear him if you do not? And Vandra – would you leave her alone in Wilsons in a time of deadly peril? You are needed right here, Les. Let the others go. There will be enough danger here, enough for us all.'

10
A TRAP SPRUNG

The membrane to disguise the colour of Danny's eyes was surprisingly comfortable. He hardly knew that it was there, although when Duddy said it was made of 'fish intestine marinated in cuttlefish ink' Dixie made a face and mimed throwing up in the corner.

'There is only one thing that you have to remember,' Duddy said. 'You absolutely must not cry. The concentrated salt in the tears will dissolve the membrane.'

'Don't forget,' Devoy said, 'you are exchange students. I wish we had more information to give you on the kingdom of Morne, but all I can say is that it was known as a place of intrigue and some little danger, although there are dire warnings in the Treaty about how students should be looked after. There is some protection in that.'

Danny and Dixie were given an hour to put a bag together. They raced back to the Roosts. All the other pupils were asleep. When Danny had grabbed his toothbrush he went to Les's cubicle to find the bed empty, pillows under the blankets.

That's odd, he thought.

'Perhaps he's gone to the infirmary to see Vandra,' Dixie said when he met her outside.

'We've just got time to get there,' he said. 'I want to see Vandra before we go anyway.' They raced off.

Les knew Danny and Dixie would not go without seeing Vandra, so when he left McGuinness he made his way to the Apothecary's. It was dark and spooky as he mounted the stairs. In the anteroom he could see the dim shapes of organs and other anatomical specimens preserved in jars. Above his head the vast skeleton of a Messenger, hung from wires as though in flight, cast a sinister shadow on the tiled floor. Les moved quietly, lost in thought, considering the detective's advice. Ever since he'd heard that the others were to be sent on a mission he had plotted and planned and listened at doors, knowing that Fairman was the only way they could cross the border, and figuring out how he would sneak along and appear triumphantly when they had arrived in the Upper World. That wasn't going to happen now, he thought bitterly. He would never get the chance to see the Upper World.

He was so lost in thought that he forgot to turn on the light when he got to the ward where Vandra was sleeping. The Messenger was light-footed and made little noise as he crossed the floor. It was only at the last minute that the figure crouched over Vandra with a pillow in his hands realised that Les was there. Whoever it was ran straight at him. Les threw himself aside as a knife flashed in the darkness. He hit the flagstone floor hard and felt the air being forced from his lungs. He was winded, helpless, his lungs on fire as he gasped for breath, but his attacker did not stop, fleeing into the night.

As he gradually got his breath and attempted to sit up he caught a fleeting hint of a scent, an expensive aftershave perhaps, hanging in the night air. He forced himself to his feet and stumbled over to Vandra's bed. She was still sleeping peacefully. He bent to pick up the pillow that the attacker had dropped. There was a strong medicinal smell, and the minute he bent to it his head began to swim. He staggered backwards, into the arms of the Apothecary, Mr Jamshid. The small man, wearing heavy glasses and a white coat stained with nameless matter, caught Les with one hand and the pillow with the other. A frown wrinkled his large domed forehead and he flung the pillow with great force across the room and into the embers in the hearth.

The fire blazed up, huge flames and great gouts of black and dirty green smoke billowing up the chimney.

'Psychochloroform,' the small man spat, 'deadly in twenty seconds. The victim never wakes up. Give me one reason why I should not slit your throat here and now!'

'It . . . it . . . wasn't me,' Les gasped. 'Someone was going to hold it over Vandra's face!'

'Are you sure?' Jamshid said. 'It's a long time since I dissected the corpse of a Messenger.'

'I'm sure!' Danny's voice rang out. 'Les would never hurt Vandra.'

Dixie, who was beside Danny, disappeared and reappeared between Jamshid and Les, pressed tight up against the Apothecary on an eye level with the larger stains on his coat.

'Interesting,' she said, studying something green and globular adhering to his lapel.

'If you insist,' Jamshid said coldly, releasing Les.

'What happened?' Danny asked.

Les quickly explained what he had seen.

'Death is stalking this place,' Jamshid said darkly, sounding like Toxique. As if to underline his words, a raven fluttered across the light and disappeared into the shadows of the roof.

'Whoever it is must know Wilsons like the back

of their hand,' Danny said. 'They're able to get about without anyone seeing them.'

'But why Vandra?' Les said.

'Because if I was planning to poison people in Wilsons,' Danny said, 'I'd make sure the only Physick in the place was out of the way.'

He realised that his voice had taken on an edge and the others were looking at him strangely. There was a harsh, almost eager tone, as though the dark side of his nature had taken over and it relished the very wickedness of the plan.

'We have to stop him, I mean,' he stammered.

Dixie looked at him with one eyebrow raised.

'I'm sorry,' he said. 'I tried to fool you. I should have said we were going on the mission – it's been brought forward.'

'That's all right,' Les said. 'I was intending to sneak along with you from the start, only I got caught. Mr McGuinness says that Toxique and Vandra need to be looked after, and he's right. You two go on your own.'

Dixie hugged him.

Les grinned at Danny. 'You take care of him, Dixie,' he said. 'He thinks he's the most cunning of the lot, but I know different.'

Les looked suspiciously like he was going to give Danny a hug too, but to Danny's relief Blackpitts interrupted.

'Caulfield, Cole, at once!'

Danny glanced down at Vandra. She looked so young and vulnerable. Without really knowing what he was doing he took the gold ring out of his pocket, the ring that the Dead had given him. Without the others noticing, he slipped it on to her finger.

'*Look after her,*' he whispered, not knowing whether he spoke to the Dead or some other being. With a last glance at her face, he turned to Dixie.

'Let's go,' he said.

Les and the Apothecary stood looking after them.

'Hope they make it,' Les said.

'You think they won't?' the Apothecary said anxiously. 'I couldn't bear it if Caulfield was killed somewhere else. He's a promising specimen – I'm very much looking forward to dissecting his corpse.' The Apothecary turned to face Les. 'Don't look at me like that, young Messenger. They say he is the Fifth. Is it not likely in these turbulent times that many will wish him dead? All I want is that if he is assassinated I get the chance to use my knives on him in the interests of science . . .'

Les gave the man a disgusted look and hurried from the room. Things were bad enough already, without all this talk of assassination. He would spend the night in the summerhouse, his refuge when he didn't want to talk to anyone. He went outside and turned left at the shrubbery.

At least everybody's asleep, he thought as he followed the path towards the summerhouse, yawning as he went.

Danny and Dixie were at the back of the college with Devoy, nervously waiting for Fairman, but they were not the only souls awake. The door of the boys' Roosts opened without a sound and a figure in a trenchcoat slipped in, closing the door behind him. The fire in the stove had died down and the room was dark, but the tall man moved cat-like down the centre of the room. He stopped at the cubicle where Les slept and swiftly drew a gun from his shoulder holster, a gun equipped with a bulbous silencer. He aimed it at what he thought was the sleeping Les and squeezed the trigger three times, each shot sounding like a muffled cough, three small holes appearing in the blanket at chest height. Silently the Unknown Spy holstered his gun and slipped quietly from the room. He might have forgotten his name, but he had forgotten none of his skills. His wife had been avenged.

Danny watched Fairman's taxi approach.

'I sent you out once before,' Devoy said, 'withholding much of what I knew about what you would be facing. This is different. No one now lives who knows much of the kingdom of Morne. We do know that it is always hidden by extreme weather, so look for great storms, floods and other natural phenomena. Protect the Treaty Stone if you can, steal it if you must, but do not let it be broken!'

The taxi rattled to a stop. Devoy opened the back door. The pair threw their bags in and climbed in after them.

'I have told Fairman to bring you to your house,' Devoy said. 'At least you know the territory there. After that you're on your own.'

Danny was going to object, but stopped. The people he had known as his parents had cheated him, yet one part of him yearned to see them, while another part longed for revenge.

'Go with care,' Devoy cried, 'go like shadows in the night, go like spies.'

The cab engine roared. Dirty smoke billowed from the exhaust. The cab trundled off into the night, merging with the darkness all around.

Many miles away in the fortress of Grist, deep in the Lower World, Ambrose Longford reached for the decanter and poured another glass of honey-coloured dessert wine for Nurse Flanagan. The remains of a meal sat on the table in front of them. Longford lit a cigar from the candelabrum on the table.

'Is the trap sprung?' Nurse Flanagan enquired languidly.

'I believe so.'

'Conal was a fool sending Seraphim to attack the boy's house,' Nurse Flanagan said. 'Everything could have been lost.'

'Perhaps,' Longford said, 'but it keeps the Cherbs in line – they now know that brute force is not the way.'

'No,' Nurse Flanagan said, raising her glass. 'Your way is always the best, Ambrose – subtle and devious.'

'A compliment indeed,' Longford said, raising his own glass in return.

'We shall have the boy this time,' Nurse Flanagan said, 'and the Treaty will be broken.'

'Even though I say so myself,' Longford said complacently, 'it is an excellent idea.'

11

Macari's Original! Really Nourishing and Excellent!

The taxi hurtled throught the night, swaying from side to side and jolting. Dixie tried to engage Fairman in conversation, but gave up after ten minutes of grunts.

'Where are we?' she asked Danny, peering through the glass into the darkness beyond.

'I think they're called the Darklands,' Danny said. He had made the journey before and knew it was long and uncomfortable. He wedged himself into a corner and tried to doze. But in a few hours he would be back home, facing the people who had pretended to be his parents. Dangerous as Wilsons was becoming, he began to long for its shadowy halls.

'I like adventures,' Dixie said. 'Do you like adventures? I think they're the best thing in the whole world.'

'Put a sock in it, Dixie,' Danny said. 'I know you're excited, but there's a limit.'

On and on the journey went, the back of the ancient cab getting colder as the night went on. Danny was warm in his trenchcoat but he could see his breath in the air, and Dixie's lips were turning blue. He took the coat off and spread it over both of them.

'That's cosy,' Dixie said. 'Do I get a story?'

'I don't have any good stories,' Danny said shortly. Suddenly Dixie sat bolt upright.

'You're going to Morne as a student of the Lower World, aren't you?'

'Yes.'

'But they forgot to tell me what I'm supposed to be a student of!'

'You'll think of something,' Danny said.

Dixie stared out of the window, frowning.

'I know,' she said. 'I'll be a student of the Upper World! So tell me about the Upper World then.'

So Danny told her everything he could think of, including cars and planes and telephones and televisions, and Dixie's eyes grew wider and wider, her expression more and more childlike. When he told her about tanks and warplanes and atom bombs her hand crept out from under her blanket and took his.

'Do people in your world really do such terrible things?' she asked. 'Please don't tell me any more.'

In a moment she was asleep. It took Danny a lot longer, but in the end he too was lulled by the endless motion of the cab.

They were awakened with a jolt that threw them forward so that they slid off the seats and on to the floor.

'What . . . ?' Danny cried as his head slipped into the foul-smelling space under the seats, Dixie on top of him. Daylight and cold air flooded in as the door beside him opened. With a groan he straightened and crawled from the cab, Dixie tumbling behind him. He raised his head and found himself staring at the front of his house, or at least something which resembled his house. The whole front wall was scorched, the brickwork hacked as if by tearing claws. The slates had been blasted from the roof. The snow still lay deep on the ground.

There was a thud as their bags hit the ground beside them. They looked up. It was the first time Dixie had seen the dark caverns that were Fairman's eyes, and she flinched. The cab driver bared his great yellow teeth. 'You're here,' he growled. He clambered back into the cab and sped off, soon becoming a tiny spot in the distance.

'Doesn't look like there's anyone here,' said Dixie, and Danny felt a chill.

Then, 'Look,' Dixie said, reaching up and taking down a huge feather stuck in a crack of the wall. She smelled it and shivered.

'Seraphim?' Danny said.

'Conal,' she replied.

Cautiously they stepped through the wreckage and into the main body of the house. Leaves blew along the corridors and everywhere there were signs of the Seraphim's attack, for they had smashed things wantonly as they went.

They had just reached the hallway when a familiar voice rang out.

'Stop right there or you're dead.'

'It's me,' Danny said. 'It's me – Danny!' He almost added 'Mum' to the sentence, and felt sadness wash over him. He was shaken out of his sorrow by a loud crack. A splinter of wood flew from the door frame beside him and scored his cheek.

'Hit the deck!' Dixie yelled. 'She means it.'

Danny dived for cover as another shot whistled over his head.

'It's me, Danny!' he shouted again.

'It's enough that he's gone, without being taunted about it.'

He lifted his head and saw his mother in the door of the downstairs bedroom. Her face was gaunt, the cool poised woman he remembered was gone.

'It's me, Danny.'

She did not lower the gun. Danny raised his head.

'Danny, don't!' Dixie warned. But Danny slowly stood up, his eyes on the barrel of the gun.

'It looks like Danny,' the woman said, as if to herself, 'but the eyes . . .'

'It's a trick,' he said. 'Look.' He bowed his head and blinked hard to let the membrane fall into his hand.

'Danny . . .' the woman breathed. She dropped the gun and ran forward, and for a moment it was as if they were truly mother and son.

Fifteen minutes later they were sitting on a scorched sofa in front of a fire made from broken-up dining-room chairs. Dixie had found a saucepan and was busy boiling water for tea over the flames while Agent Pearl told them what had happened since Danny had left. Dixie and Danny exchanged a glance when they heard about the attack by the Seraphim and how they'd been repulsed by the ravens. Agent Stone's wound had got worse. For days he had hovered between life and death while Pearl tended to him, and when he slept she guarded the house, dreading the return of the Seraphim.

Now, she said, he was weak but recovering. 'He sleeps for most of the day, but he'll be so glad to see you, Danny.'

Danny looked away. Part of him wanted to put his arms around her; part of him wanted to wound her, to repay betrayal with betrayal.

'But there are other things to talk about,' Pearl said.

Danny glanced sharply at her.

'We have had no communication from the outside world. We used to be summoned regularly to meetings to report on you, Danny, but recently we have heard nothing. The radio speaks of a big freeze. The schools and airports are closed. They are even saying that the sea is turning to ice in places. We have to do something.'

'It's a pity you have to wait to hear from your handlers so that you know what to do with me.'

'I didn't mean that,' Pearl said. 'I meant that there could be danger here for you . . . for all of us.'

Dixie's eyes flickered from one to the other, her face serious for once. 'You should listen, Danny,' she said.

Danny's eyes flashed.

'The cold seems to be centred in the mountains about twenty miles north of here,' Pearl said.

158

'Then that's where we need to be,' Danny said. 'That will be where Morne is currently located.'

'Is that where the Fifth needs to be?' another voice asked.

Danny stood up and spun round. Agent Stone stood in the doorway. His shoulder was heavily bandaged and his face was the colour of parchment, but his voice was strong.

'What do you know of the Fifth, and the . . . ?' Danny stopped.

'The Lower World? Only a little – what I could find in old books and manuscripts. Much of the team couldn't accept that such a world existed in tandem with ours. Sometimes it seemed like a dream, even to me.'

Stone shuffled further into the room, grimacing.

'Then I saw them! Those wonderful Seraphim! So much more dramatic than they ever looked in the old paintings.'

'They don't smell too wonderful close up,' Dixie said.

'Allow me to introduce you, Dixie,' Danny said sarcastically. 'This is the man who pretended to be my father.'

'I don't blame you for being bitter, Danny,' Stone said, moving into the circle of the fire, 'but the truth is, we did come to think of you as our own.'

'When you were here,' Danny said.

'Your fa . . . Agent Stone spent all his time in old libraries and research centres trying to find out who or what you were,' Pearl said.

'And Pearl spent weary days and nights protecting you, seeking to learn about those who gave us the mission of looking after you, and why. Do not judge things you don't know, Danny.'

Danny wanted to reply but a small cold voice told him not to. *There will be time to show them what you know and don't know*, it was saying.

'Anyway, Danny,' Stone went on after a moment, 'I had started to disbelieve the whole idea of the Lower World, when I saw the Seraphim and knew my theory was correct. There *is* a Ring of Five and there *is* a Fifth!'

Danny looked at him. How much more did he know about him? Pearl held up a hand. They listened. In the distance there was the faint hum of an engine.

Pearl went to the window and peered out. 'I spoke too soon about our not having contact with our handlers,' she said. 'They're coming for us.'

'Whatever happens,' Stone said heavily, 'they mustn't find Danny.'

Danny went to the window and looked out. Two Jeeps were coming down the snowy road. Both carried hard-faced men with guns.

'I'll hold them off,' Pearl said. 'There's a Land Rover in the garage. Can either of you drive?'

'I can,' Dixie said, to Danny's surprise, 'but we're not leaving you behind.'

'Don't be stupid,' Pearl said. 'What can you do?'

In answer Dixie disappeared and reappeared at the other side of the room.

Pearl blinked and looked confused, but Stone muttered to himself, 'The quality of Indeterminate Location. Staggering.'

'Staggering it might be, but it won't stop a bullet,' Pearl said. 'Get going.'

Danny didn't move. There was so much more he wanted to know, but Dixie was pulling at his sleeve. 'The Treaty Stone is more important.'

Danny saw Pearl taking up a firing position by the window, Stone struggling painfully to join her. Abandon them and they'll die, he thought. Exactly! The word came from another part of his brain.

'Okay,' he said, 'come on.' And without a glance back at the man and woman who had been the only parents he'd ever known he stalked out of the door.

Dixie hesitated, then followed. At the door she turned. Pearl was looking at her.

'One day he'll understand,' Pearl said sadly. 'Look after him. Remember the Ring has its agents in the Upper World as well.'

As Dixie and Danny ran for the garage they heard gunfire behind them. Dixie paused, but Danny grabbed her.

'Come on!' he said. 'Leave them to it. It's what they deserve!'

'They're giving you a chance to get away. You should be grateful.'

'They're giving me a chance to put myself in the way of even more danger,' Danny snarled. 'I don't have to thank them for that!' For a moment he looked as if the harsh Cherb part of his nature had taken over.

They wrenched open the garage doors as a line of bullets stitched up the snow beside them.

'Quick!' Dixie scrambled into the driver's seat and looked blankly at the controls. 'It looks different!'

Danny leaned over and turned the key. The engine caught as wood splinters cascaded from the walls of the shed, torn by bullets. Then the engine roared to life.

'We can't go out the front,' Danny said. That wasn't to be a problem. Dixie pulled at the gear lever and stamped on the pedals. The Land Rover shot backwards. With a great rending noise the back of the garage collapsed and the vehicle shot through into the snow. Dixie pulled at the gear lever again. With a gout of black smoke from the exhaust, the Land Rover started to move forward. More bullets struck the garage and flames started to lick at it. Dixie gunned the engine and the tyres dug into the hard-frozen ice on the road. Lurching at first, then building up speed, the Land Rover pulled away from the house. Looking back, Danny could see orange muzzle flashes, then drifting black smoke from the burning garage obscured the battle.

Dixie knew how to point the Land Rover in the right direction and put her feet on the pedals, but she didn't know anything else. She gripped the wheel determinedly, oblivious to street signs and road markings, and Danny was glad there was no other traffic about. As the Land Rover ate up the miles, Danny forced himself to think about what might be waiting ahead.

'Stupid,' Dixie said.

'What?' Danny said.

'Not you. Me. We don't know where we're going, but I have the Globe – the GIPIEP. Take it out!'

Danny rummaged in her bag until he found the Globe. Instantly two tiny figures appeared on it, moving side by side, as they were in the Land Rover.

'I wonder . . .' Danny said.

'Wonder? Of course you wonder. We all wonder what's going on,' Dixie said.

'That wasn't what I meant,' Danny said. He held the Globe up and spoke into it.

'The kingdom of Morne!' he said. For a moment nothing happened. Then the Globe darkened as though a tiny storm blew through it. When it cleared Danny could see the two figures again, and in front of them a tiny castle. The kingdom!

'Up there,' Danny said, pointing into the distance where the peaks of a mountain range were obscured by sullen snow clouds. 'That must be it!'

A few minutes later they met their first car, crawling through the snow. Dixie waved vigorously at its driver, so vigorously that the Land Rover brushed against a lamp post.

'Keep your eyes on the road, Dixie,' Danny said.

'I am,' she said happily, bumping over a footpath and narrowly missing a post box. They were in the suburbs of a small town now, and the next hour was a nightmare as Dixie drove through red lights, veered on to footpaths and, when she spotted a playground, drove straight through it, waving happily at the small band of bemused children who had braved the weather. Danny was convinced that they would have been arrested if it wasn't for the fact that the police had more to do than worry about terrible driving.

Blizzards and fallen power lines had resulted in an evacuation of the area at the foot of the mountains and housing had to be found for all the displaced people. The police were busy dealing with the refugee camps that had sprung up in the town centre.

Danny struggled to stop Dixie being distracted by flashing shop signs and people walking dogs – all normal things to him, but which Dixie had never seen before. Her delight and surprise contrasted with Danny's mood as he twisted in his seat to look back towards a gunfight that he could not possibly see. So he didn't notice the police barrier at the edge of town, warning of the dangers of the snowy roads ahead. He turned just as the front bumper of the Land Rover caught the barrier and crashed straight over it.

'Now the front is as battered as the back,' Dixie said with a dizzy grin as they passed a sign saying 'Newcastle 10', and she gunned the Land Rover towards the evacuated town.

The town of Newcastle lay between the sea and the mountains. It looked as if it had once been a holiday resort, but had fallen on hard times. There were closed amusement parks on the seafront, and a frozen boating pond with half-sunk boats stuck in the ice. The sea had started to freeze, and chunks of ice washed backwards and forwards in the sullen waves.

There were small cafes and pizza restaurants along the front, but they were all closed, some of them derelict. The Land Rover came to a halt, half-jammed against a telephone box, and they got out.

'This looks like a fun sort of a place,' Dixie said.

Danny said nothing. The Globe was pointing unwaveringly towards the cruel-looking snowy mountains. It was getting dark, but could they afford to wait till morning? The Treaty Stone might already be lying in pieces, the forces of the Ring streaming across the border.

Dixie followed his eyes. 'If you're thinking of tackling the mountain,' she said, 'I'm not doing it on an empty stomach.'

Danny realised that they hadn't eaten all day. His own stomach was beginning to rumble.

'Look,' Dixie said.

At the end of the street, a neon sign winked on and off. As they approached they saw it was an old-fashioned fish-and-chip shop. The neon sign read: 'Fish and Chips. Macari's Original! Really Nourishing and Excellent!'

'Someone wasn't evacuated,' Danny said.

The smells of frying fish and chips reached their nostrils as they approached. Dixie was so hungry that she disappeared and reappeared right outside the door of the chip shop.

'Don't do that, Dixie,' Danny said, looking nervously around. But the street was deserted.

When he got to her she had her nose pressed up against the menu.

'Starving . . .' she said, and disappeared again, reappearing just inside the door of the chip shop.

Danny groaned inwardly. If, as Pearl had warned, the Ring had agents in the Upper World, then Dixie's behaviour might as well have put up a sign to say who they were. He pushed the door open.

It was an ordinary chip shop. There was a counter with a fryer behind it, a jukebox in the corner and a few wooden tables and chairs. The air was full of good smells. Yet Dixie wasn't paying any attention to the food. She was staring, awe-struck, above the counter.

'What's wrong?' Danny whispered, glancing nervously behind the counter, where he could see a man slicing potatoes.

'That . . . that!' Dixie breathed. 'What is it?'

'That? It's a television. Do you remember I told you about it? It's showing the news.'

'There are people inside . . . no . . . don't be silly . . . Are they real . . . ? I mean, or are they moving paintings? Look. A river!'

'They're pictures of real people, Dixie. You just

point a camera at them and put it on film, then the TV people send a signal through the air . . .'

Dixie looked at him as if she only half believed him. Danny smiled inwardly. It *did* sound a bit unlikely when you thought about it. As he watched, Dixie's mouth made a perfect O as she gazed at an aerial shot of a snow-clogged motorway. Danny delved into his pocket and came out with a fistful of notes. Better buy some food quick and get out of here before Dixie in her excitement disappeared and reappeared in the fish fryer. He could see the snow-covered mountains through a side window. They would have to go on foot, he thought. The snow would be too deep for the Land Rover.

There was a cough from the counter. Danny looked round to see Macari, the chip-shop proprietor, standing at the counter. He was a small, swarthy man with a well-cared-for moustache and one eyebrow raised, a half-smile on his face as if there was something amusing in the sight of two hungry strangers.

'Er, could we have two fish suppers, please?' Danny asked.

'Certainly, certainly.' The man had a foreign accent – Italian or something, Danny thought vaguely, as two pieces of cod were slipped into the hot oil.

'Look, Danny,' Dixie said breathlessly. 'It's here!'

Danny followed her eyes to the television set. The

screen was indeed showing an aerial view of the town, and of the mountains beyond. The news announcer was relating how, after weeks of cold weather, an evacuation plan had had to be carried out for towns at the foot of the mountains as food and fuel ran short. That's odd, Danny thought again. Why would a chip shop be open if the population had been evacuated? He turned back to the counter to question the owner and found himself, to his shock and dismay, staring at a large and extremely deadly-looking crossbow in the hands of a now unsmiling chip-shop owner.

'So,' Macari said softly, 'what are the boy and the disappearing girl doing in the evacuated town?'

'Whoops,' Dixie said.

'We came back,' Danny said, with as much confidence as he could muster. 'We left Dixie's auntie behind in the rush. We were afraid that she would be frozen. She has no food.'

Danny was amazed how easily the lie slipped off his tongue, even with an arrow pointed at his heart.

'She's not very well,' Dixie added, with an expression of wide-eyed innocence. 'She's kind of forgetful and she's very fond of cats . . .'

'And we have to find her,' Danny cut in, stopping Dixie's flow of information about her imaginary aunt.

'I see,' the man said. 'And where does this aunt live?'

'Up there,' Dixie said, pointing towards the mountains. 'Right up near the top.'

Macari smiled, but his eyes were cold.

'It is a lonely place for an old lady, no?'

'She's very independent,' Dixie said. Macari slipped out from behind the counter, keeping the crossbow fixed on Dixie and Danny. He locked the door and turned the sign so that it showed 'Closed'. 'It is time to learn the truth,' he said grimly, beckoning them into the back room with the crossbow. Unlike the warm front part of the chip shop, there was nothing cosy about the back room. The walls were damp cold stone, and the floor was earth. It felt and looked like a dungeon, and at the back of it a dark passage led away.

'Now,' the man glowered, 'we have places to put snoopers and sneaks like you two. And there are ways to get truth from you as well. Many good ways.' Swiftly he seized Dixie's wrists and secured them to a set of manacles on the wall. He did the same with Danny.

'Try to disappear now,' he sneered. He opened a rough wooden cupboard and removed two long steel implements with what looked like small horseshoes at the end.

'We haven't done anything to you,' Danny said. 'Let us go!'

'Like hell I let you go,' the small man said. 'I find truth.'

Danny watched as the man took the steel implements into the shop area, where the fish was still sizzling in the hot oil of the fryer. He opened the front of the fryer, revealing the red-hot coals that heated the oil. He thrust the two implements into the coals and partially closed the door on them.

'What's he doing?' Dixie whispered.

'I think I know,' Danny said, 'and I don't like the look of it.'

He twisted in his manacles. There was a gun in one of his inside pockets, if only he could reach it, but the fetters held firm.

'I should be able to disappear out of these,' Dixie said, 'but the metal is stopping me. I don't understand how. Who is he anyway, and what does he want? Is he part of the Ring or something?'

The man took the metal implements out of the fire and examined them. The ends were glowing a dull orange. He thrust them back in again.

'Danny, he isn't going to . . . brand us with those things, is he?' There was a note of terror in Dixie's voice. She was a free spirit, not made to be tied. Danny could feel cold fear in his heart, and knew it was worse for Dixie. He made himself clear his mind. There had to be a way out.

He called out to the man. 'You don't have to torture us – we'll tell you the truth!'

'Sorry,' Macari said, coming back in and looking genuinely remorseful, 'you see, torturers never believe the first thing they're told. The victim always holds something back, even if they don't mean to. I'd have to give you a little tickle with the hot irons anyway, so you might as well save it for then.'

Danny could hear Dixie gulp beside him. Use your brain, he told himself; use your cunning.

'Dixie,' he said quickly, 'did you notice anything funny about this place, something not quite right when we were coming in?'

She shook her head. In the front of the shop, the swarthy little man took the irons out of the fire again. They were almost white-hot. He spat on one, and the spit sizzled and evaporated before the irons were thrust back into the heat.

'Have to think . . .' Danny muttered. There had been something that didn't quite fit. He closed his eyes and tried to recall how the front of the chip shop had looked. The peeling paint, the grease-stained menu in the window, the neon sign . . .

'What did the sign say?' he demanded. 'The chip-shop sign?'

'I don't remember,' Dixie moaned. 'What does it matter? Do something, Danny!'

Macari took the irons from the fire and looked them over. They were white hot. He touched one of them carefully to the hairs on his forearm. The smell of burning hair filled the chip shop. Dixie had her eyes shut tight and was shaking like a leaf. Danny looked around desperately. There was no weapon within reach. He peered over the approaching Macari's shoulder towards the street, hoping against hope that he could call out to a passer-by. But all he could see was the neon sign blinking on and off. Macari's Original. Really Nourishing and Excellent. It was an odd thing for a sign to say. It didn't even make a lot of sense. 'Really Nourishing and Excellent' . . .

'Morne,' Danny shouted. 'It's Morne!'

'What are you talking about, Danny?' Dixie said.

'It's Morne!' Danny said. 'Macari's Original Really Nourishing and Excellent. M, O, R, N, E – Morne!'

'Have you gone completely daft?' Dixie said, but Macari had paused, the two brands still white-hot in his hand.

'What do you know about Morne?' he demanded.

'We're students,' Danny said, 'sent from the Lower World. Under the terms of the Treaty!'

'Are you sure?' Macari peered at them suspiciously. The smell of hot metal from the branding iron reached Danny's nostrils.

'Absolutely sure,' Danny said.

'Certain,' Dixie added.

'I'll have to check the book,' Macari grumbled. He shoved the irons back into the fire and took a well-thumbed book out from under the counter.

'Who sent you?' he demanded.

'Er, Mr Devoy,' Danny guessed.

'Devoy . . . Devoy . . .' Macari flicked through his book. 'Ah. Here. "Two souls for instruction." Your names?'

'Danny Caulfield and Dixie Cole.'

'Of course, of course. I'll have to have a word with the court about this. What a way to treat visiting students!'

Macari hurried to untie their shackles, unobtrusively closing the chip-shop door with his foot as he did so that they could no longer see the branding irons.

'I'll have to have words about this. You see, once the others came through, I thought that was the end of the students.'

Others? Dixie and Danny glanced at each other as they rubbed at the painful welts left by the shackles.

'What is this place?' Danny asked.

'It's the gateway to Morne,' Macari said. 'Welcome, young students.'

Macari's eyes were twinkling now, but Danny was cautious.

'The kingdom travels to various locations,' Macari said, folding his hands and reciting as if from a guidebook, 'hidden by the weather. Sometimes a sandstorm in the sunbaked desert, sometimes a typhoon in the storm-tossed ocean. The kingdom is always on the move, always watchful, for it is the guardian of the peace between the two worlds!'

'But where is it now?' Dixie asked.

'Above us in the mountains. The passage behind you leads to it. We always have a disguised entrance into the world. Makes things much easier. We just close up the chip shop when Morne is elsewhere. But enough talking, my young friends. You must be tired and hungry after your journey. Let me take you to Morne!'

Macari gave a great bow, sweeping out his right hand to show that they should go first. With an edgy glance at each other and a nervy disappearance by Dixie from one side of the tunnel to the other, they set out for the kingdom of Morne.

12

ASSASSINS

The college was in uproar. After the Unknown Spy had, as he thought, killed Les, he wandered through the shrubberies until he met Detective McGuinness. He had handed his gun to the detective and said mildly, 'I believe I have killed someone. Perhaps you would take me into custody.'

McGuinness had escorted the Unknown Spy to the Roosts and seen immediately that he hadn't killed anyone, merely ruined a good pillow, but not before both Roosts were wide awake and rife with rumour and speculation. The Unknown Spy had repeated his belief that Les had killed his wife, but Smyck immediately tied this to Danny's disappearance during the night.

'Maybe Caulfield did it instead.'

'Don't be daft,' Les said.

'Well, why'd he run away then?' demanded Orelia Detestes, a particularly nosey cadet with bright brown darting eyes and a sharp face, which, as Les said, if you added whiskers, would resemble that of a particularly obnoxious rat.

McGuinness did not comment, other than to say he was taking the Unknown Spy into custody for his own protection.

Les skipped breakfast and went to see Vandra before class. She was sleeping, and Les did not wake her. He looked out of the window. The long black car that had brought Toxique's father was still parked at the front of the building. When Les arrived late for geography class he saw that Toxique was missing. He assumed that he had been called to see his father but when the class ended Les found Valant waiting outside.

'Master Devoy wishes to know if you have seen young Toxique,' he said.

'No,' Les replied.

'Then perhaps you have some idea where he might be found?'

'No,' said Les, lying this time. Toxique was in enough trouble already. When classes finished for lunch he slipped away, but not before he had been stopped by Exspectre.

'You seem to be losing your friends,' the pale boy said. 'A bit careless of you.'

'At least I got some friends to lose,' Les said, but Exspectre's comment had hit home. It was a bit strange with Vandra ill, Danny and Dixie gone to Morne and now Toxique not in class. But I do know where to find him, Les thought, as he made his way through the shrubberies.

His instinct was accurate. Toxique was sitting in the old summerhouse, moodily feeding crumbs to a column of black ants.

'No poison in that bread then, Toxique?' Les said.

'No,' Toxique said, 'that's the problem. A real Toxique would be working out all sorts of new ways to poison ants. I just don't feel the need.'

'Valant was looking for you.'

'My father put him up to it, I suppose,' Toxique said despairingly, 'but I can't face him. For a start, I didn't try to kill the Messenger with the poison dart, but I can't admit that I haven't even tried to assassinate anyone. And if I say that I did do it, that's worse – failure isn't tolerated.'

'Which is the worse problem?' Les said.

'They're both bad,' Toxique said, 'but failure is worse. It's an automatic death sentence.'

'Then we've got to prove that you didn't fire the dart,' Les said firmly. 'After that we'll worry about your assassination record.'

'What about my father?'

'Maybe he's not that mad at you,' Les said.

'How do I find out without facing him?' Toxique said, dread in his voice.

'How about we try a little spying?'

Toxique stood up.

Les slapped him on the back. 'That's better,' he said.

'You're about to get bitten by the ant you just sat on,' Toxique said absently-mindedly.

'Ooh! That hurt,' Les said, rubbing the bite. 'We'll show them there's more to a Toxique than assassinating people. Let's go.'

Les guessed that Toxique's father would be in the room that Devoy favoured: the library of the third landing. Cadets were forbidden from entering it upon pain of an Eighth Regulation offence, but Les had a plan. He dived under the summerhouse and came back up with a worn-looking leather attaché case.

'Where'd that come from?' Toxique said.

'Oh, you know,' Les said vaguely. He was quite proud of his abilities as a thief, but not everyone shared his view.

The two boys ran back towards Wilsons. They scrambled up to the Roosts where Les rooted in his bedside locker. He produced the Beetles of Transmission and put one into the leather case.

179

Toxique waited outside the main hall while Les took the case in to Valant.

'Yes?' Valant enquired archly.

'In all the excitement Mr Devoy left his briefcase in the Roosts. He asked it to be brought up to the library of the third landing.'

Les made as if to dart through the door beside Valant's desk, but Valant stepped in front of him.

'No you don't,' Valant said. 'I'll take care of that.' He grabbed the case from Les.

'But Mr Valant, it's urgent . . .' Les said.

'All the better if I take it then,' Valant said firmly. 'You know you're not permitted in the library of the third landing without one of the instructors.'

Les ran down the steps outside. 'We got a result,' he said. 'Valant's going to bring the case up.'

Les and Toxique found a quiet corner of the shrubbery and waited. At first they could only hear Valant's feet and the creak of the bag. They held the big beetle belly-up and waited. They heard a knock and then Devoy's voice.

'Come in.'

'One of your cases was left downstairs,' Valant said. Les held his breath. Would Devoy be suspicious? He could almost feel the Master's eyes on the bag.

'I don't recognise it,' Devoy said. 'It might

belong to Brunholm. Just put it down, Mr Valant, please.'

'Would you and Mr Toxique like some tea?' Valant asked.

'That would be very pleasant, thank you,' Devoy said. The door closed as Valant left.

'Where were we?' Devoy said.

'My son,' a cold, silky voice said.

'Of course,' Devoy said. 'Well, as you know, there is nothing to connect your son to the attack on the Messenger.'

'The attacker used Toxique darts,' Toxique senior said. 'That is proof enough for me, and the fact that the Messenger survived appals me.'

'I have to say I am glad one of the persons in my care survived,' Devoy said.

'You know as well as I, Devoy, that assassination is a necessary and honourable branch of spying. And assassins have to be trained. The boy must be blooded. And if he is not capable of fulfilling the role he has been born to—'

'I must confess,' Devoy said, 'that I find your creed a harsh one, Mr Toxique.'

'The Toxiques deal in matters of life and death, Mr Devoy,' the cold voice went on. 'There is no room for sentiment.'

Les glanced at Toxique. His friend's face was pale

at the best of times, but now he looked as if all the blood had been drained from his body. Through the beetle they heard a knock on the library door and Valant returning.

'I have never had the advantage of a son,' Devoy said, 'but my assumption was that such matters went beyond mere sentiment.'

'Not for the Toxiques,' the other man said. 'Different rules apply.'

A sound escaped Toxique junior. Les looked round in alarm as his friend leapt to his feet and raced off through the shrubberies towards the main building.

'Toxique!' Les yelled, running through after him. Les, hampered by his wings, wasn't a fast runner, and Toxique had disappeared through the front door by the time he had cleared the shrubberies. Panting, Les ran up the steps and into the hallway, where a dazed cadet was clambering to his feet.

'What way did he go?' Les gasped. The cadet pointed to the stairs that led towards the library of the third landing.

As Les scrambled up the first flight of stairs, a raven cawed mockingly from the shadows of the rafters above his head. Far ahead he could hear running feet. Les found himself sprinting across the floor of the Gallery of Whispers, the great domed room where, if you asked a question, you would receive an answer after your question had travelled round the room, although the answer was frequently strange and hard to decipher. Questions flitted through his head as he ran. Would he catch up with Toxique before he reached his father? Which of Toxique's father's words had sparked this uncontrollable rage? Suddenly he was on the third landing and could see Toxique launching himself at the library doors. They crashed open. An unearthly sound escaped the young assassin as he threw himself into the room. There was a mighty crash from the room, followed by silence.

Les slowed as he reached the library, not knowing what carnage was waiting inside. Toxique was on the floor at his father's feet. The man stared down at his son with cold fury. Devoy looked on, expressionless as usual, while Valant gazed in horror at the broken china strewn across the floor.

'The tea,' Toxique gasped. 'It's poisoned!'

His father bent down to pick up a shard of the cup which had been dashed from his lips. He smelt it carefully.

'No odour of any sort,' he said.

'There wouldn't be, surely,' Devoy said. 'If someone was trying to poison a poisoner, they would hardly make it so easily detectable.'

Toxique senior took a small case from his inside pocket, opened it and scrutinised the array of brushes and powders inside.

'What would such a poisoner use?' he said, looking down at Toxique. 'Answer me, boy.'

'If it was me,' Toxique said, 'I would use Tasmin arachnoid.'

'Colourless and odourless,' his father said softly. 'We shall see.'

He dipped a brush in one of the powders and dabbed the damp surface of the teacup. After a moment the surface turned cobalt blue.

'Tasmin arachnoid it is,' the man said. He looked down at his son but his expression did not soften.

'It appears that your son's gift of anticipation has saved both our lives,' Devoy said.

If Toxique senior was grateful he did not show it. 'At least it lured him from whatever hole he has been hiding in,' he said, his eyes fixed on Toxique's face. Les stepped forward, his cheeks burning. How could the man speak to Toxique like that after what he had just done? But Devoy held up his hand to silence Les before he could say a word.

'It is worth reminding you that our only Physick is out of action following the dart attack. There would have been nothing to save us, Mr Toxique.'

Toxique senior got to his feet. 'I have to question

those in charge of this institution who permit poisoners and murderers to roam the corridors openly,' he said, his voice like ice. 'And as for my son, he knows what his duty is, and if he is proved to have failed then he knows the price he must pay.' The man gathered his cloak around him and swept angrily out of the room.

'That's a bit much,' Les said indignantly, stooping to give Toxique a hand as he got shakily to his feet.

'People like Mr Toxique set very high standards for themselves,' Devoy said, 'and they expect the same of others, whether they have the capability or not. There is a weight of family history on his shoulders as well. In time he may come round. As for me, young Toxique, I am indeed grateful and will remain eternally in your debt.'

'I just felt it as we were . . .' Les kicked Toxique hard on the ankle before he could mention the beetles, '. . . walking through the shrubbery.'

'You boys are late for class,' Devoy said. 'You had better go. And, Mr Knutt?'

'Yes.'

'Please take your briefcase with you. I'm sure the beetle feels a little confined.'

Red-faced, Les grabbed the briefcase and headed for the door, followed by Toxique.

Devoy turned to Valant as the door closed behind them. 'It is a good thing they were listening,' the

Master said. 'Otherwise I might well be dead. We must find whoever is responsible, before someone else is killed.'

Outside the door, Les turned to Toxique.

'How did he know we were listening?' he said.

'Maybe it's something to do with the fact that you've got the other beetle in your hand,' Toxique said.

Les looked down at the beetle still gripped tightly in his right fist, its legs waving feebly in the air. 'Bit of a giveaway, all right,' he said with a smile. 'How are you feeling?'

Toxique gave a shrug. 'He won't accept me until I carry out an assassination. He told me once that my grandad was the same to him.'

'We won't worry about that for the time being,' Les said. 'We've got a killer to catch.'

'Knutt and Toxique,' Blackpitts's voice said, 'when you are finished with rescuing visitors from deadly toxins, please get yourself to Inks class, where no doubt latecomers will be suitably punished.

13
The Kingdom

The passage wound upwards into the mountains for what felt like miles. Danny's thighs ached with the climb. Macari had given them some fish and chips before they left, so they weren't hungry, but Danny was desperately tired. Each section of the passageway was lit by flickering torches, but between them it was dark, and he had slipped and fallen several times. In his head he ran over his new identity. He was there to study the history of the Lower World. They had decided that Dixie would pretend to be a student of the Treaty. That way she could ask to see the Treaty Stone. If the others, whoever they were, haven't broken it already, Danny thought.

Danny felt a sudden strange sensation in his head, as if for a moment his thoughts were not quite his own. He shook his head and walked doggedly on, but the feeling persisted. Not that someone was trying to get into his head, but that they were thinking about him, and in doing so had connected with him in some way.

He remembered the time he had joined the Ring of Five, how he could feel and hear the thoughts of other members of the Ring in his head. It was a little like that, only very far away. As if someone was trying to find out what was happening wherever Danny was. Longford. It was him! The very second he thought of the name the sensation vanished, as if Longford had sensed Danny's presence and cut him off. And yet in his eagerness he had left something of himself behind – more than he had intended, a part of his thinking, like a lingering scent in Danny's mind. Danny stopped dead.

'What is it?' Dixie asked. She grasped his arm. He shook his head to show that he was all right, but fear swept over him. If Longford's thought was a scent, then there was a foul undertone to it. For he knew, from the fragment that Longford had left, that a trap had been prepared for him in the kingdom of Morne. He searched his mind for Longford's thought, but it was gone.

'Do your worst, Longford,' he murmured to himself, but the brave words were lost in the cold damp tunnel as he resumed his climb.

*

After another half-hour's climb the packed earth and stone underfoot became paving, and the rough stone walls gave way to smoothly pointed limestone with paintings and rich tapestries hung every few yards. Other passages ran off to each side. From some rich scents drifted, from others came snatches of voices, or music. There was the impression that lots of things were going on just out of sight. Up ahead stood two young men. They looked like medieval courtiers, richly dressed in embroidered doublets and hose. They were absorbed in whispered conversation, and when they saw the small party approaching they gathered up their cloaks, pulled the hoods over their heads and hurried off in opposite directions.

The corridors widened, ceilings lost in the dark. Small groups of people stood in opulent rooms off the corridor, many turning their faces away as Danny, Dixie and Macari approached. The women wore silk dresses, the men rich velvet tops and hose. Both men and women had powdered wigs.

'What's going on?' Dixie said. 'Why is everybody standing around acting secret? Has something happened?'

Macari turned with a grin. 'No, nothing unusual. Morne is always like this. They're always scheming and gossiping and trying to catch the eye of the Vizier and the court. No one here trusts anyone else. They're always trying to do each other down. Treacherous as sin, the whole lot of them, and the more charming they are, the worse they get.'

Danny remembered the hot irons in Macari's hand and thought that he didn't trust him either.

'Now,' Macari went on, 'orders are that you're to be presented to the Vizier and the court – it's an honour accorded to all visitors, not that there are that many.'

'Who's the Vizier?'

'The Vizier is the Supreme Authority, Lord of Lords, Master of All Domains Pertaining to and Congruent with the Realm and Kingdom of Morne, Lord High Protector and Beloved . . .'

'He's got a lot of names,' Dixie said.

'Seven hundred,' Macari agreed, adding, 'It takes a good two hours every Saturday to get through them before the Royal Bath, which is followed by the Royal Nap and then the Royal Tea . . .'

'We get the picture,' Danny said hastily. Macari came to a halt in front of a set of extremely large doors covered in gold leaf. Two soldiers in golden armour with spears in their hands glared at them. From a small plain kiosk beside the doors a rotund man wearing a scarlet robe emerged. He was holding a clipboard.

'Let me see,' he said, turning a lively if careworn

face towards them, 'this can't be the delegation from the Lower Tower or the petitioners from the Southward Gallery, or the Keyholders Guild of the Keepers of Secrets.'

'We're students,' Danny said, 'from the Lower World.'

'This is Chancellor Noinrum Camroc,' Macari said, 'Master of Ceremonies and Etiquettes, Songbird of the North, Holder of the Divine Flute—'

'Does everybody have such long names?' Dixie asked.

'We'll dispense with titles since they're from the somewhat . . . er . . . lax Lower World,' Camroc said. 'We'll just have time for the formalities before the evening ceremonies begin.'

He turned to the golden doors and rapped sharply three times with the golden flute he carried on a chain at his waist. The doors were flung open on a high-ceilinged chamber, dimly lit by great candelabra. They saw rich hangings, velvet curtains, the glint of gold. There were many people in the room, once again richly dressed. The people were gathered in knots in various parts of the room, scheming and conspiring against each other, the men glancing around before leaning forward to whisper in a companion's ear, the women hiding their mouths behind fans as they exchanged gossip.

All eyes turned towards the door as Camroc led them in and whispered comments followed in their wake.

'What are they wearing? . . . Is that the best the Upper World has to offer? . . . At least they could have washed themselves properly before meeting the Vizier . . .'

'Why do they hate us?' Dixie said, for she could feel the waves of resentment flooding towards them.

'They're jealous,' Camroc said. 'Some of them have waited years for the opportunity to be presented to the Vizier, and here you are, just walking in off the street, so to speak, and being brought straight to him.'

Danny felt his mind roam coldly over the assembled throng. Without even thinking about it he was weighing up the alliances, the intrigues, the treacheries. He felt drawn to the faithless crowd by the part of him that wanted to spy on others, to betray. He took a deep breath and tried to shut out the whispers.

They drew near to a great dais. The shadows grew darker. Candles flickered in the gloom and figures of men and women parted then closed behind them. Then suddenly, without ceremony, they found themselves not in front of the gorgeous throne that Danny had expected but facing a wooden chair with carved arms in the shape of ravens' heads. Nor was the man sitting on the chair what Danny had expected – a proud ruler, richly dressed and perfumed. The Vizier was an ordinary-looking man with grey-flecked brown hair and shrewd eyes, simply dressed in plain black hose and tunic.

'Welcome, young students,' he said quietly. 'It is many years since we had students from the Lower World, so it is doubly gratifying to have two parties at the same time.'

Danny had the uncomfortable feeling that the man knew exactly why both parties were here and he had to force himself to meet the steady gaze.

'You have picked very serious subjects,' the Vizier went on, 'and I have considered long and hard how to make your visit a little more interesting for you. I thought that an element of competition might add to your pleasure.'

There was a murmer of approval from the courtiers pressing around them.

'The winners will be given the information they most desire about their chosen subject, a piece of knowledge that may well have been lost and is preserved only in the kingdom, for we are the keepers of knowledge.' Was it the flickering light, or had the Vizier glanced at Danny with the smallest of smiles?

'Now,' the Vizier said, 'it is time for the newcomers to meet their rivals.'

Danny looked up. He had only just noticed the two figures standing in the gloom behind the Vizier's chair . . .

'Step forward,' the Vizier commanded, and they did. The smaller of the two was a Cherb. The features were unmistakably those of the Wilsons deadly enemies: the pixie-like ears and dark hair, one eye blue, the other brown. The Cherb boy looked at Danny with a mixture of malice and amusement. The taller figure was a girl. Her long blonde hair hung down her back. He face was long and fine-boned and her eyes a cold piercing blue, but her smile was shy and a little uncertain. She turned to the Vizier.

'May I ask a question, My Lord Vizier?' Her voice was low and husky.

'Of course.'

'You mentioned what might happen to the winners of the competition. But you did not mention the losers.'

'The losers?' The Vizier smiled. 'A good question. A good competition must have a good prize. Equally, I think, there must be a real jeopardy for the losers. So the unsuccessful candidates will stay here to serve in the shadows.'

'What does that mean?' Danny said, as Dixie gulped beside him.

'As the living have servants, the dead also have to be tended to.' The man's tone was light, but his eyes were dark and burning.

'That seems fair,' the girl said calmly. 'And what is the nature of the test that we are to be set?'

'It is simple. You merely have to find out what the mountain says.' They all looked at him blankly. What did the question mean? How could the mountain say anything?

There was a murmer of approval from the bystanders and some applause.

'They're not clapping because it's an easy task,' Dixie said sourly.

The blonde girl stepped forward. 'My name is Lily,' she said, putting out her hand.

'Danny,' he said. Her grip was cool and firm and her look direct. He felt, strangely, that she was not necessarily the enemy just because she had been sent by the Ring.

The Cherb boy broke into Danny's thoughts. 'Come on, Lily,' he growled. 'They'll be bait for the dead by the time we finish with them.'

'You can rest tonight and begin in the morning,' the Vizier said silkily. 'You may deploy fair means or foul, you may use guile or be plain-spoken, the choice is yours. There is nowhere in the kingdom closed to you, but you may find that people defend their territory jealously.'

Macari brought them to a comfortable room off a main corridor. Like the rest of the buildings the furniture was ornate and there were silk hangings on the walls. There were silver salvers of beef and chicken on a table, which they fell on. When they had finished Dixie threw herself down on one of the beds while Danny explored the room.

'Look,' he exclaimed. Behind curtains there were two great glass doors that led out on to a balcony. They stepped out and looked on to the snow-covered mountainsides, the great peaks rearing above them, the lower slopes still under the moonlight far beneath them. They stood there for several minutes, lost in the cold beauty of the landscape.

The kingdom of Morne was all around them, a series of interlinked castles and keeps and towers, spreading up the mountain as far as you could see.

Dixie shivered 'I don't trust one brick of this place. I wish I was back in Wilsons.'

Danny knew what she meant. Wilsons could be strange and tricky, but it was homely, and you had the feeling that, for most of the time anyway, most people were on your side.

'We need to find the Treaty Stone and get out of here,' Danny said.

'There's the challenge as well,' Dixie said. 'Forgot that? I don't fancy ending up as a servant of the dead.'

She disappeared in a way that managed to be moody and a minute later he heard water running in the bathroom. When she reappeared abruptly a few minutes later she was wearing a silk nightdress that shimmered as she moved.

'There's a pair of goldy PJs in there for you as well,' she said with a tired grin. She clambered into bed and within seconds was asleep.

Although he was tired, Danny's mind was racing and sleep felt a long way off. He opened the great windows quietly and slipped out on to the balcony. The cold air seared his lungs. He looked up at the silent bulk of the mountains rearing above the strange kingdom, the snow-clad valley below him. It was beautiful but treacherous.

He saw a flicker of movement at the far end of the valley. He narrowed his eyes. A small black shape was just visible against the mountain, moving swiftly towards him. A raven! The bird flew fast and high without deviating until it reached the first turret of Morne, then it dipped and turned right so that it was flying along the facade of the building. It passed straight in front of him, then slowed, coming to a rest on a balcony a few hundred metres away. It cocked its head on one side and peered down.

It's trying to show me something, Danny thought. He followed the direction of the raven's gaze. From the balcony below a small figure dressed in black jumped lightly on to the parapet and from there leapt on to the next balcony down. It was the Cherb boy. The raven looked back up at Danny. He realised it wanted him to follow. With a quick glance in at the sleeping Dixie, he pulled his trenchcoat tight around him and slipped over the parapet, swinging his legs inwards so that he landed on the one below. As he did so, the dark figure reached the ground.

It was easier than it looked to climb down the front of the building using the balconies, though people were still awake in some of the rooms and once Danny had to crouch, not breathing, while on the adjoining balcony an unseen couple spoke together in whispers.

'We are surrounded by snakes on every side,' a man's voice said.

'Then we have no hope. What is to become of us?' replied a woman's voice, full of despair. Danny waited until the voices moved back inside, then resumed his downward progress.

When he reached the ground he could see footprints in the snow leading upwards along the front of the building. He looked around. The windows of Morne were all dark. Pulling the collar of his coat tight around his neck, he set off. The snow was crisp and firm and the tracks were easy to follow, moving purposefully and without deviation. The two Ring students were a day ahead of Danny and Dixie and could well have found the Treaty Stone by now. Perhaps the Cherb's mission now was to shatter it. Danny felt alive out here, all of his senses primed. To be out alone in the dark, on the trail of an opponent who did not know he was there, touched the devious part of his being. Knowing that he should have wakened Dixie added a extra forbidden pleasure, that of deceiving a friend in a small way.

The footprints turned away from the building and towards a small stand of snow-covered pine trees in the shadow of a crag. Danny slowed. It was dangerous to follow an opponent into the trees, where an ambush would be possible. A gust of wind sent ice crystals scudding across the surface of the snow. He looked up. Dark cloud had started to gather around the mountain peaks, the clouds moving with alarming speed across the moon. He hesitated. He should either go back or seek the shelter – and danger – of the trees. He brushed a snowflake from his lapel and moved cautiously in under the trees.

Danny crept forward, glancing up from the footprints to the dark canopy of trees. In the darkness a night creature stirred and he jumped. It was a small stand of trees, but the darkness was almost total. The wind stirred the peaks of the pines. Danny came to the far end of the copse. The footprints emerged from the trees and doubled back towards Morne. A flurry of snow blew into his face and as he stepped from the trees a blast of frozen air hit him. Morne was already hidden by the drifting snow. The Cherb had led and like a fool he had followed. He staggered as the wind struck him. He'd been tricked and now he was alone in a snowstorm.

Danny put his head down and began to follow the tracks. As far as he could tell they pointed back towards the walls of the kingdom, but he couldn't be sure. The prints were filling with snow, and before he had gone a hundred yards they had faded completely. Danny trudged on, his head down against the driving snow. He hadn't been that far from the walls of Morne. If he found them he could work his way along. And yet, no matter how far he walked, he did not reach them. It was getting harder and harder to see. The sound of the wind had increased to a shriek and the snow blew horizontally. Ice formed on his eyelashes and in his hair. Danny stepped in a hole hidden by the snow and found himself sprawled on his front. The excitement of the chase was gone. His limbs felt tired and heavy and he had to force himself to get to his feet and go on.

Snow clung to his shoes and made each step hard work. His coat kept the snow out, but it didn't protect his face or his frozen feet and he found himself thinking about stories of frostbitten explorers losing ears and fingers. He cursed himself for falling for the Cherb's trap, and for not waking Dixie. He stumbled on a rock and fell again. The snow cushioned his fall. He felt a great weariness steal over him and he closed his eyes. A memory of being at home in bed crept into his mind. It was time for school and he was being called, but the bed was warm and deep and he only wanted to snatch another few minutes . . .

'Danny! Danny! Wake up!' Someone was shaking his shoulder.

'Just one more minute,' he murmured. As if in a dream he felt two small hands grip his. He was pulled into a sitting position, then forced to stand.

'Help me, Danny!' The voice came from far away. His arm was draped over slender shoulders. He took one step forward, then another. All he wanted to do was to lie down, but the voice urged and cajoled him until, in the end, the howling of the wind died away, the snow ceased and he fell to the ground.

Danny opened his eyes to see flickering shapes dancing on a stone ceiling. He turned his head. A fire blazed in a small grate and a figure moved in the shadows around it, a figure that looked familiar.

'Dixie?' he said.

'Wait a moment. I have a hot drink for you.'

It was a girl's voice, but it wasn't Dixie's.

'I don't think I could have carried you much further,' the voice went on. It was Lily, the girl chosen by the Ring to destroy the Treaty Stone.

14

FAMILY

He stared at her, then at the proferred cup.

'Don't be silly,' she said. 'If I wanted to bump you off, all I had to do was leave you out in the snow. I wouldn't have to poison you.' He took the drink. It was hot soup.

'Where are we?'

'Must be a shepherds' hut,' she said. 'They left a few tins of soup and stuff in it.'

Danny sat up and sipped the scalding liquid, feeling life flow back into his frozen limbs. His brain was starting to unfreeze as well. Why would one of his enemies lead him into a trap and the other rescue him from it?

Lily had turned away to the fire. 'I know what you're thinking,' she said, 'and I would probably think the same. Why did she do that, after I've been led into danger?'

'Why did you do it?' he said, his voice sounding harsher than he had intended.

'I know you have no reason to trust me,' she said, her voice very low, 'but until you do, I can't tell you.'

The room fell silent, save for the crackle of the fire and the distant roar of the wind.

'I don't have to trust you,' Danny said carefully, 'but I do need to thank you.'

She turned and gave him a sad smile.

'That's a start,' she said. 'We'll wait here until the storm's over, and then we'll make our way back to Morne.'

'What are you studying?' Danny said, trying to make his voice sound casual.

'Upper and Lower World relations,' she said. 'What about you?'

'Early Lower World history. What do you think of Morne?'

'It's a strange place. I think the Vizier rules it by setting people against each other. They're so busy fighting and squabbling that they don't have time to challenge him.'

'You're probably right.'

They were talking cautiously, like a chess game, Danny thought, each of them trying not to give too much away. He knew that Lily was on a mission to find and destroy the Treaty Stone, and she probably knew that he was on a mission to find and protect it.

This was what Danny the Spy enjoyed best. Playing mind games with a cunning opponent.

'How long are you staying?' Danny asked casually.

'Oh, as long as it takes,' Lily said airily, 'but I don't agree with the Vizier.'

'No?'

'I think people pulling together is the only way to achieve anything.'

What was she playing at? Was she saying they should work together? The Ring of Five and Wilsons on the same side? It didn't seem possible. She had to be up to something, Danny Spy thought. But what if she's not? the real Danny countered. Should she be trusted?

His head starting to hurt, he drank the last of the soup. 'I think we should both try and get some sleep . . .' He was interrupted by a great noise, a noise that sounded like some ancient being beset with sadness and regret, a sound of terrible longing that echoed through the ages.

Almost against their will they got to their feet and went to the rough wooden door and opened it. Outside the snow had stopped, the moon staring down again, drifts piled in weird shapes. The storm was retreating, great clouds streaming back through the high mountain passes, and as they did, by some trick caused by the speed of the storm or the shape of the mountains, a great voice seemed to speak from the mountain peaks. Danny held his breath, awestruck, as the voice boomed and rumbled over the silent snowfields.

'A-L-O-N-E,' the voice mourned, and Danny felt his blood turn to ice. 'A-L-O-N-E!' The sorrow of millennia echoed from the mountain peaks. Again and again it boomed out. Then, as the last wisp of cloud raced through the last pass, it stopped. Danny realised he had been holding his breath. He looked down. Lost in the terrible sorrowing of the mountain, Lily had taken his hand and was holding it tightly. When the sound faded she quickly released his hand and headed off into the snow.

'We'd better get back,' she said over her shoulder.

'Wait,' he said, running after her. 'What did you mean earlier? When you said you can't tell me why you helped me until I trust you.'

'That's what I meant.'

'You realise,' Danny said, 'that we both know what the mountain said?'

'Yes.'

'And that if we don't both answer the question at exactly the same time then one of us ends up serving the dead?'

'I realise that too.'

'Well,' Danny said slowly, 'that means that either one of us goes straight to the Vizier and condemns the others, or we trust each other and deliver the answer together.'

'And?'

'I'll trust you, Lily,' he said. 'I won't go to the Vizier if you won't.' He stopped in the snow and held out his right hand. After a long moment of hesitation she shook it.

'Right,' she said. 'Follow me.'

She took them along the wall of Morne to a small picket gate. There was a heavy iron lock on it, but she took a clip from her hair and with impressive speed and dexterity had it open.

Inside was a jumble of old furniture and faded oil paintings, sleighs with one runner and broken beach umbrellas. Moonlight streamed in through a high barred window in the wall.

'It's just a storeroom,' Lily said, 'but you can get back into our rooms from it.' She hesitated.

'What is it?'

'You said you trusted me. It's time for me to trust you.'

'Trust me with what?'

'With this.' She turned away from him and bent over. He couldn't see what she was doing, but her hands were at her eyes. She turned round to face him.

'Let me move into the light.' She stepped into the shaft of moonlight. At first all he saw was the paleness of her skin, the raven hair streaming back. Then he saw her eyes. He blinked and looked again. One was blue, the other brown.

'Yes, Danny. Just like you.'

'How?' he said. 'I thought I was the only one . . .'

'That's what everyone thinks, Danny,' she said, 'but you're not. You were never alone. They tried to hide it from you, but you have a sister.'

'You?'

'Yes, Danny,' she said, turning towards him and raising her head so that he could see the shape of her face, and the strange brown and blue eyes. 'I'm your sister.'

The next hour went past in a blur. Danny had got used to being alone and had worked at building up a hard skin to protect himself. Now he felt more vulnerable than ever before. He couldn't think of the right questions to ask. It seemed that Lily knew little more of their parentage than he did, having also been brought up by strangers, in the shadows of the fortress of Grist.

'I was always hidden from the Ring of Five,' she said. 'I was never allowed out without contact lenses so they never knew about my eyes. But I was smart, like you, Danny. I studied hard, spent nights in the library of Grist, reading about the Fifth. The Ring were clever, Danny. They went through all the books and tore out the pages about the Fifth, but they didn't check the baptismal records. Twelve years ago a pair of twins was registered, the colour of their eyes noted as one brown and one blue. Our first names were there – Danny and Lily – but the second names had been scored out, as were the names of the parents. I found out about this a year ago and I've been looking for you ever since.

'I got into spy school in Grist. I lied, cheated and betrayed my way to the top, Danny. When it looked as if someone else would get this mission I made sure she fell down the stairs and broke her ankle. I knew they would send you, if you were still alive. I knew it!'

Danny looked at her dumbfounded. He had a sister and a family!

'Do you know where . . . who our parents are . . . where they are?'

'No,' she said. 'I didn't get that far. But I have a few leads in Grist. The answers are there – I'm sure of it.'

'And do you know why they think that I – or we – are so special?

'I know that the Ring want you – there was great excitement when you joined them the last time. That they needed someone of mixed Cherb and human blood. But there is something more going on that I don't understand. We need more time.'

'We?'

'You must come back with me, Danny. In disguise as you are now. Together we can find our parents.' She lowered her voice confidentially. 'I know that you're on a mission here – to find the Treaty Stone, the same mission as I have.'

'Yes,' Danny said, 'but our mission is not the same. Mine is to save the Stone. Yours is to . . .'

'Destroy it,' Lily said eagerly. 'I thought about this. I must not fail, or else . . .'

'Or else what?'

Lily made a contemptuous noise. 'Rufus Ness said he'd kill both of us – me and the Cherb – if we failed, but that's not what matters—'

'Of course it matters . . .'

'Shh. Someone's coming . . .'

They ducked behind a pile of packing cases. The door opened and a servant came in, a big man with a thatch of blond hair. He was carrying a box of what sounded like broken crockery. He set it down heavily just inside the door, straightened to turn, then something caught his eye. Fresh snow on the floor, and wet footprints leading from the door. He moved forward slowly, scratching his head as he looked from the now locked door to the footprints. He didn't look very bright, and Danny thought they would do better to stay hidden in the hope that he would go away. Instead, Lily sprang out from behind the cases with a heavy brass candlestick in her hand. She struck the man behind the ear and he fell with a sickening thud. Suddenly there was a knife in her hand. She grabbed the man's hair and pulled his head back so that his throat was exposed. As her knife hand swept back Danny grabbed her wrist.

'What are you doing?' he cried.

'We'll slit his throat and leave him in the snow,' she said matter-of-factly. 'They won't find him until we're gone.'

'You can't do that,' Danny said. 'He hasn't done anything to us.'

'Course he has,' Lily said. 'He could ruin everything.'

'Wait,' Danny said, rummaging in the cases behind them. He brought out a dusty bottle of whiskey. He unscrewed the top and splashed whiskey over the man's clothes, then poured the rest into a drain.

'There, they'll think he was drunk and fell.'

'Not bad,' Lily said, 'but my way would be permanent.' Danny had only had a sister for half an hour. How could she kill a man just like that?

'Look.' Lily pointed. The first light of dawn was showing in the window above their heads.

'We'd better get back to bed,' she said. She led Danny up a winding stone staircase, which opened on to the bedroom corridor. She kissed him gently on the cheek.

'I've dreamed of this moment all my life,' she said. 'But we mustn't let anyone know.' She pointed out of the window towards a tall tower with a shining silver roof.

'I'll meet you there tomorrow. We'll be able to talk more then.'

One quick hug and she was gone. Danny opened the door to his room quietly, Dixie lay in bed breathing softly. He threw off his coat and got into the other bed. A sister! He could still feel the dry touch of her lips on his cheek, and a warmth he had never felt before flooded his heart. At the same time he remembered how she had pulled back the servant's head to expose his throat. That gave him a certain warm feeling as well, warm like spilled blood. His other self stirred, and he knew that this was the side of Lily that Danny the Spy liked. Could he trust her? Was she really his sister? Every fibre of his being wanted to believe it. He decided to say nothing to Dixie. He told himself it was to protect her, but part of him thrilled at the deception.

15

THE UNEXPECTED

Les and Toxique had gone back to Vandra's bedside after class and the three friends had spent the evening trying to figure out who the killer of the Unknown Spy's wife might be. It was later than they had realised when Blackpitts's voice had cut abruptly across their thoughts.

'Cadets Knutt and Toxique, you are forty-five minutes late for bedtime. Tell Master Brunholm that you have incurred a Third Regulation offence! Now go to bed!'

Les and Toxique looked at each other. Les had a few choice words that he was tempted to apply to Blackpitts, but he knew that the anouncer had uncannily good hearing except when he was asleep. A Third Regulation offence was a harsh punishment for being late for bed, but if Blackpitts was in a bad mood he could easily increase the punishment.

'Come on, Toxique,' Les said. 'Vandra's almost asleep anyway.'

The two boys made their way out of the infirmary, beneath the skeleton of the Messenger and through the silent college.

'Blackpitts,' Les called. 'Blackpitts, wake up!' There was no reply.

'What are you doing?' Toxique demanded.

'Trying to see if Blackpitts is awake or not.'

'Why?'

'Well, the only person this mystery assassin has managed to actually bump off is the Unknown Spy's wife. So I think we should have a look at his room while he's safely under lock and key.'

Toxique moaned. 'Blood and murder! We're in enough trouble already,' he said.

'Well, then, a little more won't hurt.' Les said firmly.

'McGuinness will already have searched it,' Toxique objected.

'Stow it, Toxique,' Les said. 'Come on!'

There was no sign of Valant in the entrance hall and the main door was closed from the inside. They crept down the corridor towards the Unknown Spy's room. But they were to be disappointed. The door was locked and nothing Les could do with his lock picks could open it.

Toxique looked relieved. 'We'd better get to bed.'

'Not yet,' Les said. 'Hear that?' The faint sound of

music reached their ears. Les slipped down the corridor, Toxique following reluctantly. They peered through the glass doors of the ballroom. Les stifled an exclamation. As well as the Messengers, who were fond of dancing, all the staff were there. Exshaw, Valant, Brunholm, Duddy, Spitfire . . . all of them. McGuinness stood on the stage with a saxophone in his hand. His wife stood beside him with a double bass. And at the back of the stage, looking every inch a cool jazz man in a black polo neck, Devoy sat at a drumkit. As they watched, McGuinness counted into a dance number, and Duddy and Brunholm took to the floor.

'If I hadn't seen it with my own two eyes . . .' Les muttered.

'McGuinness isn't bad on that thing,' Toxique said, 'and Devoy's technique is impeccable.'

'Didn't know you liked jazz,' Les said.

'It's good for calming yourself after a . . . you know, a killing. All the Toxiques are well known in the best jazz clubs.'

'Well, it gives us a great chance,' Les said.

'To do what?'

'Have a chat with the Unknown Spy.'

For the second time that night, Toxique groaned.

Fifteen minutes later they found themselves on the masters' corridor, Les looking out for new traps since the attack on Brunholm. Brunholm had added security but only outside his own room, and none of it very subtle. There was the tried-and-tested piano wire stretched at neck height, and an enormous bear trap outside the door, as well as classics such as a hair, wetted and placed across the crack between door and frame so that it would come off if someone entered. Brunholm had also covered the door in notices. There were 'Keep Out!' signs, 'Beware of the Dog!' and 'Warning: Armed Response!'

'Fat lot of good that'll do,' Les whispered. 'Any tricky stuff? What does your gift tell you?'

'Nothing,' Toxique said, 'but it doesn't always work, you know. A lot of the time I can't foretell stuff.'

'We'll press on,' Les said. 'I think we're safe enough.'

The barred window of the little cell in the master's study was dark. Les peered in. As he did so, the dim light in the room picked out the Unknown Spy's pale face, his eyes fixed on Les. As the face got closer Les knew that the man must be walking towards him, but he had the impression of a haunted head floating through the air in his direction. The face came to a halt at the bars.

'Who are you?' asked the Unknown Spy.

'My name's Les Knutt,' Les said, 'and this is

Toxique. We're trying to find out what . . . what happened to your wife.'

The Unknown Spy's eyes narrowed.

'Er, condolences on your loss,' Les said hastily, wondering if he had been too blunt.

'I didn't kill you then?' the Unknown Spy asked.

'No,' Toxique said. 'It was a pillow you shot.'

'A pillow?! Can't believe I fell for that old one,' the Unknown Spy said. 'Do bear in mind that I haven't finished with you yet, won't you?' Something about the mild way he said this chilled Les's blood even more than bloodthirsty threats would have done.

'Wait a minute!' Les said. 'I had nothing to do with—'

Before he could go on, Toxique had pushed in front of him. 'If this Les Knutt killed your wife,' he demanded, 'then why? There had to be a reason. Can you think of anything?'

The Unknown Spy stared at them, or rather stared through them, searching his ruined memory for an explanation.

'Is there anything she knew that no one else knew?' Toxique asked. 'Or something she was an expert at?'

'She was awfully smart, you know,' the Unknown Spy said brightly. 'She invented lots of spying techniques. She had started to remember things too. She was writing them down in a book.'

'Is that what the attacker was looking for?' Toxique asked.

'Possibly. What was her finest technique?' Les asked.

'There was one,' the Unknown Spy said. 'It was named after her, but I can't remember her name. Isn't that odd? I can remember the name of a technique but I can't remember my own wife's name.' A single tear trickled down his cheek.

'What was it called?' Toxique said softly. 'Tell me what it was called.'

'What was it again? Oh yes, the Sibling Strategy.' The two boys looked at each other in confusion. 'It was called that at the start, *before* her name was put on it,' the Unknown Spy went on.

'What was it?' Toxique asked eagerly. 'What did it do?'

'I don't know,' the Unknown Spy said mournfully. 'I can't remember.'

The next day Vandra was well enough to leave the Infirmary. Toxique and Les told her about the Unknown Spy and what he had said about his wife.

'Doesn't really get us any further,' Toxique said gloomily.

'I know,' Vandra said. 'Why don't we tell McGuinness about it?'

The other two looked at her.

'It's not like telling Brunholm,' she said. 'McGuinness is pretty straight. It might mean something to him. It can't hurt anyway.'

'We should be in class,' Toxique said.

'You can say you were helping me back to the Roosts. I can barely climb up there on my own anyhow.'

It was true. The powerful poison had not yet worked its way out of Vandra's system. She was finding it hard to walk in a straight line and her friends kept intervening to prevent her from veering into the shrubbery. But they never had a chance to use their excuse. As they passed under one of the decorative arches in the gardens a speaker coughed into life.

'Out on your rounds again, Knutt and Toxique?' Blackpitts said coldly. 'A Fourth Regulation offence this time, I think.'

'At least he always used to give you a chance of an excuse,' Les said despairingly.

They found McGuinness at the parade ground. The tunnel that the Cherbs had opened the previous year when they tried to invade Wilsons was still full of water. Water plants had started to spring up around the edges, and it made a pleasant pond. He was sitting on a dusty bench, seemingly dozing in the sun, but when they approached him he opened one eye.

'Next time you come to Monday-night jazz club, I'll expect you to dance or sing, not lurk outside the door.'

'How did he see us?' Les whispered furiously.

Toxique looked taken aback. 'Slaughter and guts, he must be able to see through walls.'

McGuinness opened the other eye. 'This looks very much like a delegation,' he said. 'What's on your mind?'

They plunged into the story of the visit to the Unknown Spy and his wife's book and the Sibling Strategy. McGuinness's eyes gleamed under his hat.

'Well done, Toxique,' he said. 'You've got more out of him in five minutes than I managed in many weary hours. I'll have to look into this Sibling Strategy.'

A faint flush spread over Toxique's waxen features – a flush that might, in anyone else, have been a blush of pleasure.

'I'm not sure where the information gets us at the moment, however,' the detective went on, 'but the art of investigation is the art of making links, of joining one piece of information to the next.'

'But we haven't got any other pieces,' Les said despairingly.

'There's always something,' McGuinness said, 'even if you don't know you have it – or if you've seen or heard it.'

'But what do we look or listen for?' Vandra said.

'I can't tell you that since I haven't found it,' said McGuinness, 'but I'll tell you one of the rules I use for myself. I watch out for something that's different, for unexplained change, something familiar that doesn't seem quite right all of a sudden. Now it's time you were resting, Vandra, and you two went back to class.'

McGuinness closed his eyes again and tipped his hat forward so that they could no longer see his face. The three friends looked at each other and started to make their way back to the main building.

'It's hard to notice what's different about this place when things are odd most of the time anyway,' Vandra said.

'I know,' Les said gloomily.

Just as they passed back under the garden archway, Blackpitts's speaker burst into life again. 'Make that a Regulation Five offence.' There was a note of malicious delight in his voice.

Les rolled his eyes to heaven. 'As if things weren't bad enough,' he said, then brightened. 'Maybe the assassin will bump us off – that way we won't have to take a Fifth Regulation punishment.'

'Don't be daft, Les,' Vandra said. 'Don't joke about things like that. What's wrong with you?'

Toxique's normally pale face had turned a shade whiter and there were two spots of red high on his cheeks. His dark eyes glittered with excitement. 'McGuinness told us to look out for something different, didn't he? Something familiar that has changed? Well, something familiar has changed, and McGuinness was right – it's been staring us in the face all the time!'

16

THE RING OF FIVE ROOM

The first thing Danny saw the following morning was Dixie's face, an inch from his own.

'Wake up, for goodness sake! I've been shouting at you for ten minutes.'

Danny shook his head, groggy with lack of sleep. The night's events came flooding back. A sister!

'Come on, Danny,' Dixie said. 'We've got to find out what the mountain says, whatever that means. And find the Treaty Stone. *And* stop the other two from doing any harm to it. And I'm starving and I want some breakfast.'

As they walked along the corridor they were aware of people stopping and whispering behind their backs. Once they heard a sneering laugh. Dixie disappeared and reappeared right beside a couple who were whispering and pointing, sending them scuttling down a side corridor.

After walking through several hallways, each more gorgeous than the last, they found a dining hall, where wigged and powdered servants carried silver salvers from kitchen to table, whipping off the lids to reveal bacon and sausages and eggs and fried mushrooms and toast. For a few minutes they forgot their quest as they ate greedily, asking for seconds and more, their cups of sweet milky tea being replenished from enormous teapots.

Danny had taken the edge off his appetite when he spotted something likely to spoil it altogether. The servants were clearing the dishes from a small table for two, one that looked as if it had been abandoned a while ago. He asked one of the servants, who confirmed that Lily and the Cherb had left long ago. Sister or not, he thought, he didn't trust her Cherb friend at any rate. He bolted the last of his food and took a swallow of tea.

'Come on,' he said.

They practically ran from the dining room. For the the first few hours they prowled the corridors of Morne, finding the place ever more labyrinthine as the morning went on. They found themselves in throne rooms, galleries, anterooms, bedchambers and endless corridors. Everything looked different and yet the same, and there was no sign of a treasury or a strongroom where a treasure might be kept although once they stumbled upon a room so glittering with gold and jewels that they had to shield their eyes, and a crypt so deep and dark and lined with sombre tombs of the great that their hearts quailed. Everywhere they went there were knots of courtiers, and Danny had no doubt that reports of their progress or lack of it were going back to the Vizier. By mid-afternoon, tired and hungry, they collapsed on a red velvet divan and realised that they were no closer to achieving their quest.

'You know,' Dixie said, 'there's probably an easier way of going about this.'

'I'm sure there is,' Danny said sarcastically. 'We could grow wings like Les and fly over the place, and the Treaty Stone would be sitting on the roof so all we would have to do is pick it up and fly away.'

'No,' Dixie said seriously, 'I think my way's a little easier than that.'

She stood up and walked over to a passing courtier. 'Excuse me,' she said, 'would you mind telling me where the Treaty Stone is kept?'

'Certainly,' the courtier, a handsome young man, replied. 'Take the third corridor on the left and keep going until you reach the Hall of Secrets.'

'Thank you,' Dixie said, as Danny looked on open-mouthed.

'Would you like me to take you there?'

The courtier's name was Louis and he was

twelve years old. He had black curly hair and always seemed to have a smile on his face. Unlike the other inhabitants of Morne, he wasn't secretive or suspicious.

'I'm only half-Morne,' he said with a smile. 'My mother was from the Upper World.'

'Can anyone just walk in and see the Treaty Stone?' Danny tried to sound casual.

'Yes, of course,' Louis said. 'The provisions of the Treaty have to be seen so that people can read them.

'Could somebody not just walk out with it then?' Danny said.

'Ah, that's a different matter,' Louis said cheerfully.

The corridor they had joined opened out into a wide concourse. For the first time they saw groups of young people, sitting around on marble benches or walking towards the vast iron doors that stood open at one end.

'Who are all the young people?' Dixie asked.

'Students,' Louis said. 'There are many great wonders displayed in the Crypts.'

'The Crypts? Where they keep dead people?' Dixie asked.

'That's right,' Louis said, 'but don't worry about them. They won't harm you unless you try to steal or harm any of the exhibits.'

Danny and Dixie exchanged looks. Having the dead running about the Butts – in secret and in the dark – at Wilsons was one thing. But here . . .

The entrance hall of the museum soared above their heads. There were the usual trappings – statues of important-looking people, portraits of battles on the walls . . . It was the staff who were different. A pale and ghastly-looking woman in a uniform was taking coats at the cloakroom. The security man at the main entrance was skeletally thin, his skin stretched over his bones like yellow tissue paper, his eyes bulging in their sockets.

'Lovely day, kids,' he said cheerfully. 'Enjoy yourselves.'

In the museum proper they ran into a tour party. Their guide was a young woman, pale but pretty with long dark hair.

'The Oligarchic period of Morne history under Vizier Kolum was known for its bloodthirsty pogroms. On your left you can see the golden goblet from which he drank the blood of his victims, claiming that it would make him immortal . . .'

The guide was walking backwards as she spoke and she collided with Danny.

'Oh, I'm so terribly sorry,' she said, turning around. 'That was clumsy of me.'

'Don't worry,' Danny started to say, but then her breath hit him. It smelt of the grave, of earth and decayed flesh and mould. He reeled away, gasping for breath, but she merely smiled apologetically and turned back to the group.

On they went, deeper into the museum. Many exhibits were boring, crumbling stone urns or exhibits with labels like 'Agricultural Implements of the early Upper period'. But there was a lot more to look at in 'Battle Instruments of the Upper–Lower Wars'. There were vicious-looking wing knives for Messengers, and Cherb fire throwers. There were torture instruments, which reminded Danny of the ones in Wilsons, though here there was a section devoted to Seraphim and Messengers, with feather pluckers and wing stretchers.

There were bombs devised to be dropped by Seraphim, which sent flailing knives through the air, and cruel-looking knives and small arms that were described as 'Miscellaneous Cherb'.

Danny noticed a small black door. As he approached he saw a sign over it: 'The Ring of Five'. He tried the door but it was locked.

Louis took him by the arm. This time he wasn't smiling.

'We don't go in there,' he said, steering Danny away. Danny glanced uneasily back towards the door, feeling the familiar tug, the need to be part of what was secret and malicious.

'Now,' Louis said, 'here we are. The Treaty Stone Room.'

The first part of the room was full of photographs from before the negotiation of the Treaty. There were aerial shots of the destruction wrought by the conflict: miles of burned-out houses, desperate refugees. Then there were photographs of the negotiation and signing of the Treaty: serious-looking men and women posing for the camera. In one, Danny saw a much younger-looking Devoy, then, in the main photograph, an unsmiling Longford, bending over a table with a small etching instrument in his hand.

Finally in a room of its own, the Stone. A single spotlight focused on a single black stone, much smaller than he would have thought. Its surface was etched with minute gold writing You viewed it through a sheet of heavy bulletproof glass, and there were red lights blinking here and there, doubtless showing the presence of all sorts of beams and pressure sensors – the kind of system that galleries used to protect valuable paintings.

'How are we going to get near that?' Danny said in a low voice.

'Do we need to?' Dixie asked. 'It looks pretty safe where it is.'

Danny's heart gave a bound. On the other side of the room he saw Lily standing with a group of students who were scribbling in notebooks as their teacher rumbled on about the Treaty and conflict resolution. Lily wasn't writing – her gaze roamed over the security. Danny could tell she was noting the positioning of the beams and pressure points. Behind the students her young Cherb companion was using a small pair of binoculars, apparently to study the fine etched print on the stone, but every so often he swung them to the ceiling.

'It might look safe,' Danny said, 'but I don't think it is.'

Dixie followed his eyes.

'We don't have the expertise or the gear to get it out of there,' Danny muttered.

'But they do,' Dixie said, 'by the look of things.'

'They're acting that way,' Danny agreed.

Dixie sighed, then, 'Dixie, you're a genius!' she said. 'Danny, pat me on the back.'

'If you insist,' Danny said, 'but why are you a genius?'

'I've figured out how to get our hands on it.'

'How?'

'We let them steal it, then we steal it off them!'

'You might have something there,' Danny said slowly.

'If we can deal with the other thing first,' Dixie said.

'What other thing?' Danny saw Lily looking at him. A smile of pure delight spread over her features. Danny tried to keep his face straight.

'You know,' Dixie said. 'Only the thing that condemns us to serving the dead for the rest of our lives – that little thing?'

'Oh, that,' Danny said, his eyes still fixed on Lily. 'That's okay. I already know that.'

'You already know it?' Dixie said slowly. She was looking at Danny with a serious expression on her face, an expression he'd never seen before.

'What are you saying, Danny? How do you already know it?

'I . . . went for a walk last night. After you went to sleep. I heard it.'

'You went for a walk, but you never mentioned it?'

'It slipped my mind.'

'You found out how to stop us spending the rest of our lives looking after dead people and forgot to tell me?'

'Er, something like that,' Danny said.

'Am I missing something here?' Louis said, looking worriedly from one to the other.

'What did the mountain say?' Dixie had her hands on her hips.

Danny had never seen her look really angry before. 'It said . . . It said . . .' He was stuttering. The good part of his mind wanted to protect Dixie, but the spy part of his mind was cold. Let her find out for herself!

Dixie looked long and hard into his eyes. 'Never mind, 'she said softly. 'I'll find out myself what the mountain says.' Then she linked arms with Louis. 'Come on, Louis. Show me some of this kingdom of yours.' She turned on her heel and walked off, half dragging Louis with her.

Danny watched miserably as they disappeared into the throng of students. Then he realised that part of him felt glad. Danny the spy was happy to get out from under Dixie's watching eye. He looked back across the room. Dixie was gone. No matter, he thought, he would catch up with her later. In the meantime there was something he wanted to do.

A few minutes later he was standing at the Ring of Five door. He had passed one of the security staff sitting at a desk a little way down the corridor. He walked back there, keeping his gait casual. The guard was an attractive girl with black curly hair, barely out of her teens.

'Yes?' she said brightly. 'Can I help you?'

'It's the Ring of Five room,' he said. 'I'm a student from the Lower World and the Ring is a really important part of my research. I wonder if I could just have a look.'

'Oh no, sir,' the girl said. 'There is a key, but the Vizier himself must be asked for permission.' As she spoke Danny watched with horrified fascination as a long pink worm emerged from her nose and dangled down over her top lip.

'I'm surprised,' the girl said confidentially, 'that he even lets us keep the key here.' She sniffed and the worm was sucked back up. Danny put one hand on the desk and the other to his head.

'Are you okay?' said the girl.

'Yes, just feeling a bit faint is all.' Danny wasn't really feeling at all faint, but it wasn't hard to act it after the worm.

'I'll get you a glass of water,' the girl said sympathetically. As she left the desk Danny saw two bulletholes in her back surrounded by dried gunpowder and old blood. What had happened to her? Was it considered impolite to ask?

Still feigning faintness in case anyone was watching, he slumped into the chair behind the desk, fumbling in his coat for his lock picks. It was odd how the coat always had the thing you needed in the first pocket you tried, rather than, like most coats, in the last.

One-handed, he started to go through the desk. The drawers that were open he didn't bother with. In the three that were locked he found weapons and some syringes and tablets. He had no idea what the dead girl used them for, but shuddered at some of the images that went through his mind. But no sign of the key. He felt underneath the desk. The girl would be back at any moment. Then his hand touched a small metal clasp. He fumbled with it. There was a click and a little velvet box fell into his hand. It had to hold the key.

As he slipped the box into his pocket, the dead guard returned with a glass of water.

'Thanks,' he said gratefully, gulping it down.

'That's okay,' she said a little wistfully. 'Wouldn't mind a glass of water myself, but, you know . . .'

'Yes, of course,' Danny said, not really knowing at all. If she took a drink, would the water leak out of the holes in her back?

'Never mind,' she smiled kindly. 'Must look on the bright side, isn't that right?'

Danny thanked her profusely and walked away. He hoped she wouldn't get into trouble for the missing key, though a sneering voice in the back of his mind reminded him that she was already dead, so what could the Vizier do to her anyway?

The little black door was only slightly off the main part of the museum, yet he felt a long way from the rest of the visiting parties. It was as if the room was instinctively being given a wide berth. When he was sure that no one was watching, he opened the little velvet box. He had been right. Inside was an ornate metal key. Just as he was about to fit it to the lock he became aware of someone behind him. He wheeled round. Lily. Her smile was cat-like.

'I wanted to get this door open too,' she said, 'so I reckoned you would be here. I wouldn't have got the key so fast though. Go on. Open it.'

17

THE DIARY OF
MATT SCALPLE

The key turned easily. They found themselves in a small, ill-lit room. The room was dominated by a portrait of Longford on the back wall. There were photographs of Rufus Ness, Nurse Flanagan and Conal and dusty robes in glass cases – robes which had once been worn by the Ring, according to a faded card underneath the glass case.

'Why the big secret about this room?' Lily said. 'There's nothing here.'

'No,' Danny said, disappointed. 'I thought there might be something to tell us who our parents were.'

'What's this?' Lily said suddenly. There was an old notebook in a small case. The case was locked, but it took only a few seconds for her to open it. She blew the dust off the cover.

'"The Diary of Matt Scalple",' she read. 'But it's burned and some of the pages are stuck together – it's hard to read it.'

'Let me see.' Danny flicked through the pages. Parts of it were illegible, but it appeared to be an account of events leading up to a battle between the Ring of Five and the defenders of Wilsons Island. At first things went well – Cherb attacks were being repulsed. But then it became clear that a great terror was abroad. Matt Scalple referred to rumours of villages being destroyed, of armies devastated. Then came the final page, torn and burned.

'"... they've found out what it is ... the terror ... it's coming now ... nothing can stand in his way ... the power of the Fifth ..."'

The page was torn and dirty with what appeared to be bloodstains on the paper. After that there was nothing.

'The Power of the Fifth?' Lily said, gazing at Danny with something like wonder.

'I don't have any power,' Danny said.

'Are you sure about that?' Lily said excitedly. 'We'd make them all sit up if you did! Think about it, Danny. What we could do – if the Fifth has powers ... We could take over anything, both worlds if you wanted!'

'I don't want to take over anything,' Danny said, 'and I'm telling you I don't have any power.'

'That's the difference between us,' Lily said, a little mournfully. 'I want to take over things. I think we're a mixture of black and white, good and evil, you and me, Danny. I think the good is on top in you most of the time, and the bad is on top in me . . . most of the time.'

Danny wandered around the dim room. He didn't want to leave it. For the first time in his life he had real family, and, although they hadn't got any clues as to who their parents might be, the truth must be close. The members of the Ring looked down on him from their portraits and he could feel the tug again, as if they were telling him that they were his real family.

Lily sat on a low seat by the wall. 'You know what my mission is,' she said wearily, 'to break the Stone, or Rufus Ness will kill me. Will you trust me, Danny? I know it's difficult. We've only just met . . .'

'I have to bring the Stone back, protect it . . . the Treaty . . .'

'You're right, Danny,' she said. 'Wilsons is more important. The Treaty . . .'

'But you're the only family I've got.' Danny sounded desperate.

'I know.'

'If the Stone is broken . . .'

'If the Stone is broken,' Lily said suddenly, sitting up, it doesn't mean war. Not if you take your proper place at the head of the Ring of Five. You can stop them from attacking Wilsons and trying to invade the Upper World.'

'Do you think so?' Danny asked. 'Do you really think so?'

'Yes!' Lily said. 'We can do this!'

'I'm not sure if I want to go back to the Ring,' Danny said, uncertainty flooding through him.

'Well, there is another way,' Lily said slowly.

'What?'

'If you are the Fifth, then I can also be the Fifth. I could join the Ring in your place. With you in Wilsons, and me in the Ring . . .'

Danny turned it over feverishly in his mind. It could work. After all, if the Treaty survived this time, the Ring would keep coming on after the Stone – they were bound to succeed eventually. This way he could control events . . .

'You see,' Lily said, watching him carefully, 'it could work.'

'I have to think,' Danny said.

'Just don't take too long,' Lily said. 'it's my neck on the line, after all. And talking about necks on lines, we'd better get out of here before they miss their key.'

'I have to think about what to do,' Danny said, 'but there's one thing I don't have to think about. You *are* my sister, Lily. I know it in my heart.'

They left the room, closing and locking the door behind them. When they got to the guard's desk, Lily expertly distracted her while Danny slipped the box back. As they were walking away Danny glanced back at the little black door.

'I still don't see why it should be locked,' he said. His eye passed over a little brass plaque, almost invisible under generations of dirt, in the shadows to the left of the door. If he had read it he would have known why the room was kept locked. Underneath the grime, the plaque read:

This is a rare example of a Room of Malign Intentions. In such rooms foolish or evil thoughts are intensified, while good and wise choices are pushed to the background. It was thought that this was a fitting place for a display about the Ring of Five. The room was locked by order of the Vizier after a series of attempts to overthrow him inspired by visits to the room.

When Danny got back to the bedroom he found that Dixie's gear was gone. He went out into the corridor where he met, as if by accident, the courtier Louis.

'Where's Dixie?' he demanded.

'She thought it would be better to have a room of her own,' Louis said. 'Hers is just down the corridor. But I think she's gone to the library to work.'

Danny eyed the boy suspiciously, wondering if he could really be as wholesome as he seemed.

He spent the rest of the day searching for Dixie without success. There were vast libraries on the north side of the kingdom and he went through every one of their cavernous disused rooms, with their books mouldy, or stuck together with damp. It had been a long time since students from outside had visited the libraries of Morne.

No one bothered Danny, although people still whispered behind his back and he had the feeling that reports were going back to the Vizier.

Finally, as evening drew on, he caught sight of Dixie in the distance.

'Dixie!' he called. She was intent on a book, but when she heard his voice she looked up and disappeared. When he got to the spot where he had seen her the open book was lying on the ground, but there was no sign of Dixie, no matter how much he called her name. He picked up the book. It was an old, leather-bound tome and the title was engraved on the cover in faded gold letters – *On Treachery*. Danny had the uncomfortable feeling that he had been meant to find it.

The next few days went past without event. Dixie was obviously disappearing every time she saw Danny, and her room was always locked. He didn't know what to do with himself. He went to the storeroom both nights, but there was no sign of Lily. He saw her during the day, but she was always with the Cherb, who glared at him if he got too close.

On the third day he met Chancellor Camroc in the corridor. Camroc was bustling along, but stopped when he saw Danny.

'Are you still here?' he said in surprise.

'Yes, well, I'm, er, still studying,' Danny said, 'and I've still got to tell the Vizier what the mountain says.'

'Of course,' Camroc said. 'I'm getting so forgetful. That'll be during the Leaving Ceremony.'

'The Leaving Ceremony?' Danny asked, puzzled.

'Yes,' Camroc said. 'There will of course be music and the singing of the old songs.' He looked off into the distance and hummed a few bars and Danny realised for the first time that there was a strong smell of red wine from Camroc.

'What is the Leaving Ceremony?' Danny asked.

Camroc looked at him in surprise. 'It's when the Kingdom of Morne moves to a new location. It's coming in two days. The rainforest, I think, this time. Canoeing on the Amazon to look forward to, boy!' Camroc burst into song, a strange harsh noise in a unknown tongue, not without a certain wild beauty.

Danny stared at him. He had two days to make up his mind – should he steal or destroy the Treaty Stone?

Many miles away Agent Stone rubbed his tired eyes, put down the book he had been studying and sighed.

'What is it?' Pearl asked.

'It should be one of the great discoveries,' he said, 'the existence of a whole new world, separated from ours by space and time. The old legends begin to make sense, the stories of the gods and the Underworld – so why am I so worried all the time?'

'Maybe because both worlds now rest on the shoulders of a small boy,' Pearl said, 'and that boy is . . .'

'Our son?' Stone said.

'Don't say things like that,' Pearl said. 'It isn't true.'

'Perhaps not in a strict sense,' Stone said, 'but he has no one else.'

'He might have been better without us. With us around he didn't have to look far to find the meaning of betrayal. We cheated him from the start.'

'Then we must make up for that,' Stone said.

'If we can,' Pearl said, sitting down and staring into the ashes of the fire. 'If we can.'

18
The Iron Maiden

Try as they might, Vandra and Toxique could not get Les to tell them what familiar thing he thought had changed in Wilsons.

'I have to think about it,' he said. 'What if I'm wrong? It would be terrible if I was wrong. I have to talk to someone on the staff.'

'Who would you talk to?' Toxique asked.

'Not Brunholm anyway,' Vandra snorted. 'And Duddy's not much use.'

'What about Valant? Or Spitfire?'

'No,' Les said with a frown. 'I'll have to go right to the top.'

'To Devoy?' Vandra said.

'To Devoy,' Les said grimly, then, as if to himself, 'but what if they're all in on it?'

It was no surprise to Vandra and Toxique when Les got out of bed that night and sneaked out of the Roosts. They had concealed themselves on the roof of the girls' Roosts to watch out for him. He was so lost in thought as he passed them that they could have dropped something on his head and he wouldn't have noticed. Once he had descended the stairs they jumped softly down and followed him. He made a beeline for the main building. Vandra and Toxique had learned much about tracking in Wilsons, but they didn't need any of their skills, Les was so wrapped up in his mission.

They followed him through the front door, past Valant's empty desk and into the gloomy corridors that led to the heart of the building. In the shifting shadows of the Wilsons interior they soon lost sight of him, and when they came to a fork they debated which branch to take until a raven flew over their heads and into the left-hand branch.

'I think that settles it,' Vandra said, and they followed the raven. On they went, passing one of the interior courtyards where the Messengers exercised, the lighting getting dimmer and dimmer, until they were almost in darkness.

'I don't like this,' Toxique said, his voice rising. 'I think someone's going to att—!' The lights went out. Toxique shrieked as a wiry arm wrapped itself around his neck. Vandra fell heavily against the wall, but managed to grab a torch from her pocket. When she turned it on, it was to see Les choking Toxique.

'Les!' she shouted. 'It's Toxique!'

Slowly he released his grip. 'You're right,' he said. 'I thought it was . . . never mind. You better come with me now. But stay outside when I'm talking to Devoy.'

They jumped at a clanging noise which came from nearby.

'What's that?' Toxique whispered, a note of hysteria in his voice. They heard the sound again.

'Take it easy, Toxique,' Vandra said, but there was something sinister about the noise.

'It's this way,' Les said. He set out determinedly. With a glance at each other, Vandra and Toxique followed.

The noise was coming from the other side of the teachers' common room. The Unknown Spy watched them silently from his barred window as they crept through it. They could almost feel his eyes on them as they tiptoed past.

They were approaching the front of the house. Toxique looked terrified.

'The noise,' he said, 'it's coming from that room – you know the one.'

'The torture chamber,' Vandra said grimly.

'There could be work ahead for you tonight, Physick,' Toxique said.

'I'm in no condition to help anyone.'

Reluctantly they moved along the corridor towards the torture chamber. The boom rang out again, a horrible melancholy noise. Vandra glanced at Toxique, hoping he wouldn't suddenly shout out. But he merely rolled his eyes.

'I know what it is,' he said. 'I know what we're going to see.'

The three friends reached the door. Vandra and Les lay down on the floor and inched forward so that they were looking into the room from ground level – it was one of the concealment techniques they had learned in the previous term; you put your body where the person you are watching doesn't expect to see it. They had a clear view into the room, and all three hearts sank when they saw what was going on. A man stood with his back to them. He was oiling the hinges of the iron maiden, the steel coffin with the spiked lid. As they watched he swung it backwards and forwards, then slammed it shut as if to test the hinges. They heard the booming noise again as the lid closed. Then the man turned and they saw him in profile. It was Devoy.

The three cadets wanted to leave, but a horrified fascination rooted them to the spot. They watched Devoy polish the thumbscrews, check the tensions on the rack and dust the teeth pullers and bone crushers. The expression on his face did not change – it never did – but there was something demonic about the calm way he moved from instrument to instrument.

It was Vandra who broke the spell, drawing Toxique and Les away from the doorway. They walked back through the common room, still observed by the Unknown Spy. In silence they went through the unpeopled corridors of Wilsons and did not speak until they were out in the open air.

'If it was Brunholm,' Les said at last, 'it wouldn't have been so bad. You would have expected it. But Devoy?'

'Yes,' Vandra said, 'and who is he planning to torture? All that stuff is ready to use.' Toxique said nothing, but made a snuffling noise. Vandra put her hand on his arm.

'I don't know about you,' Les said, 'but I don't really feel like bed.'

'Me neither,' Vandra said. 'What about the summerhouse?'

'Okay,' Les said. 'I got some tea there, and some muffins maybe we could toast.'

The friends made their way down the gardens and on to the forest path leading towards the summerhouse. The night was calm, cold and quiet and they moved without making much noise. A casual observer would have thought that everyone at Wilsons was safely in their bed, but the night at Wilsons was sometimes busier than the day, and at least one pair of eyes was watching them. The siren, Vicky, was in a bad mood. For weeks now she had been aware of another presence in the building – someone else using her own secret routes for getting about the place unseen. This other didn't seem to care very much about concealing their tracks. Manhole covers were left askew, hidden passages didn't have their secret entrances properly replaced after use, and food and tools and all sorts of trash were strewn along her own well-maintained routes. For all that she was vicious, amoral and untrustworthy, the siren of the North Shore was also extremely tidy. She might have tolerated sharing her secret world with someone who tried to keep it shipshape, but she wasn't going to put up with mess.

She had tried laying traps for the intruder, but he was cunning and the traps had been contemptuously thrown aside. There was nothing for it but to use the siren songs that in years gone by had lured innumerable ships on to the rocks and sent scores of sailors to a watery grave. Her technique had got rusty, so she had spent a week in the woods refining it. First she had charmed the birds from the trees. She had tempted spring flowers into opening, then left them to blacken and die in the frost. She had charmed blind moles from the ground and by the end of the week she was able to lure foxes and weasels and all animals that were cunning and wary. She was ready.

She had picked a spot where her voice would travel along part of the network of secret passages but not penetrate the walls to lure other inhabitants of the school. She cleared her throat, tried a few practice notes and began.

The sweet beguiling music drifted through the tunnels and passageways, gathering in force until it seemed that the very stones of the passages would weep, and the creeping crawling creatures of the night stopped their business and dreamed. Vicky gave herself up to her treacherous song until it seemed that nothing, neither man nor beast, could resist it . . .

'Oi!'

Vicky blinked and her song faltered. Had she heard a noise?

'Oi, you!'

The siren's song came to an abrupt halt. Was she hearing correctly? 'Me?'

'Yes, you. Would you shut up with that bloody singing! I'm trying to get some sleep here.'

Vicky couldn't tell where the gruff rude voice was coming from. The speaker was able to use the twisting tunnels to disguise his location. 'What do you mean, "bloody singing"?' Vicky said crossly. 'That's a classic siren song.'

'Just sounds like noise to me,' the voice said, 'and it's keeping me awake.'

'I'll have you know that "noise" has lured ships on to rocks for decades . . . longer!' Vicky said.

'Must have been tone-deaf sailors then,' the voice grumbled. 'It doesn't do anything for me, so put a sock in it.'

Vicky's mouth hung open. Never in a long career of luring sailors and others to their death had she been told to put a sock in it. She put her hand in her pocket and produced a slender razor-sharp knife.

'Maybe if you told me where you are I could sing you a lullaby,' she said, in as sweet a voice as she could manage.

'Stick your lullaby!' the voice said. 'I'd rather have the ravens sing me to sleep.'

Vicky crouched to listen. The voice was either very smart or very lucky, for such were the echoes that she could not even tell the direction from which it was coming.

'Now push off,' the voice said.

Almost crying with vexation, Vicky retreated. She had never been so insulted. And, as if to add insult to injury, extremely loud snoring began to echo from the passageway behind her.

★

Despite the cold, the summerhouse always felt welcome, as if its old planks retained the warmth of distant summers. Les busied himself making hot milky tea, while Vandra toasted the muffins. Toxique lit some old candle stubs.

'There's nothing we can do about Devoy at the minute,' Vandra said firmly, 'but if Les still won't tell us what or who he suspects . . .'

'In case I'm wrong,' Les said, looking torn.

'. . . then we'll have to go with what we have. Which is what the Unknown Spy told us – that one possible reason for his wife's murder was that she was the inventor of the Sibling Strategy. But what was the strategy? And why was she murdered for it?'

'To tell you the truth,' Les said, sounding a little ashamed, 'I don't even know what a sibling is.'

'A sibling is a brother or a sister!' A cloaked figure carrying a revolver stepped into the circle of candlelight. Toxique stifled a scream. Les cursed out loud and Vandra jumped to her feet. The figure threw back its hood. It was Starling.

'Phew!' said Les. 'I thought you was a Cherb.'

'If I had been, you'd all be dead,' Starling said. 'You could be heard and seen for miles.'

'So much for the Gift of Anticipation,' Les muttered at Toxique.

'Don't look at me,' Toxique said. 'I told you it doesn't work all the time.'

'Just keep better watch the next time,' Starling said. 'Your carelessness will cost you though!'

They looked at her nervously.

'A cup of tea and a muffin,' she demanded with a laugh. 'Now, what's all this about the Sibling Strategy?'

'We just wanted to know what it was,' Vandra said.

'It's simple enough in principle, though it requires a lot of skill and experience,' Starling said. 'All you do is use a close relative against the subject. There are variations, of course. There's the double-sibling strategy, the older and younger variations, the fake-sibling variation . . . McGuinness has been researching it. It appears that the Unknown Spy's wife first developed it after she had been betrayed by her younger brother. This betrayal haunted her all her life.'

'But what would she use it for?'

'That's what I don't know,' Starling admitted, her voice muffled by the muffin, melted butter running down her chin.

Vandra turned the S and G ring on her finger, feeling that something in their talk was vital to Danny. But what?

19
WHAT THE MOUNTAIN SAID

The following day Lily came to Danny's room early.

'I didn't mean to wake you,' she said, 'but I haven't been sleeping all that well. We need to decide what to do, Danny.'

'Where's the Cherb?' Danny said, peering up and down the corridor.

'He's busy with the final preparations for stealing the Treaty Stone,' Lily said. 'We have the day together. Whatever you decide, Danny, we'll always have this day.'

As they set off together Danny saw Dixie disappearing at the end of the corridor. Why can't she understand that I've found my sister? he thought, the Room of Malign Intentions distorting his thoughts so that he could only see things from his own point of view.

But for that day there was nothing to do but to walk in the gorgeous halls and corridors of Morne, ignoring the courtiers muttering in corners. Danny and Lily climbed upwards to where the towers of Morne met the soaring granite peaks. It was beautiful and silent. They had brought a picnic from one of the dining halls, and as they ate Danny told of his upbringing by two secret agents who had pretended to be his parents. Lily said that her upbringing had been hard. There had been no pretence that the couple who reared her were her real parents. She'd been abandoned, they said, usually adding that they weren't surprised, since she was lazy and no-good, despite the fact that she worked from dawn to dusk, cleaning the cheap boarding house that they kept.

'Think about it, Danny – when we rule the two worlds we'll be able to find our real parents!'

It was dusk before they returned from the high peaks, walking slowly. They parted outside Danny's door. When Lily reached the end of the corridor, she turned and gave him a long steady look.

He went into his room and sat down on the bed. He had made up his mind. He could not let his sister be at the mercy of the Ring. If he had been able to think about it properly he could have found another way out. He could have taken Lily back to Wilsons with him. He could even have joined the Ring again and protected her that way, but the influence of the Room of Malign Intentions still hung over him, fogging his judgement, an influence that was still there when Dixie appeared right in front of him.

'I wish you'd stop doing that,' he said sourly.

'"Hello, Dixie" would have been nicer,' she said. She looked tired. There were dark shadows under her eyes. 'Danny, we need to do something about getting the Treaty Stone. If it's broken—'

'If it's broken, then so what? Devoy isn't right about everything, you know.'

'I can't believe you've gone over to . . . to the Ring, just like that.'

'I haven't gone over to the Ring!'

'Well, what is going on then? Who is that girl? Why are you hanging around with her?'

Danny wanted to scream at Dixie to stop being so stupid, that Lily was his sister. But the fog of Malign Intentions stopped him, and somewhere in that fog prowled spy Danny.

'Just leave her out of it,' he mumbled.

'I can't leave her out of it,' Dixie said. 'I don't trust her—'

'That's enough,' Danny said. 'I do.'

'Danny, we're friends,' Dixie said. 'Tomorrow we have to stand up and tell the Vizier what the mountain says, and after that we have to get out of here with the Treaty Stone. We're a team, Danny.'

But a voice inside Danny's head said, 'She's wrong.

You and Lily are a team.' He felt a wave of cunning sweep over him, warm and sickly.

'Its all right, Dixie,' he heard himself say. 'We'll get the Stone. I'm just getting close to the girl so that I can get the Stone off her once the Cherb has stolen it.'

'Are you sure, Danny?' Dixie looked at him closely.

'Of course,' he lied. 'Sorry, I should have told you of my plan. You get used to not trusting people.'

'You can say that again,' Dixie said, looking a bit more cheerful. 'This Louis character – I don't think I'd trust him as far as I could throw him. Or any of the people here.'

'I'm getting tired,' Danny said, faking a yawn.

'I'll let you get a bit of kip then. Big day tomorrow. I think I've worked out a route out of here, by the way.'

'Brilliant,' Danny said.

'Okay, I'm off then,' Dixie said. 'By the way – do you definitely have the word? What the mountain says?'

'Yes, I'm sorry. I should have told you sooner.' Danny hesitated. 'The mountain says . . . storm.'

Dixie smiled at him. 'I knew you wouldn't leave me as a slave for the dead. Night!'

One minute Dixie was there, next she was gone. Danny stared miserably at the spot where she had been standing. Why had he told her the wrong word? And why had he not told the truth about Lily? He went to the window and looked out on to the snowy mountains. He could tell Dixie the real word tomorrow. He could pretend it was a joke. He wouldn't let his friend fall into the hands of the dead.

He lay down on the bed and fell into an uneasy sleep.

The following day though, it wasn't easy to get close to Dixie. She always seemed to be in the distance, and whenever he approached her the boy Louis appeared to engage him in conversation on some pretext or other. The Leaving Ceremony was due to begin that afternoon, and Danny was becoming increasingly desperate. The people of Morne, in even greater finery than usual, flocked into the hallways around the Vizier's court. Camroc walked through the crowd looking around with great satisfaction and humming snatches of obscure songs. Danny found himself face to face with Macari, in bright blue silk and a hat with a peacock's feather.

Macari winked at him. 'Glad I didn't have to leave my mark on you.' He laughed.

Danny wasn't sure whether being branded with a red-hot iron was funny, but he grinned mirthlessly back.

A hand plucked his sleeve and drew him aside. Lily. Her face was taut with anxiety.

'The Cherb will steal the Treaty Stone during the festivities,' she whispered. 'We can get out by the storeroom. Danny, I . . . I need to know . . .'

'I'm coming with you,' he found himself saying. 'We've been let down enough.'

'What about your friend?'

'Don't worry about her – she's taken care of.' Danny barely recognised his own voice. He remembered the time he had taken voice dye and had acquired the tones of a gravel-voiced dwarf. That was what he sounded like now, with a hint of treachery added in.

More and more people crowded into the hall. The great doors to the court opened and they surged forward. Danny was separated from Lily. At the edge of the throng he could see the Cherb boy slipping away.

Macari took hold of his arm. 'Your presence is required, my friend.'

Across the room he saw Lily being escorted by Camroc, and Dixie, her arm in a metal cuff – presumably to stop her disappearing – held by a not-so-friendly-looking Louis.

The crowds parted as the three of them were led towards the dais where the Vizier sat, his gaze resting on each of them in turn. The room fell silent.

'Where is our little Cherb friend?' he said quietly.

Camroc paled and looked around wildly.

'Never mind,' the Vizier said, his voice cold. 'We'll deal with that lapse later. He would have been little use to the dead anyway, being treacherous and untrustworthy.'

He motioned to Camroc, who handed them each a quill and parchment.

'Each of you will write down what the mountain says and hand your answer to Camroc,' the Vizier said.

Now is the time! Danny thought. You have to tell Dixie!

'I require you not to speak, on pain of death,' the Vizier said smoothly as though reading his mind.

Dixie smiled confidently at Danny. He stared at her, his mind frozen.

'Write down the word,' the Vizier said.

Dixie knelt and rested the parchment on her knee. Danny watched his friend as if she was signing her own death warrant.

'Write!' the Vizier commanded.

Lily bent to her parchment. Danny watched his own hand write as though it was being controlled by someone else.

'Turn and show the word to the subjects of Morne.'

Lily turned first. She held up her parchment, a single word written on it: 'Alone'. Dixie looked confused, then looked at Danny. Of course Danny had given her the right word! She held up her parchment. A great sigh ran through the crowd. Louis shook his head slowly and smiled. Treachery! Danny thought, then realised with shame, and a strange dark sense of accomplishment, that his was by far the greater treachery. He held up his own parchment. 'Alone'.

'Take the girl,' the Vizier said quietly. Two of the dead appeared as if from nowhere and grabbed Dixie's arms in the metal cuffs before she could disappear. With a cry and a look of disbelief, she was pulled off into the crowd. Danny looked after her, stunned. Her parchment landed face up on the ground. 'Storm'.

There was a long silence in the room, then Louis, with a thin sneer on his face, began to clap. The applause spread out in ripples until the whole room was clapping. The applause swelled. Then the Vizier held up his hand and the clapping stopped. Camroc coughed, cleared his throat and emitted a long ululating wail. It was the signal for the festivities to begin. Jugglers and fire-breathers poured into the hall. The ceiling flowered with brightly coloured trapeze artists. Great tables groaning with food appeared in alcoves around the hall. Danny looked about him, bewildered, as the hall exploded in flames and firecrackers and music. He prowled the edges, looking for his sister, but she was nowhere to be seen. Dixie's frightened face kept coming into his mind, but somehow he was able to thrust it away without too much difficulty.

Finally a frantic Lily found him.

'Where have you been? I've been looking for you everywhere. Nala is ready, but the minute he gets his hands on the Stone we'd better be ready to go!'

Nala? Danny hadn't even thought of the Cherb as having a name.

They slipped out of the hall and raced through the empty corridors to the museum. The dead girl wasn't at her desk.

'That was a good move, throwing your pal to the dead,' Lily said. 'They'll be distracted with her for a while.'

A shudder ran through Danny but it was far away, as though he wasn't in touch with his own feelings, and he was able to ignore it. They ran on into the Ring gallery. Lily stopped in front of the Treaty Stone. Danny gasped. Nala had woven a cat's cradle of strong golden thread in and around the Stone. The gold shone in the spotlights.

'It's Thread of Independent Motion,' Lily said. 'You tell it where to go, and it'll go there. The best thing is that it's very strong. You can even climb on it. Go, Nala!'

The Cherb, who had been hidden at the side of the gallery, leaped up and grabbed one of the golden threads. Hauling himself arm over arm he climbed upwards. Danny could see that the thread had been positioned to avoid the many beams and security fixtures around the Treaty and he could only marvel at the intricate way it had been strung up around the Stone. Obviously the Morne people had complete confidence in their security, but they hadn't reckoned on Nala. With breathtaking nimbleness the little figure swung in and around the security beams. Danny held his breath as the Cherb got closer and closer to the Stone. Once he slipped, only just hanging on to avoid the pressure sensors on the floor below him.

It took half an hour, but finally Nala reached the Stone. Danny felt a hint of admiration for the little Cherb, his bravery and skill. He watched as Nala went behind the Stone, where he took an ordinary stone of the same size and shape as the Treaty Stone from a pocket. With one swift movement he unhooked the Treaty Stone and propped the plain one in its place.

'Weight sensors,' Lily said, her eyes not leaving the Cherb. 'Hurry, Nala.' He began the long climb back, doing everything in reverse. Nala was at the limit of his strength, sweat running from his face, his limbs

263

beginning to falter, but still Lily urged him on. It was bound to happen. Nala made a lunge for the final golden thread, his hand slipped and he tumbled to the floor. Alarms started to sound, loud and mournful. There was a great rumbling at the entrance to the Ring gallery as a massive gate started to slide across the entrance.

'Hurry!' Lily shouted. Nala hobbled towards them holding the Stone. Lily grabbed it and began to run towards the entrance. The gate was already halfway across, and gathering speed. Danny took the stone off Lily. It was surprisingly light. They had almost reached the gate when they heard a cry behind them. Nala had injured his leg when he fell and he was limping heavily. He stretched out his arms for help but Lily pushed Danny impatiently. They both stumbled through the shrinking gap and then the gates closed with a clang behind them. Nala gripped the bars. He said nothing, but his eyes were fixed not on Lily but on Danny.

'Leave him,' Lily said. 'He's played his part.' Danny followed her, but he felt the Cherb's eyes drilling into his back.

They heard running feet in front of them, but Lily had planned her route well. They ducked down side corridors and unused maintenance tunnels. Within minutes they were in the little storeroom. Lily opened the outer door and pushed Danny through. They stood in the snow, the evening shadows lengthening. They were free of Morne. They had stolen the Treaty Stone, and Dixie was a prisoner, betrayed and abandoned.

20

A DISCOVERY

For some days Les had felt that the mood of his fellow pupils wasn't good. There was a general grumbling noise when they were having their meals in Ravensdale, and in the Roosts.

Vandra had noticed it too. 'Have you noticed that everybody seems to be on some sort of punishment detail?' Les, who had spent all of his spare time that week scraping ancient raven droppings from one of the disused buildings in Ravensdale with Toxique, as part of their Fifth Regulation punishment, realised that she was right. Everywhere pupils were engaged in difficult, sometimes dangerous cleaning jobs, or studying long into the night. There had been several fist fights among the boys, and cliques had formed in the girls' Roosts.

'Who's handing out all these punishments?' Toxique asked.

Les looked tight-lipped.

266

Vandra watched him carefully. 'Hang on a second,' she said. 'I know what you're thinking.'

'What?' Les said defensively.

'It's Blackpitts, isn't it? It's him that's handing out all the punishments. He's the familiar thing that has changed!'

'I didn't want to say,' Les said miserably. 'Blackpitts was always dead good to me. I can't understand what's happened to him. He's been got at in some way, or blackmailed or something.'

'We have to find him and make him talk,' Vandra said.

'How do we do that? None of us have ever seen him.'

'I suppose,' Toxique said, 'we find a wire and follow it.'

Finding a wire and following it proved harder than they expected. There were miles of ducting, and the wires were well concealed in the ducts. When they did find one it was difficult to separate it from all the other wires. All they could really discover was that all the wires led upwards towards the roof.

'I'm not sure if I want to tangle with that Roof Man,' Les said, remembering Danny's run-in with the guardian of the roofs.

'I don't think we have a choice,' Vandra said.

'But how do we get there?' Toxique asked.

Help came from an unexpected quarter. The others went back to the Roosts but Les, on his way to Ravensdale, ran straight into Vicky who had just landed on the ground, having leapt from a ledge above his head.

'Sorry, Vicky,' Les said hastily as the siren glared at him.

'Just be more careful next time,' she said.

'You don't look very happy,' Les said.

'Things aren't the same way around here,' she said darkly. 'Not at all the same.'

'What's up?' Les fell into step beside her.

'There's a sneak about,' she said. 'I keep looking for him, but he stays out of my way.'

'A sneak? Listen,' Les said carefully, 'you're only one person. Another few pairs of eyes might make it easier to find him. I wouldn't mind helping you. The roof would probably be the best place to look, don't you think?'

'Would you look?' Vicky said suspiciously. 'I wouldn't be able to pay you.'

'That's perfectly all right,' Les said. 'Glad to be of service. The only thing is how to get to the roof.'

'That's no problem,' Vicky said airily. 'I'll show you.'

*

Four hours later Les, Vandra and Toxique found them-selves climbing up the inside of an extremely dirty and wet drainage pipe with Vicky dancing in front of them, seemingly able to negotiate the dirtiest and tightest spaces while remaining spotless. When they got out of the pipe they had to crawl through a venti-lation duct, then up a series of back stairs and decrepit ladders with missing rungs. Looking back, Les could see the pale, determined faces of Toxique and Vandra climbing grimly through the dark behind him.

After what seemed like hours Vicky threw open a rusty iron door and they all emerged. There was a strong cold wind blowing across the peaks and valleys of the Wilsons roof, and Les gulped great lungfuls while trying to rub the cobwebs and dust off his face and out of his eyes.

'We'll spread out in a line,' he said, 'and try to see if we can find Blackpi— I mean, an intruder.'

They crisscrossed the vast roof area for an hour, but didn't see anyone else, although they stumbled across all sorts of rusting and abandoned equipment: pumps, compessors, and old spy tools such as broken telescopes and satellite dishes. It wasn't until they reached the front of the roof that they found something odd – a little nest that had been concealed with camouflage netting. Inside was a pair of binoculars and a microphone with a large dish around it.

'It's a directional mic,' Vandra said. 'You can listen to far-off conversations with it.'

'And whoever was here had a perfect view of everyone who was coming and going from Wilsons.'

'Something's going on.'

They hunted across the roofs until dusk. The wind had turned cold and they were tired. Les had slipped on a broken slate and cut his knee. As he sat with his trouser leg rolled up, Toxique came over.

'There's nothing else here,' Les said.

'You're probably right,' Toxique said, 'but with Danny and Dixie gone, we've got to do something. I wonder how they're getting on?'

They were about to give up when Les spotted something. The evening light had cast strong shadows across the rooftops, so that the leading and slates showed different tones.

'Look.' Les pointed. Leading up to an old wooden door that they had tried earlier, a path had appeared, where walking feet had, over a period of time, left a trail. It had been invisible earlier on. They followed the path. The door looked as if it hadn't been opened for years, but Toxique rubbed his finger around the battered lock and sniffed it.

'Oil,' he said. 'Somebody's been keeping it lubricated.' All four of them went for lock picks and hairpins but Vicky was the first. In a flash she had the lock picked and was through the door, a long hairpin in her hand. The others followed cautiously.

The room was a prison cell. The windows had been barred. There was a bare wooden bunk in one corner. On the floor was a tin mug half-full of brackish water, and beside it a tin plate with a few crusts. A figure lay on the bunk. It was dressed in a dirty paisley dressing gown with what had once been a silk handkerchief in the pocket but was now a pathetic rag. A few scraps of hair clung to the skull – a feeble attempt had been made to smooth them across the head. Underneath the dressing gown were Indian trousers, stained to the point of being virtually unrecognisable. The person's uneven breathing was only just audible.

'Who is it?' Les breathed.

'I do believe we've found Mr Blackpitts,' said Vandra.

Blackpitts was unconscious. Vandra examined him.

'There's nothing I can do for him here,' she said. 'He's got malnutrition. Whoever's been keeping him here hasn't bothered to feed him very often.'

'What's this got to do with my intruder?' Vicky demanded.

Vandra rounded on her crossly but Les intervened. 'Could be everything,' he said. 'The person who's giving you a hard time could be the same person that's keeping Blackpitts here.'

'We need to get him to the Apothecary,' Vandra said.

'I need him to talk,' Vicky said.

'In that case, you'd better help us,' Vandra replied. Vicky sprang up on to the bed and scooped the unconscious Blackpitts up into her arms as if he weighed nothing at all. She was out of the door like a shot. The others ran to catch up as the siren leapt lightly across the roof peaks.

Even Vicky couldn't carry Blackpitts down the way they had come, although his emaciated body weighed very little. Instead she led them to a small hut on the roof which opened to reveal a rickety-looking lift. The cage was broken and the flywheel was rusted. The cable had great threads of wire hanging from it. Vicky jumped on board. The others followed, with Les looking nervously at Toxique.

'You getting any feelings about this?' he whispered.

'Nothing,' Toxique said, 'but that doesn't mean the cable isn't going to snap.'

'Thanks, Toxique,' Les said, then grabbed the side of the cage as it felt as if the ground had just been snatched away from under his feet. With a cacophony of shrieks and groans the ancient lift shot down into

272

the building. Sparks and flakes of rust flew from the cable. Toxique's mouth was moving but Les couldn't hear him. Even the normally calm Vandra was clinging on to the side of the cage. Vicky looked unperturbed. She punched a button with her fist. The lift came to a halt as if it had hit a brick wall. Toxique groaned and fell over. Les felt as if all his internal organs had been hurled upwards and squashed into his head. The door screeched open and Vicky skipped out, still holding the unconscious Blackpitts. Les staggered to the door. They were outside the infirmary. He made his way in just in time to see Vicky dump Blackpitts on an autopsy table in front of a surprised Jamshid.

'Fix him,' she said.

An hour later Blackpitts was in bed, sleeping peacefully. Vandra had ingested a glucose solution that Jamshid had prepared and had injected it into Blackpitts's veins. Blackpitts had whimpered a little and held up one frail hand, murmuring, 'No!' before collapsing back on the bed. There were bruises and marks of beatings all over his body. Vandra looked furious. Les bit his lip. He knew what he would like to do to whoever had done this. Jamshid shooed them out of the place.

They made their way towards the stairs, not willing to chance the lift. As they set foot on the first step a familiar voice sounded from a hidden speaker.

'My three favourite cadets,' it sneered, 'and with the beautiful if somewhat treacherous siren in tow. Another Fifth Regulation offence this time, I think. Latrine duty for the little Messenger. You'll be picking filth out of your feathers for a month.'

They looked at each other. Whoever it was obviously hadn't discovered that Blackpitts had been rescued.

'Toxique,' Les whispered, 'I've got a plan. Go to the Roosts. Get as many people as you can and line them up as if they're welcoming a visitor coming up the front drive. Quickly.'

Toxique looked at him in puzzlement, then realisation dawned. He hurried off.

'Come on,' Les said. 'I didn't want to risk Toxique screaming out when we're sneaking up, but I want you to stay in the background, Vandra, when we make our move. Let's go!'

They got to the roof in the lift, the way up being no less terrifying than the way down. When the lift arrived at the top, it fell back about six feet, then shot up again, striking the interior of the little hut with a crash.

'Foulness and corruption,' Toxique muttered as his head thumped against the wire cage. They followed Vicky out of the lift. The wind cut through their clothing like a knife. They found the shelter of a chimney and huddled behind it. Only Vicky was unperturbed as usual. She produced a nail file and started manicuring her nails.

It felt like hours before they heard cheering coming from the direction of the front drive. It wasn't very loud cheering, and in fact sounded more like the grumbling of a large number of people who would rather be in bed. They waited another few minutes, then crept cautiously out of hiding. The rooftops were slippery from frost and they had to move slowly, though the wind and the creak of aerials and dishes and battered old surveillance equipment at least covered the sound of their advance as they moved towards the nest at the front of the building.

As they got close to the edge, Vicky held up her hand. They could just see the outline of someone crouched in the nest. Moonlight glinted from binoculars. Down below there was another forced cheer from the gathered cadets.

They approached the nest along the edge of the roof, not daring to look to their left where the crumbling parapet had given way in places so that there was nothing between them and the sheer drop below. There was a flash of steel in Vicky's hand. Closer and closer they crept. Les stopped Vandra. He didn't want her getting caught up in a struggle. The figure in the nest was intent on what was going on below and didn't move. They were almost at the edge of the nest when disaster struck. A small door was flung open and Brunholm strode out on to the roof.

'Hey!' he shouted. 'You cadets! What are you doing up here? Get down right now!'

Things happened very fast after that. Brunholm stepped on a patch of ice and with a howl of anger and pain he flew into the air and landed on his back. The figure in the nest whirled round, features contorted in fury. Les felt fingers like iron hawsers around his throat and found himself staring into a pair of red-rimmed eyes. Eyes that burned into his – one brown, the other bright blue. Rufus Ness, the spymaster of the Cherbs.

Ness gasped and his grip lessened. One hand went to his shoulder, where bright red blood appeared on his tunic.

'So Cherb blood is red after all,' Vicky said, wiping her knife fastidiously with a lace handkerchief.

Ness bellowed with rage and charged at her, but Vicky skipped out of the way. Les stood up, but swayed, light-headed, dangerously close to the parapet. Down below, the crowd of cadets listened in silence to the combat on the rooftops, trying to make out in the darkness what was going on.

'Don't move, Ness,' Brunholm said. He had

recovered his balance and now levelled a revolver at the Cherb.

Ness spat on the ground and ran lightly along the parapet. Vandra tried to get out of his way, but she slipped. With a contemptuous grunt, Ness swung an arm at her. Vandra staggered towards the brink, seemed to regain her balance, then the crumbling stone beneath her feet gave way. There was a gasp from below, and a horrified intake of breath from Les as Vandra, without a sound, fell from view.

It was Toxique who told what happened next. Toxique, who had found his fellow cadets asleep and who had bullied and cajoled them out of bed by threatening to slip a mild but potent emetic into one of their meals over the following days if they didn't come. Toxique, who had led them to the driveway and ordered them to cheer. He watched as Vandra turned in the air, her fall taking an age, almost graceful as the ground rushed towards her. A scream died in his throat. There was nothing to be done. Then, moving with the speed of an arrow, a small shape flew across the facade of the building. As Vandra sped towards certain death she was seized by a pair of frail arms. The watchers held their breath as Vandra's little rescuer struggled to hold altitude, the weight too much for the small body, the ground approaching too fast. At the last second the rescuer found strength from somewhere, slowed, hovered in the air for a second then fell straight into a patch of gooseberry bushes.

'Now, my dear,' the elderly Messenger Daisy said, picking herself out of the bushes and attempting to remove several thorns from her legs, 'one good turn deserves another, don't you think?'

On the roof, Ness had disappeared in the confusion. Brunholm began to fire shots in the darkness. A ricochet struck the chimney beside Les's head, and he had to wait until Brunholm had emptied the revolver and the hammer was clicking on an empty chamber before he dared emerge from cover.

'Where's Vicky?' he asked.

'Gone after that murdering scum,' Brunholm growled, pocketing his gun. A skylight in the roof was open and there was fresh blood on the entrance to it.

'Let them go,' Brunholm said callously. 'Neither of them would be any great loss.'

An hour later Devoy and Brunholm sat in the library of the third landing while Les, Vandra and Toxique told him what had happened.

'The levels of punishment were severe, I see that now,' Devoy said. 'My thoughts were with Danny and Dixie, so I wasn't paying attention to what was happening right under my nose. It shakes me to the core to know that Rufus Ness had infiltrated Wilsons. He was obviously responsible for the assassination attempts on Les and on poor Daisy.'

'And me,' Brunholm put in. 'That crossbow is a Cherb trick all right.'

Devoy had been standing in front of the fire. Now he moved across the room until he was standing in front of the Mirror of Limited Reflection, which showed his face but none of the room behind him. He was indeed shaken to the core by the fact that Ness had been at large in Wilsons, and might even still be there. He looked up at the portrait of Longford. It had been an achievement to get Ness into Wilsons in itself, but Longford always had a larger scheme up his sleeve.

'What about the Unknown Spy's wife?' he asked.

'Ness, without a doubt,' Brunholm said. 'It was done to turn the Unknown Spy against Knutt.' He looked at Les with dislike. 'Though why he would go to so much bother to get rid of a mere messenger boy . . .'

'Quite,' Devoy said. 'No offence, of course,' he said to the reddening Les, 'but it seems unnecessarily complicated. If he wanted to kill Mr Knutt (and we are all glad of course that he did not), why did he not just kill him and be done with it?'

'Unless,' Vandra began hesitantly, 'it was a double bluff. What if we were meant to think he killed the Unknown Spy's wife as a way of getting the Unknown Spy to kill Les, whereas in fact the attempt on Les's life was a cover for getting rid of the Unknown Spy's Wife, if you know what I mean . . .' she concluded lamely.

'Excellent,' Devoy said. 'Now you're starting to think like a spy!'

'Yes,' Brunholm said, 'it makes sense, but why?'

'Why, indeed?' Devoy said. His mind was full of questions. How did Ness get into Wilsons? He couldn't have done it on his own. Blackpitts is the announcer now, but before that he was an exceptionally efficient and cautious agent. Ness would have needed help to overpower him and to take over his position in a convincing way. Devoy would have to deal with it all . . .

'Excuse me,' Toxique said, 'but we did find something out. We know that the Unknown Spy's wife was an expert at the Sibling Strategy, but we don't know much about what that is.'

Devoy's expression did not change, although it came closer to changing than it had for many years. His eyes gleamed. Longford always had another motive, a hidden agenda. And these children had stumbled upon it. The Sibling Strategy? How could he have been so blind?

21
CRYING

The walls of Morne towered above Danny and Lily. Danny sprawled in the snow panting, then leapt to his feet.

'We'd better run,' he said. 'They'll be hunting us!'

'It's all right,' Lily said. 'They don't leave the walls of Morne. Ever. That little door we came through is for visitors.'

'What about Macari?'

'His chip shop is part of the place. He never actually left.'

'Still,' Danny said, 'we need to get going. Night's coming on. We have to get to the shelter of the town.'

The urgency of his own voice surprised him. It was as if it was urging him to get away before he became fully aware of what he had done. That moment wasn't far off. Beyond the walls of Morne, the influence of the Room of Malign Intentions was wearing off quickly.

There was a loud rumble, almost like distant

thunder. The ground around them shook a little. A small piece of masonry fell from the wall above them and landed at his feet.

'What's happening?' he said, alarmed.

'It's the kingdom getting ready to relocate,' Lily said. 'It's breaking free of the mountains.'

There was another loud rumble, and this time a tiny maze of cracks appeared along what had looked like a seamless join between the castle and the bedrock it stood on.

'Will it come back here?' Danny asked.

Lily shrugged. 'According to Louis, not for eighty or ninety years, maybe even a hundred.'

Danny stared at the castle. The full realisation of his betrayal of Dixie came crashing down on him. If he had not put out a hand to steady himself he would have fallen down. Nausea gripped his stomach. He had given her to the dead. He would never see his friend again.

'What is it, Danny? Are you okay?'

'I have to go back,' he said, his voice thick and strange.

'Are you crazy?' Lily asked. 'It'll take you with it. I'll never see you again.'

'I have to go.'

'Don't,' she said desperately. 'Really, Danny. Don't forget we stole from them.'

'If we go now,' he said, 'we'll have time to get Dixie out.'

'No . . . I can't.' Lily's face was white. She clutched the Treaty Stone tightly to her chest.

'Lily, come on . . .'

'I can't.'

Danny moved back towards the door as another shudder sent snow cascading from one of the castle roofs.

'Wait here for me then.'

'Danny, you have to come with me. We're a family. We don't have room for anyone else.'

'She's my friend. That's important too.'

'Not as important as family. She'll come between us. She doesn't like me. Let's go.'

She took hold of his sleeve and looked imploringly into his eyes. A large tear ran down her cheek, then another. She held Danny with her gaze, daring him to pull away. Her eyes brimmed with unshed tears, their true colour disguised by the blue membrane, the membrane that Duddy had said could resist everything except salt tears . . . As the tears welled in her eyes, the colour turned milky, a single blue tear ran down her cheek and one brown eye emerged, one brown and one blue as it should be if she was Danny's sister, except that there wasn't one brown and one blue. As the membrane dissolved completely Danny found himself staring into a pair of liquid brown eyes. Lily saw the expression on Danny's face. Her sleeve came up to wipe her eyes, and came away blue. She stared at it, then looked back at Danny. Danny stepped back from her. She looked shocked, then a smile spread across her face, a smile he had never seen before and did not like.

'So,' she said softly, 'it had to be, didn't it, Danny? I really had you fooled.'

Her voice was different too, the gentle girlish tone was gone. This was a woman's voice, sure of itself.

Danny felt as if an abyss had opened at his feet. 'Lily . . .' he began.

'Is not my name,' the other said, looking him up and down. 'So you are the Fifth. You're not very cunning, if you don't mind my saying so.'

'Who are you?' Danny said, feeling sick.

'It doesn't matter now. The important thing is that I have the Treaty Stone. I had hoped to string the whole thing out a little longer.'

'What whole thing?' Danny said.

Her voice changed

'You and me, Danny,' she said, in Lily's voice once more, 'we can do anything we want. We can control the Treaty—'

'Stop,' Danny said, holding his head.

'Yes, I'll stop.' It was the woman's voice this time,

harsher now. 'After all, I have the Treaty Stone. I'll be able to hold Wilsons and the Upper World to ransom.'

'I thought you were working for the Ring,' Danny said.

She laughed. 'So did they. They inserted me and Nala into Morne. But they are interested in conquest, and I am interested in myself. And now, with this Stone, I can change everything. Longford and Ness think it is good enough to keep their agents in poverty and send them into danger time after time. No more! They shall have their Stone, but I will set the price!'

Behind Danny the kingdom walls shook again and more snow was dislodged. From high up the valley came a low rumbling sound, from the place where Danny had walked with the person he had thought was his sister. He stared at her in despair. Whoever this person was, she had taken everything, every scrap of trust he had in the world. He did not know what she saw in his eyes, but she took a step backwards and a gun appeared in her hand. For the first time her voice was uncertain. 'I'm not afraid to use this, you know.'

Danny said nothing. He kept on staring at her. There was a low buzzing coming from Morne, or was it coming from inside his own head? With all his being he wished that she would disappear, that it would be as if she had never been.

'I warn you!' The woman's voice rose to a shriek. 'I'll shoot if I have to.'

Danny said nothing. All he knew was that he wanted her obliterated. The buzzing noise in his head had become a wild screech. He was dimly aware of the trigger of the gun being pulled, of a shot flyng past his head. Then he was staring into her eyes, eyes filled with terror. In that moment he knew he had the power to obliterate her, and that he would. In the moment of unleashing the terrible power that had gathered within him, a small voice spoke from within his mind, a voice that asked if he could live with it for the rest of his life. At the very last second, as a force he could not understand burst from him, he wrenched control to himself, tried to contain the deadly power. He did not have the strength. There was only one place to focus.

The Treaty Stone in her hands vibrated. She cried out as it began to warm, then became hot, then white-hot. She dropped it into the snow. A great hissing cloud of steam rose where it fell. There was a loud cracking sound. Without looking, Danny knew that the Treaty Stone was irreparably broken. They both stared in horror as the snow cleared and the Stone emerged, sitting in a pit on the bedrock where it had burned through, splintered into many pieces.

Danny felt numb. The enormity of what he had done weighed on him like a millstone. The Treaty Stone was smashed; the Upper World lay helpless to invasion from the Lower. Countless lives were in danger. And he had done it all because someone had lied about being a member of his family. He felt weak and realised he was on his knees. The power that had been unleashed had drained him. Lily, or whatever her name was, had backed away from him, afraid that this time he really would kill her.

He was vaguely aware that the rumbling sound from the mountain had increased. More snow fell from the roofs. The rumbling grew louder and louder. He looked up the mountain and saw a vast plume of white moving towards them, a plume travelling faster than a man could run, picking up speed as it came. He shouted out to Lily but she couldn't hear him. He beckoned to her urgently, but she shook her head. She would not approach him. He shouted a single word, her betrayal forgotten.

'Avalanche!'

She turned too late. The avalanche was almost upon her. She just had time to turn back to Danny, her face a mask of horror, before the snow struck. Danny pressed himself back against the wall as fine powdered snow filled his nose and his mouth. There was a roar as if a hundred express trains were thundering down the mountain, and through it all he heard a distant shriek. The power of the snow's passing threatened to suck him away from the wall and he clung to the door handle behind him for hours it seemed, his whole world white and cold and filled with noise.

The silence, when it came, was almost louder than the snow. Danny blinked and rubbed snow away from his face. The landscape in front of him was piled high with new snow. There was no sign of Lily. And there was no sign of the fragments of the Treaty Stone. For a long time he stood at the door, waves of remorse and of loss running through him. He had been given a sister and had her taken away. He had betrayed his friend and failed in his mission – worse, he had helped to destroy the very thing he had been sent to save. The building he lay against shuddered and shuddered again and once he thought he felt it lift from the bedrock before settling down once more. Danny slumped back against it, and as he did so, iron formed in his soul. He had failed in everything, but he would not let his friend go to a living death with the dead. And if he could not stop it he would go with her. He straightened, his mind suddenly hard and cold. No one would get under his guard again. But he had betrayed a friend, and that was a wrong that had to be righted. He grabbed the door handle and wrenched it open.

Danny ran through the empty storeroom and up the stairs beyond. To his surprise the courtiers of Morne were in work clothes and were busily engaged in packing away their exquisite objects and fastening their paintings to the walls with wire. Furniture was being secured and even the pillars were being checked. Danny ducked into a side room and found a pair of overalls and a cap. He put them on, pulling the cap down over his eyes, put his overcoat over the top and then moved stealthily along the corridors. He saw Camroc coming towards him, so he scooped up a piece of statuary and slung it over his shoulder to hide his face.

He got to the museum and, for the first time in Morne, he had a stroke of luck. The dead girl he had stolen the key from was standing by her desk. It had been turned upside down and ransacked. She was crying as she went frantically through a pile of paper and files.

'What's up, love?' he said, making his voice deeper.

'Nothing's up,' she said. 'Only lost the most important key in the place. They're threatening to send me to the crypts for ever!'

'What would you do to get it back?'

'Anything,' she said, crying bitterly.

Danny leaned close to her so that she could see his face. He lowered his voice. 'I can get it for you – a key for a key.'

She looked at him, then recognised him. 'You! You took the key!'

'Shh,' Danny said. 'Will you do it?

'Depends,' she said. 'What key do you want?'

'The girl,' he said, 'the one the Vizier sent as a servant to the dead . . .'

'Her? I don't know . . .'

'What are the crypts like anyway?' Danny said. 'I've no problem if you want to go there.'

There was something hard in his voice that caught her attention.

'Well?' he said.

'Okay,' she agreed in a small voice. 'I hear she's not much good as a servant anyway.'

The entire building gave a lurch that almost threw Danny off his feet.

'Quickly,' he said. 'You go first.'

The girl set off immediately, Danny following. A raven flew overhead. If it had any opinion as to how the slight boy had so cowed one of the dead, it did not express it.

She opened a small metal door and they went

290

down a spiral staircase, the air getting colder, an odd musty odour in the air. There were lanterns to start with, then the only light was supplied by an unpleasant green mould on the walls which gave off a sickly glow. A mould, Danny thought, that you might find on the inside of a coffin. They were in the realm of the dead now, and everything in the darkness spoke of it. There were rustlings and slitherings and foul odours and sickly, sweet-smelling grave-flowers growing in niches in the wall. How could he have left Dixie here?

At last, when he had despaired of ever reaching his destination, he heard a distant voice singing in quavering, reedy tones.

'You all smell foul
You're a bunch of old ghouls
You want me to serve
I'll stick your dead head in the toilet
And push it round the curve . . .'

Dixie! Danny hurried forward, pushing the dead girl in front of him, then snatching his hand back as it touched the damp suppurating bullet wounds in her back.

The passage opened on to a row of cells with iron doors. Water ran down the dank walls.

'Hello?' A voice came from one of the cells. 'Is anybody there? Can a dead person be anybody? I'll rephrase. Is nobody there?'

'Unlock the door,' Danny said.

'The key . . .' the girl said.

'Unlock it!'

The girl took an iron key from a hook in the wall. Around them Danny could feel the building shudder.

'Hurry.' The cell door was flung open. Danny stepped forward. Dixie was sitting on a low bed. She was filthy and her hair hung lankly about a wan face. She peered up at Danny.

'It's not another trick, is it?'

'No, Dixie,' he said, 'it's not another trick. We're going home.'

He grabbed her by the hand. It felt cold and clammy, as if contact with dead flesh had contaminated her.

'The key!' the dead girl demanded.

'When we get out!' He dragged Dixie down the corridor. As he did so something made him glance through the spyhole in one of the other cells. He saw Nala sitting on his own on a bench. He went to walk on but stopped. He couldn't leave him to the mercy of the dead, even if he was a Cherb and an enemy. He unhooked a key from beside the door and unlocked the cell.

Nala looked up.

'Come on,' Danny said.

The Cherb's expression didn't change, but he rose and followed.

The climb up was a nightmare. The building swayed from side to side with grinding and rending noises as it began to tear itself loose from the mountains. Although they hung on to the rail they were flung from one side of the stairs to the other so much that Danny feared the dead girl's arm would be ripped right off. As soon as they got to the top he threw her the key to the Ring gallery, in its velvet box. She took it without speaking and ran.

Danny looked around him. The floors were tilting. Here and there Morne folk who had been caught out were hastily lashing themselves to the nearest solid object with belts and bell pulls. Dixie faded a little as if she was trying to disappear, then reappeared, looking even more exhausted. Danny lifted her in his arms and raced towards the storeroom, Nala the Cherb keeping pace with him.

As they reached the storeroom the whole building shot upwards four or five feet. Dust flew from the floor and the walls.

'The door, Nala!' Danny yelled. The Cherb threw the little door open and held it as Danny charged towards it and dived through, Dixie in his arms. He hadn't realised that the kingdom had already lifted off. They were fifteen feet from the ground. Danny tumbled down, losing his hold of Dixie. He landed in a snowbank, with Dixie beside him. Nala fell but landed lightly on his feet. They gazed upwards in awe as the massive bulk of the kingdom of Morne rose above their heads, hovered, gigantic chunks of masonary and slates and huge slabs of ice and snow falling from it. It filled the entire sky for what seemed like an eternity, then it started to whirl, faster and faster, growing smaller and smaller until it took on the dimensions of a doll's house, then disappeared, leaving them alone in the frozen landscape.

22
FLIGHT

Danny stood up. Nala regarded him warily, but Danny ignored the Cherb. He was more concerned about Dixie. She was shivering already, and when she tried to stand her legs gave way beneath her. A snow flurry blew down from the high peaks. Danny shivered too.

'We can't stay here. There could be another avalanche. Can you walk, Dixie?'

She shook her head. Danny tried to help her to her feet but it was all he could do to get her upright. She couldn't walk at all. He looked around helplessly. They would die on the frozen mountain, either from the next avalanche or from cold.

'I'll carry her.' It was the first time Nala had spoken. Without waiting for a reply he stepped forward and threw Dixie over his shoulder, then set off down the mountain, moving quickly on the soft snow. Danny, caught by surprise, took off after him.

As the night grew darker and colder Danny

walked in Nala's footsteps. On and on they went, but the mountains were high and they still had not got to the lower reaches. The wind rose and the moon disappeared behind swirling cloud. Nala was tireless, but Danny did not know how much further he could go. Then the snow began to fall. A few flakes at first, then heavier, until in a few minutes they were walking in a full-blown blizzard. Danny kept losing sight of Nala and after ten minutes' walking in the blizzard he had lost him completely. A Cherb, he thought, and you trusted him! He forced himself on, though all he wanted to do was lie down in the snow and go to sleep. Ice had formed on his eyelashes and in his hair and he could barely make out where he was going, so when he saw a red glow ahead he had to rub his eyes several times to make sure of it.

He made his way towards the glow and saw it was a fire, lit in the partial shelter of a huge boulder. Nala had laid Dixie beside it and he was busy digging in the snow for furze branches to feed to the blaze.

Danny slumped gratefully down beside the fire.

Nala jerked his head at Dixie. 'The girl needs shelter,' he said. 'The fire isn't enough.' He fed some more branches into the flames, then sat down a little way off, looking out into the blizzard. Danny looked down at Dixie, already half-covered in snow. He tried to think, but the day's traumas had drained him. He realised that he was still wearing his coat. At least he could cover Dixie, he thought, and started to take it off. Then a sudden distant memory came to him. A statue falling from a niche . . . McGuinness rescuing him . . . the coat! McGuinness had been impressed that he owned Steff Pilkington's coat. He remembered how the detective had laid the coat on the ground and started to work on it. Danny threw the coat down and started pulling at the buttons. Strong metal rods appeared. He quickly worked out how to bend each rod in a arc and stick the ends in the ground, threading it through belt loops and epaulettes as he did so. Within five minutes the coat had formed a tent – a surprisingly roomy one. Danny looked at it in astonishment. He coaxed Dixie to her feet and got her inside. Nala was still staring out into the storm.

'Come in,' Danny said. 'Get out of the blizzard.'

Nala looked at him as if surprised to be asked, then got to his feet.

Inside the tent it was warm. (How did that work? Danny wondered.) The wind howled against the stretched fabric, but the tent held firm. The pockets of the coat were on the inside and Danny was able to fish out the torch and a few bars of choolate. They sat in silence, a silence that couldn't be described as companionable, considering that one of the company was a Cherb and that loss and betrayal haunted them.

But despite that, first Dixie fell asleep, then Danny, and finally even Nala slept.

Danny woke to sun streaming through the tent flap. He looked out to see Nala gazing down the valley. Dixie was still asleep. He crawled out. The blizzard had paused but the tent was half-buried in snow and there were ground mounds and hills of soft snow piled everywhere.

'Not good,' Nala said. 'You can't walk in that.'

'I have to get back,' Danny said. He had to warn Wilsons that the Treaty Stone was broken. The Ring might already be moving against them!

Dixie stirred and stuck her head out of the tent. 'Morning,' she said. 'Have they stopped serving breakfast?' She grinned at Danny and he knew that things would be all right. He would have to explain himself to her, but the glint in her eyes told him that she would forgive him. Dixie's loyalty pushed all thoughts of cunning and treachery from his mind. He would get back to Wilsons and warn them. But how? He leaned back against the exposed side of the tent. It was frozen taut as a drum and his hand slid off it so that he nearly fell in the snow. Dixie laughed, but Danny got up and stared at the tent.

'Get up!' he said.

'What?'

'Get out of the tent, Dixie!'

Working frantically, Danny pulled the ends of the steel rods from the ground. He was glad to see that when Dixie found herself in his way she was able to disappear and reappear several yards away.

He lifted the whole coat-tent out of the ground and turned it upside down on the snow. He grinned to himself. It looked like a little cloth boat, with the steel rods forming the ribs of the boat and the coat fabric the hull. It was stiff with frost and rocked gently when he touched it.

He hauled it out of the dip where they'd camped and looked down the mountain, picking out a route.

'Hop aboard!' he said.

'What?' Dixie said. Nala eyed him dubiously, then came over and clambered gingerly into the boat.

'Hurry up, Dixie,' Danny said. She disappeared and reappeared beside Nala. Danny pushed them to the edge of a slope, then pointed the boat downwards and started to push. He pushed as hard as he could. Soon the makeshift sled started to pick up speed. Danny had misjudged it. The half-frozen canvas made a perfect surface for sliding over the powdery snow. The sled's momentum was carrying it away from him. He stumbled and almost lost his grip. He stretched out a hand. Nala looked at him, his strange brown and blue eyes impossible to read.

Now would be the moment, Danny realised, to shun his despairing hand, to leave him floundering in the snow. Nala looked at him for what felt like an eternity, then reached out and grasped Danny's hand. With one effortless pull he hauled Danny on board.

'All is paid,' Nala murmured. 'You save me. I save you. All is paid.' Danny didn't know if that meant that they were now enemies again, but he didn't have time to think about it. As a sled the upturned tent was almost too successful. They were hurtling down the mountain at a ferocious rate, crashing over hidden rocks, one minute airborne, the next minute ploughing through a snowdrift.

'Where's the steering wheel?' Dixie yelled, but Danny was busy clinging on to one of the metal ribs to avoid being thrown out of the frail craft, and did not answer. Down the mountain they plunged, a fine spray of snow flying out behind, deadly crags that would have smashed them to smithereens if struck passing by on either side. Danny's hair was flattened to his skull and his hands ached from holding on, but a wild exhilaration was growing in him. He looked at Nala, crouched at the front of the sled, and saw his teeth bared in a grin. He met Dixie's eyes. She threw back her head.

'Yeeeehawww . . .' she yelled, and Danny, for the

first time in what felt like years, laughed out loud. A jagged rock loomed in front of them. Danny threw his body weight to one side. It was enough, if only just. Nala turned his head to avoid being split open by the rock. Almost instantly another rock loomed. Dixie disappeared from one side of the sled and reappeared at the other. Her weight wasn't quite enough to change their direction, but Nala flung himself the same way, and the sled almost capsized as it rounded the rock.

The three careered down the mountain, steering the sled with their body weight, inches from disaster at every turn, yet Danny had never felt so alive, Dixie was whooping, and even Nala, sitting in the bow, was showing his teeth in a fierce smile. It was perhaps three miles to the foot of the mountain, and they covered it at an incredible rate. Even when the ground began to level off the sled showed no sign of slowing down. Buildings started to appear, some of them just rooftops sticking up from the snow. They narrowly avoided having the bottom of the craft torn out by a road sign. There were more and more buildings as they approached Newcastle town, but they had no way of stopping.

'There!' Danny shouted. They steered towards the now frozen river that generally flowed through Newcastle. Once they hit the ice their speed picked up even more. Bridges flashed by overhead; the buildings of the deserted town were a blur.

'We're going out to sea!' Dixie yelled.

Danny's mind worked fast. Sea would be the best way to travel, but they had no way of propelling themselves. He looked down the river. In the distance he could see a riverside restaurant, its collapsed canvas awning lying over the tables and chairs.

'Dixie,' he yelled, 'could you get that?'

Dixie's eyes narrowed as she judged the distance, then she was gone. They sped towards the restaurant and they could see Dixie struggling with the awning. She was still struggling as they flew past. Danny gazed back anxiously. She was almost out of sight when she reappeared breathlessly, the canvas draped over her head. Danny snatched a loose fence post as the river suddenly widened and they slewed out of control, turning round and round until finally they hit the open water with a huge splash. The craft came to rest, bobbing about on the gentle swell.

Dixie looked around her in admiration. 'That's some coat,' she said. 'What did I get the canvas for?'

'A sail,' Danny said.

Danny set about rigging up the fence post as a mast. The pockets of the coat yielded up scissors, needle and thread, and Nala and Dixie started creating a sail.

Dixie was, in her own words, useless with a needle and thread but Nala worked like lightning and within a hour they had a makeshift sail rigged. Danny found a drifting plank and improvised a rudder. A fresh breeze had sprung up and soon they were scudding along towards the north-east.

'We're cutting straight across the bay towards the house where my . . . where I used to live,' Danny said. 'This'll save us half a day.' And indeed, the far coast was getting clearer by the minute. Danny felt his heart sink. Would Stone and Pearl be there? Were they still alive? One part of him longed to see them, but in a dark, cold, treacherous corner of his mind, a sly voice wished them dead. In the distance he could see church spires now, and the masts of boats in the harbour.

The hours passed. He looked in the pockets for food, but even the coat had its limits, and they were tired and hungry as they approached the town.

'We'll land on the beach,' Danny said. 'We'd look a bit odd sailing into the harbour in an overcoat.'

They beached on the deserted strand close to the pier. Danny undid the buttons and the steel poles withdrew into the buttonholes. Within a few minutes there was no sign of the little boat. He slipped the overcoat on again. It had been cold in the boat, but not as cold as it had felt before Morne had gone, and

303

there were signs of a thaw here – water dripping from a tree, the ice in rock pools melting.

'First we need to get something to eat,' Danny said. They walked up towards the town. Danny could hear traffic and the sounds of music from the amusements on the seafront.

'What are we going to do about him?' Dixie said, pointing to Nala. 'Those eyes are a dead giveaway.'

'So's disappearing from sight,' Danny said, but it was too late. Dixie had disappeared and reappeared beside a souvenir shop. She picked out a pair of sunglasses from a display and reappeared right beside them.

'That's better,' she said, as she put a pair of pink heart-shaped sunglasses on Nala.

'Dixie,' Danny said despairingly, 'you're supposed to pay for . . . Never mind. Let's get some food.'

He bought pizza slices and they walked up through the town eating. Danny was silent and moody. He kept seeing Lily's face as she disappeared in the avalanche. The wrenching pain of having had a family only to lose it would not leave him alone.

Dixie marvelled at everything, pointing to shop dummies and television sets in shop windows. She went into ecstasies when an aeroplane flew high overhead. Beside them, Nala stomped along in the pink sunglasses.

If the Ring has any spies here . . . Danny thought. Then he looked over at Nala. Could he be working some double cross? Perhaps leading him into the hands of the Ring? Sly thoughts filled his mind, threatening to overwhelm him. How could they lose Nala? Perhaps Danny could break a window or something and throw the blame on the Cherb so that he would be arrested. He remembered how Nala had saved him and pushed the thought to the back of his mind. It was getting late. The shops were beginnng to close. He didn't want to be caught out on the deserted streets at night. He made Nala and Dixie wait in a bus shelter while he went into a shop where he bought a mobile.

'What is it?' Dixie said.

'A phone,' Danny said.

'What's that?'

Danny looked at her, but she wasn't joking. She had no idea what a phone was. He explained it to her. She looked at him, half disbelieving.

'When we were walking down the street there were plenty of people talking into phones,' he said. 'Did you see them?'

'I thought they were just talking to themselves,' Dixie said, as if that was the most natural thing in the world. She looked on in awe as he turned on the power and, taking a deep breath, dialled Stone's number. She took several steps back when she heard Stone's voice coming through. The agent sounded tense.

'Did you succeed?'

'No,' Danny said flatly. 'The Treaty Stone is broken.' There was a long silence. Danny waited for Stone to ask him what had happened, but the question never came.

'Do you still have the Land Rover?' Stone asked.

'No.'

'Then walk to the edge of town. I'll pick you up there.'

'What . . . what about Pearl?' Danny asked.

'Alive,' Stone said tersely. 'We were well trained, Danny. We're both alive.' Danny ended the call and put the phone into his pocket.

Dixie looked at him curiously.

'Danny,' she said, 'your eyes – the brown is coming through again. Doesn't that only happen when—'

'Come on,' Danny said, cutting across her roughly. 'It's starting to get dark.'

There were hardly any people around, and by the time they got to the suburbs they were on their own, few cars out in the icy conditions. Nala looked uneasy and kept glancing upwards.

'What's he looking for?' Danny whispered to Dixie. 'Surely the Seraphim can't be here already?'

'I hope not,' Dixie whispered back. They had

reached the trees and fields where the houses petered out. Without a word Nala drew them into the shelter of some trees.

'I never asked you,' Danny said, forcing himself to address Dixie, 'what was it like . . . I mean, with the dead.'

Dixie shivered. 'I don't want to talk about it,' she said.

There was an uncomfortable silence. Nala had moved a little distance off, and was watching the sky.

'I need to explain,' Danny said. He told her all about Lily and how she had pretended to be his sister, how he had found out the truth and then watched her being swept away by the snow. Dixie listened in silence.

'So,' Danny finished up, 'I know I betrayed you, Dixie, and I know what that means. I just wanted to explain why.'

There was a long silence. When Dixie broke it there was no trace of the quirky and mercurial girl he was used to.

'There's a big struggle going on inside you, Danny. We all know it. There's a part of you that would betray all of us. We know that too. But there's the other part of you, the one we like, and the one we hope wins out in the end. When things happen – like me going to . . . going to the dead – I know it's because you're not the

307

same as the rest of us. We've just got ordinary good and bad going on inside us. You've got bigger stuff.'

She squeezed his hand, and they sat under the trees in the growing darkness until they heard the sound of a car engine in the distance.

The car stopped. They waited until Stone got out before they emerged. His face was tired and strained, but he managed a grim smile when he saw them, then a look of surprise when he noticed Nala.

'Who's this?' His expression changed when he moved closer and saw Nala's eyes.

'Surely he's a—'

'A Cherb, yes,' Danny said shortly. 'It's a long story.'

'We don't have time for long stories if the Treaty has gone,' Stone said. 'You can tell me later. You'd better get into the car.'

Eager for her first ride in a car, Dixie got in the back. Danny opened the other back door and waited for Nala, but the Cherb didn't move.

'Jump in,' Danny said, but Nala shook his head.

'Your world. My world,' he said. 'Maybe again.' Something that might have been described as a smile crossed his strange face. He glanced upwards. 'Watch out for Seraphim!' He turned and bounded off into the woods.

'That's the last of him then,' Dixie said.

'I don't know,' Danny said, getting in next to her. 'I've a feeling we haven't seen the last of Nala the Cherb.'

Stone turned the car and started to drive back towards the house.

'What was that about Seraphim?' Dixie asked. 'The Stone's only been broken a few hours. They can't have moved that quickly.'

'Think again.' Stone indicated a laptop on the seat next to Danny. 'Google "Angel Sighting".'

Danny opened the laptop. Dixie gazed in fascination as it booted up.

'Television?' she said in delight.

'No,' Danny said, 'it's a computer.' Dixie obviously didn't know what that meant, but she gazed with rapt attention as it flickered into life. He googled the words 'Angel Sighting'. There were several newspaper articles from that day alone in which people described seeing four or five large winged figures in the air. Air-traffic controllers said that unexplained objects on their screens 'could be birds', but a policeman was reported to be undergoing psychiatric examination after claiming to have seen a 'sinister winged figure' standing outside the prime minister's country residence.

'Seraphim!' Danny said.

'I'm afraid so,' Stone said, 'just checking things out, letting the few people that are aware of their existence know that the barrier between the worlds has been breached. I have always suspected that the Ring has spies in the Upper World. I expect those networks will be strengthened now. We will have to fight them. It will be a secret war, a war of spies – to begin with, at any rate.'

He turned to Danny.

'They will want their greatest asset at their side. Be careful, Danny.'

Danny was barely listening. He stared with unseeing eyes at the winter fields as they passed. He could still see Lily's face as the avalanche swept her away. Bitterness welled up in him. First Stone and Pearl had masqueraded as his parents, then Lily had pretended to be his sister. His friends at Wilsons were good, it was true, but he yearned for something deeper. If he couldn't have a family, then maybe comradeship. He had not forgotten the way his mind had joined with theirs, his thinking had become as theirs.

They all fell silent as they drove through the countryside. Dixie went to sleep on Danny's shoulder and Stone appeared to be lost in his own thoughts. Danny's mind would not let him rest. What if the Ring did conquer all? Would he not be better off as part of it? At least he would be able to protect his friends and perhaps put a stop to the worst excesses of the Ring forces. Apart from anything else, he would be able to use the power of the Ring to find out who he was.

Before he knew it, they were pulling into the old house, now scarred and damaged from the Seraphim attack.

Dixie woke up and shivered. 'Will Fairman come for us, do you think?'

Danny realised that she was far from home in a foreign world, full of strange things such as mobile phones and computers. She was homesick for Wilsons.

'I think so,' Danny said, 'although he's no longer the only person allowed to cross the border.'

They parked the car around the back. Stone and Pearl had worked hard while he'd been away. The house was fortified with sandbags in the windows and the doors.

'I've got heat and movement detectors rigged outside,' Stone said. 'We won't get caught by surprise again.'

When they went inside there was a cheerful fire burning and a smell of baking pie. Pearl came to the kitchen door wearing an apron, flour on her hands. Her face lit up when she saw Danny and she looked like a picture of a mother from an old book. But he turned his face away, and he could feel her hurt.

The pie was put out on the table and they ate hungrily. Danny was exhausted, but Stone said that he needed to talk to him. Pearl took Dixie off, clucking over her tangled hair and dirty face. Stone took Danny into the library. They sat down in front of the open fire.

'I've been researching your background for years, Danny, going through old records and libraries, trying to find out who you are. No one ever seemed to pay any attention before, but I accessed a copy of an old manuscript online, and someone was keeping an eye on it. It brought the pursuit where I got wounded, and probably brought the Seraphim.'

'What was in the manuscript?'

'It's to do with being the Fifth, Danny. I don't know how you came to be here in the Upper World, but I think I know why. The Fifth has access to a terrible power – I believe special powers are not unusual in the Lower World? It comes from the very core of the Fifth's being, and sometimes lies undiscovered until powerful emotion causes it to be unleashed, for good or evil, but mostly for evil.

'Certain influential government agencies learned of

312

the power of the Fifth and thought they could harness it to develop a new generation of terrible weapons. That was why you were given into our care, so we could keep you safe until you were old enough to be exploited.

'We're not sure what happened but they lost track of us the last time we moved. It might be that someone is protecting your identity.'

'What are you trying to say?' Danny asked.

'I'm saying you can't stay in this world. You are being hunted at this very moment.'

'I'm being hunted in the other world as well,' Danny said despairingly.

'Yes, but there they will not conduct experiments on you to find out if you have a special power and how it works. And there you have many friends. Here you only have two – me and my colleague who pretended to be your parents, an act for which I can only say I am sorry.'

Danny looked at him and for a moment longed to call this man Father, and to tell him about Lily. But the moment passed.

'The taxi, Fairman, will come for you in the morning, Danny. I have had no luck in finding out who your parents are. That is another mystery, and it strikes me that both worlds have an interest in suppressing it.'

They went back into the living room. Dixie had showered and was dressed in a Chinese dressing gown. Pearl was brushing her hair and they were talking about make-up.

'I wish I knew what was happening at Wilsons.' Dixie sighed.

'We're going back in the morning,' Danny said.

Dixie clapped her hands. 'Brilliant!' she said. 'I hope they're all okay. I'm desperate to know what's happening there.'

'The Radio of Last Resort,' Danny said, 'of course!' The Radio of Last Resort had been given to him so he could receive messages from Wilsons. It was still in his bedroom. He ran upstairs and got it, carried it down to the living room and switched it on, then sat in numb silence listening to the message which came through the speakers, a message which was played on a loop, so that it repeated again and again. It was Brunholm's voice, but there was a note of triumph in it, of bitter victory that turned the blood cold.

'Attention. Attention. This is Marcus Brunholm. Master Devoy has been suspended from his post as Master of Wilsons and is now in custody. I, Marcus Brunholm, with the assistance of Rufus Ness, Head Cherb, am now in charge of all affairs at Wilsons, pending a full agreement with the Ring of Five in relation to their participation in the running of Wilsons.'

Danny and Dixie looked at each other, frozen. Devoy overthrown, Brunholm in cahoots with Rufus Ness had taken over, and they were going to hand the school to the Ring!

23
A PLACE OF TORTURE

Les, Vandra and Toxique were pleased with their day's work but haunted by the discovery of Devoy attending to the torture chamber. They had not thought him capable of such cruelty.

'But who do we tell?' Les said.

'It's obvious,' Toxique said. 'McGuinness. He's straight. He'll help us.'

'Good idea,' Vandra said. 'In the meantime I'm exhausted and it's the middle of the night.'

They decided they would meet in the morning after class and seek out the detective. A simple decision, they thought, as they went gratefully to bed, but they would have been less comfortable as they lay down if they had sensed the pair of red-rimmed eyes that watched the Roosts from the rooftops. Ness's bloody shoulder had a rough bandage on it, but he was otherwise unharmed. He had not finished with Wilsons. Not by a long shot, and events were about to play into his hands.

The next morning the three cadets woke late and almost missed breakfast. They yawned their way through Spitfire's class (earning Les three strikes with the duster) and through a double period of deception and concealment with Exshaw, which Les thought would earn them at least a Third Regulation offence. But Exshaw merely smirked at them, and remarked that 'punishment, like revenge, is a dish best tasted cold'.

McGuinness could be elusive, but they found him with ease, sitting on one of the summer seats in the garden as if he had been waiting for them. His face darkened as they told him about the torture instruments, and he shook his head in disbelief at their account of Devoy tending to them.

'We'll have to go upstairs with this,' he said.

'Upstairs?' Vandra said.

'Well, we can't go to Devoy, so it'll have to be Brunholm.'

Les was appalled. 'We can't go to Brunholm!'

'Torture is a treasonable offence in Wilsons,' McGuinness said sternly. 'We have no choice.'

Events moved with lightning speed after that. Brunholm, it seemed to the cadets, had moved with unseemly haste against Devoy.

'I knew he would slip up somewhere along the

line,' he had cried, and had immediately summoned the other teachers. Some of them, such as Spitfire, had refused to accept Brunholm's word and Les was called in front of them to relate what he had seen, which he did, barely able to look Spitfire in the eye.

'It seems that what you are saying is true, Marcus,' Duddy said, 'and it could not come at a worse time if what is rumoured is the case – that the Treaty Stone has been broken.'

'It must be true,' Valant broke in. 'The ravens are in an awful state. They've been wheeling around in the sky over the place all day. And they attacked one of the Messengers when they saw him on the roof.'

'Devoy must be arrested at once,' Brunholm said. 'Who will come with me?'

The only person to step forward straight away was Exshaw. It appeared that he was already heavily armed in preparation for an arrest. He had tear-gas canisters and a collapsible baseball bat as well as a collection of brass knuckle dusters.

'You won't be needing any of that,' Valant said gruffly as he stepped forward. 'I'll come along to make sure nobody gets hurt.'

'And, since it's a criminal matter, I'll come as well,' McGuinness said.

*

Devoy had not accepted the charges against him and had barricaded himself into the library of the third landing and asked for a copy of the college Book of Laws. When McGuinness went to fetch it, Exshaw and Brunholm had mounted a sustained assault, despite Valant's protestations. When Devoy refused to come out Exshaw had smashed a panel in the door and lobbed in two tear-gas canisters. When Devoy at last opened the door, coughing and with tears streaming down his face, Exshaw had gone for him with his baseball bat, dealing him two good blows before a scowling Valant wrestled it from him.

The pupils were in Ravensdale having tea, the place a cauldron of gossip with cadets taking sides. Les had almost come to blows with Smyck over his role in the Devoy affair, when the lights went up on the suspended box from which teachers would address the school. There was a gasp as the pupils saw the bleeding and handcuffed Devoy, his eyes still streaming from the gas.

Brunholm and Exshaw accompanied him, and Brunholm read out a long list of charges, alleging that Devoy 'did knowingly and feloniously create a place of torture, in breach of article six of the Penal Code'.

Vandra got up. There were tears in her eyes as she said she would help Devoy with his wounds, but

Brunholm told her harshly to sit down. The lights went out again.

Afterwards there was chaos in Ravensdale. The cadets spilled out into the streets of the ancient village. There were several fist fights, with factions forming and re-forming while the ravens wheeled and cawed overhead. The cadets only calmed down when McGuinness appeared in their midst and fired a shot over their heads and threatened to arrest them all for violent assembly. Even so, there were scuffles on the way back to the Roosts, while there were rumours that the Messengers had backed Devoy and had taken over the top two floors of the main building.

Worse was to come. The following morning a clearly unwell Blackpitts announced over the intercom that the Treaty Stone had indeed been shattered, and that peace overtures with the Ring had begun. To that end, Rufus Ness had been accepted as envoy and joint head of Wilsons until a new Treaty could be put in place. The Ring had taken over Wilsons lock, stock and barrel!

Les and Vandra met Toxique on the landing.

'What are we going to do?' Vandra said. 'Rufus Ness joint head!'

'Who can we trust, is more to the point,' Toxique said. 'Seems all the teachers are on Brunholm's side.'

'What about Blackpitts?' Les said. 'He owes us one. At least we'll find out a little bit about what's going on around here.'

But when they got to the main building they found there was another obstacle. While they had been talking, Exshaw had been waiting at the entrance to Ravensdale, handing out prefect badges. Smyck had been appointed head prefect while Expectre was Close Surveillance Monitor. The girl Frieda had been appointed Monitor of Junior Messengers, Physicks and Assassins.

'I think that means us,' Les said.

'I think you're right,' Vandra said as Frieda appeared beside them and announced, in a self-important voice, that she was going to escort them everywhere and that they had to tell her their movements in advance. The rest of the morning they tried to evade her. Les and Toxique spent half an hour in the boys' toilets discussing how to lose her, but it was Vandra who came up with the solution. When the boys came out of the toilet she was waiting for them, Frieda hovering in the background.

'Quick', Vandra whispered, 'Les, fall down as if you're poisoned.'

Les threw himself to the floor, gurgling and clutching his throat.

Frieda darted forward.

'He's been poisoned!' Vandra cried, and threw herself on him. She bent over his throat for a minute and when she came up her fangs were dripping a green liquid, a liquid with a smell so vile that the two boys almost gagged. Frieda stared at Vandra, turned green herself, then dashed for the door of the ladies'.

'Quick,' Vandra said, spraying gobbits of foul green liquor around her. 'Let's go!'

'Entrails and pus, what is that stuff?' Toxique said as they ran.

'Kind of a Physick party trick I used to do when I was small,' Vandra said, wiping her chin with a handkerchief. 'It's a mixture of bile and small intestinal—'

'Stop,' Les gasped, 'or I really will throw up.'

They ran up the stairs to the infirmary. Blackpitts was sitting up in bed. He was thin and ill-looking, but he had made an effort. He was wearing a floral dressing gown and had slicked his hair over to the side with some kind of oil. On the bedside table there was a microphone which he had obviously been using to make his announcements.

'My dear young friends,' he exclaimed when he saw them, 'I am so grateful for your part in my rescue. That fiend came to me posing as a salesman of colognes and tinctures for the fashion-aware mature gent. Caught me completely unawares . . .'

'No time for that now,' Vandra said urgently. 'We need to know what's going on and how we get organised against what's going on. Rufus Ness as joint head of Wilsons!'

But Blackpitts merely gave them a resigned look. 'You must understand,' he said, 'everything has changed now. You might not like Rufus Ness being part of Wilsons, but there's nothing we can do. With the Treaty ended we must do what we can to come to terms with the Ring and the Cherbs.'

'But what about Devoy?' Les said.

Blackpitts held out his hands palm upwards. 'Again. He has breached the law and he must answer for it.'

The cadets looked at each other in despair. They heard footsteps behind them and turned to see Frieda.

'There you are,' she said. 'That'll be a Fourth Regulation offence – evading the lawful attentions of a monitor.'

Jamshid came in and glanced at Frieda with dislike.

'You have to leave the patient alone,' he said, 'and the infirmary must be cleared. Vandra, I might need a Physick.'

'What's wrong?'

'Trouble among the Messengers. It seems that one of them – Hotspur – has been an agent of the Ring all along. He's now declared himself and demanded to be made Chief Messenger. A fight broke out and several Messengers were badly injured.'

Just as he finished speaking the doors crashed open and two makeshift trolleys were wheeled in by Gabriel the Messenger and others. Each trolley carried an injured Messenger, two pitiful crumpled bodies, bloodstained wings crumpled beneath. Vandra gasped when she recognised one of them as Daisy. And gasped again when she saw the figure that strode in after them, the head Cherb, Rufus Ness.

'Take a good look,' Ness growled, 'and learn the price of rebellion.'

The cadets looked on, shocked. Ness turned on his heel and marched out.

'I can't believe that one of our own would do this,' Gabriel said despairingly, as Jamshid examined the wounded Messengers.

'Don't forget how many of the Messengers became Seraphim,' Jamshid said. 'It is in all of you, I think. Vandra, I'll take this one first – she is in most danger.' He pointed to Daisy. 'You work with the other. I think some toxin has got into his bloodstream.'

Vandra turned instantly to the injured Messenger. For a long, wearisome afternoon, Les and Toxique waited outside with Frieda watching, her eyes flickering from one to the other. In the end Vandra emerged exhausted. Her Messenger was out of danger, she said, but Daisy's life hung in the balance.

Blackpitts announced teatime and they walked slowly down to Ravensdale. In contrast to the previous evening, the mood among the cadets was sombre and they took their places without much talk, save for a few sneers from Smyck and the gang that had gathered around him. As they ate a poor tea of boiled potatoes and cabbage, the mood worsened.

The platform from where the staff addressed them was illuminated. For a moment it was empty, then four figures stepped out. First Rufus Ness, then Brunholm, then the turncoat messenger Hotspur, a tall aristocratic figure with a permanent sneer, and finally, to the cadets' dismay, Exshaw, a triumphant look on his face.

Les noticed that Brunholm was elbowed to the back of the platform. It was Ness who did the talking.

'You are all now pupils of this newly renamed institution, Longford Academy. A provisional ruling council has been appointed, made up of loyal servants of the Ring who have proved their worth over the years: Messenger Hotspur, Master Brunholm and Master Exshaw.'

The cadets stared. They did not know Hotspur, but they couldn't believe that Brunholm and Exshaw had been traitors all along. Brunholm looked a little abashed, but Exshaw could not hide his triumph.

'The Ring will assemble here in the coming days to decide what is to be done with all of you.'

Brunholm looked startled, as if he had not been aware of this. He looked as if he was about to protest, but Ness spoke first.

'The trial of Master Devoy will take place at that time. The judges will be the members of the Ring.'

The cadets looked at each other. In a matter of a few days, the Ring had taken over. They were under constant surveillance, and their teachers were helpless to do anything, it appeared.

Vandra touched the ring given to her by Danny.

'Where are you?' she whispered.

24
A TRIAL

Stone had wakened Danny and Dixie in the predawn darkness. They were exhausted but they were partly revived by a breakfast of bacon, eggs and toast, washed down with hot tea. Dixie helped Pearl with the cooking and they chatted softly at the end of the kitchen.

Stone looked at Danny with worry in his eyes. 'Try to keep in touch, Danny,' he said. 'Send messages through the taxi if you can. The more we can learn about the Lower World, the easier it will be to protect this one. I will keep searching and trying to find your real parents. I owe you that.'

Danny wanted to believe him, but he had been fooled before. He remembered the day he had spent walking with Lily in the snow. She had been laughing at him all the time. He got to his feet abruptly.

'I'm going outside to wait for Fairman,' he said. Stone watched him go.

'He's had a hard time,' Dixie said.

'I know that,' Stone said, 'and we are part of it. I worry about him.'

From outside they heard the clatter of a diesel engine.

'Looks like it's time to go and face the music,' Dixie said.

'Face the music?' Pearl said.

'Well – we were supposed to rescue the Treaty Stone, but that didn't happen.'

'I didn't dare to ask, what did happen to the Stone?' Stone said.

'I don't know,' Dixie said simply. 'I wasn't there and I wasn't told,

Dixie hugged Pearl outside the house before they got in the black cab. Danny shook Stone and Pearl's hand stiffly and there was an uncomfortable silence.

'If you ever . . .' Pearl began, but something in Danny's eyes told her not to continue. Pearl and Stone watched in silence as the taxi drove off into the snowy landscape.

'Will we see him again?' Pearl asked.

Stone took her hand. 'We will and we must be ready for that day. I cannot tell if he will come back as an avenger – worse than anything this world has ever seen – or if the other part of him will win out, the good part.'

They stayed outside watching until the taxi was

no more than a dot and then disappeared from view.

Danny thought that because it was daytime he would get to see what landscape lay between the two worlds, but a strange dusk fell as they turned off the motorway, and as the cab built up speed and started to shake and judder he could see nothing, although it felt as if it was taking longer than previous journeys. There were many changes of direction, and at times Fairman appeared to be confused as to which way he should be going.

'If I get my hands on whoever broke that Treaty Stone,' Fairman said, 'I'll break his neck. I'll break his neck and then I'll rip his throat out.'

At one point he peered upwards through the windscreen as though something was flying through the sky in front of them.

'Is it the Seraphim?' Dixie asked, but Fairman didn't reply.

Danny and Dixie wedged themselves into opposite corners against the incessant bone-jolting shaking of the cab as it sped on through the untimely dusk.

At last the shadow started to lift and they could see trees on either side of the road. The cab slowed a little and the juddering eased. Danny was able to see that they were on the outskirts of Tarnstone, the nearest town to Wilsons. Although it was now broad daylight, there was no one on the streets.

'What's going on?' Danny asked.

'They're afraid of attack from above from the Seraphim,' Fairman said, turning on to the road which led to Wilsons.

Then he asked a strange question: 'Where do you want to be dropped off?'

'Wilsons,' Danny said, 'of course.'

'That mightn't be the best idea,' Fairman said. 'You might get more of a reception than you bargained for.'

'Why?' Danny demanded, and 'What do you mean?' said Dixie, but the more they asked, the less Fairman would say.

'I'm supposed to be neutral,' he growled. 'More than my job's worth to tell you any more.'

In the end Danny told him to drop them at the outer wall of the school. They could approach through the grounds and get some idea of what was going on without being seen.

The cab screeched to a halt at the high school wall. Danny and Dixie were relieved to get out, and Danny was surprised to feel a sense of home when his feet touched the ground. The cab sped off and they were left standing by the side of the road.

'I'm getting worried,' Dixie said, shivering. 'Let's go.'

Dixie was able to disappear over the wall and reappear on the other side. Danny had to clamber over. They found one of the Paths of Infinite Return, which would lead to its destination only if you walked on it backwards. This made it difficult to move quickly. It took them twenty minutes to make their way through the overgrown grounds to a place where they could get a view of the main school.

Everything looked fairly normal. It was quiet, but it was still class time. They waited for five minutes but nothing changed.

'I think we should just walk right in,' Dixie said. 'There's Brunholm. He doesn't look as if there's anything wrong.'

Brunholm had come round the corner of the building, deep in conversation with another man. Danny was about to stand up when Dixie grabbed his sleeve.

'Look, Danny – look who he's with!' Brunholm's companion was Rufus Ness!

Their hearts beating fast, they backed into the undergrowth. Ness stopped and turned in their direction. For a second Danny could feel Ness's mind, a virile, cunning presence, searching for his. He closed his mind off. Ness looked almost to be sniffing the air as if he could smell Danny, then he turned back to Brunholm, a dog who was waiting for its master.

Once they were out of sight, Danny and Dixie made for the summerhouse, their minds racing as they tried to absorb the implications of Ness and Brunholm in cahoots. Had Wilsons been captured by force, or overthrown from within?

When they got to the summerhouse they found that they were not the only refugees. Two people had got there ahead of them. A weary-looking Starling disguised as a sailor lay on the window seat while a put-out looking Vicky tried to ignore her. Between the two of them they told a tangled story of Cherb forces massing, of Devoy imprisoned and the Ring making its way to Wilsons, where it had taken over.

'Brunholm, Hotspur and Exshaw, the traitors,' Vicky spat. 'Devoy's in the same cell as I was put in.'

Starling had been investigating Cherb movements, so Vicky was the only source of information about Wilsons, and Danny questioned her closely. Who had joined with the Ring? When was Devoy being tried and who were his judges? When was the Ring arriving? And how had the ravens reacted?

'The ravens haven't been seen since Ness declared himself,' Vicky said. Danny sat on his own for a long time, his brow creased.

'When did you say Longford and the others were arriving?' he asked eventually.

'They're due any time now,' Vicky said, and spat in a most unladylike way into the fireplace.

'I understand what's going on,' Danny said slowly.

'I'm glad you do,' Dixie said. 'I haven't got a clue.'

Danny got up slowly and opened the door.

'Where are you going?' Dixie asked. He didn't answer but stepped through the door. Dixie made to go after him, but Starling grabbed her arm and stopped her.

'Don't,' she said. 'Let him go on his own.'

Dixie stood in the doorway silently watching Danny walk towards Wilsons. 'I'm not sure if I like the look of this,' she said.

'He has a grim face on him all right,' Vicky said.

Danny crossed the gardens and made his way around the front. His mind was clear and cold. He could see what was happening laid out in front of him like the pieces in a great chess game. He knew what had to be done, and the consequences of getting it wrong – not just for him but for the two worlds.

Without breaking stride he ran up the front steps of the school. Valant was standing at the reception desk and looked up in surprise.

'Tell me when the Ring arrive,' Danny said. 'I want to greet them.'

Valant looked at him with narrowed eyes. He wasn't used to being told what to do by pupils. But something in Danny's tone brooked no argument.

Danny went to the teachers' common room. Duddy looked up as he burst into the room.

'You're back,' she said. 'What are you doing here? You should be reporting to Mr Brunholm . . .'

Danny ignored her and went straight to the small cell. He looked through the bars. Devoy was sitting on one bunk, the Unknown Spy on the other. They were talking together quietly.

'Mr Devoy?' Danny spoke quietly but Devoy was instantly on his feet.

'Danny! The Treaty Stone . . .'

'Is broken. An agent of the Ring,' Danny said, lying smoothly.

'I knew it was gone, but I didn't know how.'

'All is lost,' Danny said. 'The Treaty is no more. I intend to rejoin the Ring.'

Devoy held his eyes, then sighed. 'I have thrown

the dice and lost. Do what you must. I will go back to my talk with the Unknown Spy. I do not have long left.'

He turned away. Danny froze as he heard a familiar civilised voice behind him.

'So, Danny, you are to rejoin the Ring. I knew you would. Congratulations.'

It was Ambrose Longford. And behind him the other members of the Ring. Nurse Flanagan in a low-cut red dress. Rufus Ness. The dreadful figure of Conal the Seraphim, like a giant malignant praying mantis. Danny opened his mind to them and felt them join, Nurse Flanagan's mind voluptuous and perfumed, Conal's hard and cold with something rancid about it. And then there was Longford's, subtle and probing. Danny felt he was looking for something, and then Longford smiled.

'The power of the Fifth. You have found it and used it – to no good end, I expect. Congratulations, Danny.'

'Who was she?' Danny said bluntly.

'Was, Danny? You mean she is gone? Her real name was Euphonia Haslam, one of my best agents. She was meant to lure you back to the Ring.'

'It's called the Sibling Strategy,' Nurse Flanagan said, almost purring the words. 'An agent poses as a long-lost brother or sister in order to gain the subject's confidence. Well-used it can be devastatingly effective.'

'My plan was to have her . . . let me say . . . terminated,' Longford said, 'and put the blame on Master Devoy and Brunholm. In reaction to their crime you would join with us against Wilsons – a subtle plan, I thought, but now it seems that you have dealt with her yourself. You obviously weren't fooled by the Sibling Strategy. At least she broke the Treaty Stone before she went.'

'Enough of that,' Danny said harshly. 'What is the plan now?'

'As you see,' Longford said. 'Thanks to Brunholm and the other traitors within Wilsons, and of course the sterling work of Rufus Ness. But we need to move swiftly, Danny. Devoy must be put on trial and punished for his crimes. The trial must be open and public, as must the punishment.'

'Punishment?'

'Yes.' Longford allowed himself a swift smile in the direction of Devoy's cell. 'I have too much respect for my old adversary to permit anything sordid. I have engaged the services of the greatest in his field. Mr Toxique wll be arriving here this evening. I believe he may be eager to help. He has been deeply disappointed by the educational services his son has received at Wilsons.'

'The Toxiques never fail,' Nurse Flanagan said happily.

'But the end is always dignified,' Longford said. 'So, Danny, you are ready to take your place among us. I can feel the anger seething in you, the sense of betrayal. We know about the people who posed as your parents, of course. If Conal had succeeded, you would have been avenged.'

'It was news we very much wanted to give you,' Nurse Flanagan said, 'but it wasn't to be.'

'Now, down to business. Danny, you will join us on a panel of five judges to try Devoy?' Danny felt Longford's mind probing his, searching for any hesitation.

'Of course,' Danny said. 'In fact we should do it before any of the cadets start to organise resistance. A dead Devoy should knock any rebellion out of them.'

'Splendid,' Longford said. 'And if and when it comes to the sentence being pronounced, regrettable as that may be for a career as distinguished as that of Mr Devoy, we will grant you the privilege of giving the order!'

Danny nodded his acceptance of this honour. Devoy, who had come to the barred window, was watching him closely. Longford was smiling. Brunholm looked apprehensive. Devoy could see treachery in every face, and Danny's was no different. Suddenly a raven swooped from the rafters. It flew into Danny's face, plunged its feet into his hair and stooped over his forehead, aiming blow after blow at his eyes. He managed to get his hands up, and the sharp beak penetrated the backs of his hands time and again. He wheeled round in pain. Longford lifted a walking stick from a hat stand and aimed a careful blow. The raven squawked once and tumbled to the ground, an untidy heap of feathers. Longford kicked the dead bird into the corner. Danny examined his bleeding hands with cold eyes.

'The ravens really don't like you, Danny,' Longford said. 'Always a good thing, in my book. Now, Rufus, perhaps you will escort Mr Devoy to the ballroom. It seems as good a place as any for a trial. Might as well bring that babbling idiot, the Unknown Spy along as well. We'll kill two birds with one stone, so to speak!'

As they walked down the stairs Longford explained how Ness had penetrated the school.

'He had to kill the Unknown Spy's wife, of course. She had started to remember things so she was liable to spill the beans about the Sibling Strategy. But more importantly she was also an expert on voice recognition, and Ness knew she was capable of recognising his voice and unmasking him. It was an elegant solution to the problem of Knutt, we thought, to blame him and send the Unknown Spy after him. His brain is so addled he can't see through a simple trick.'

'What about the dart attack on the Messenger?'

'Mostly fun,' Longford chuckled, 'though it didn't hurt to turn the Toxique family against the school. And the attack on Brunholm was the most fun of all. I wish I had seen that. The real purpose, of course, was to make sure that Brunholm was seen as a victim as well, to deflect suspicion from him. Meanwhile our fake Blackpitts was busy activating our agents in Wilsons, old and new.'

'Exshaw?' Danny asked.

'There are three reasons people become traitors, Danny: money, love and anger. Exshaw was embittered for years because he had been passed over for head in favour of Devoy. We went back over the files – I credit myself with that research. Once we knew, it was a simple matter to turn him with a promise to make him head once Devoy was rightfully punished for his crimes.'

'You're going to make Exshaw head?'

'Of course not, Danny,' Longford said, lowering his voice. 'He has almost outlived his usefulness. No, Exshaw will not be head. On the other hand, if the trial goes the way we want it to, we think that *you* should be principal of Wilsons.'

Danny stopped dead and stared at Longford. Danny Caulfield head of Wilsons?!

The rest of the Ring walked past him, Nurse Flanagan entering his mind so that he could feel her arch amusement at his surprise. She patted him on the cheek. 'It would be ideal really,' she murmured. Even Conal appeared amused at his surprise.

Danny stood there with his mouth hanging open, then he hurried to follow the others into the ballroom, once more stopping short when he entered. All the cadets and Messengers and staff were crowded in. On a raised dais were five chairs, one for each of the judges. Devoy was already sitting in a single chair facing the dais. Behind the chair, dressed in black, pale and dreadful, stood Toxique senior. The four members of the Ring waited for Danny. He joined them and they filed on to the dais and sat down. Danny could see his friends' disbelieving faces below. Seen through the tall ballroom windows, serried ranks of Seraphim perched on the gable walls and rooftops of Wilsons. There would be no disputing the outcome of the trial.

Longford stood up.

'We are here to witness the trial of Master Devoy for the making and keeping of instruments of torture in breach of the Twelfth and final

Regulation of Wilsons Academy of the Devious Arts.

'In keeping with tradition, Master Devoy will defend himself. He may call any witnesses he chooses. Prosecuting on behalf of the Ring, all rise for Danny Caulfield.'

25
PARENTS

There was an audible gasp as Danny was announced as the prosecutor, then a scraping of chairs as the room got sullenly to its feet. Danny tried to keep his face still. Not only was he to pronounce sentence, but he was to prosecute!

'Remember, Danny – Master of Wilsons,' Longford whispered, then in a louder voice, 'Who is the accuser?'

'I am, if you please,' Exshaw said, rising to his feet.

'State your case!'

'I saw the defendant, Devoy . . .' Exshaw said, trying, but not succeeding, to keep triumph out of his voice, 'I saw him refurbish and renovate a museum of torture. He made the instruments workable again, tended them with loving care, obviously intending them to be used again, perhaps against cadets of this very school!'

Devoy's expression, as ever, did not change.

Every eye in the ballroom was on him, waiting for the denial, but it did not come. Spitfire half rose to her feet as though to defend him, but she was the only one and she sank back down into her seat again. Danny's eyes flickered restlessly over the crowd. He sat beside Rufus Ness and more than one person noticed the similarity, that Danny's alert pose was uncomfortably similar to the Cherb leader's reptilian stillness. If they had been able to see inside Danny's head they would have been even more disturbed. Quietly the other members of the Ring had entered Danny's mind, not speaking to him but stoking the turmoil and the hurt. *Parents. Sister.* The words were not spoken but they did not have to be. Visions of Danny at the head of the Ring, Master of Wilsons, came, unbidden it seemed, into his head. He heard his own voice without consciously forming the words.

'Do you deny the accusation, Devoy?'

'I cannot,' Devoy said, 'and it would make no difference to these proceedings if I did.'

'Come, come,' Longford said. 'We cannot convict the man just like that. There must be someone who will give some explanation.'

No one in the room stirred. Pained faces looked at Devoy. Valant, Gabriel, the storeman . . . Old colleagues of Devoy's trying to read his expression.

They knew how he felt about Wilsons, how his mind ever searched for information that would protect it. Now he had overstepped the mark. The use of torture would make them worse than those they opposed.

'Corroboration,' Spitfire cried. 'He cannot be convicted without another witness to back up this assertion.'

'Good idea!' Longford said. 'There must be another witness.'

Danny scanned the silent throng, his eyes moving from face to face. The room fell silent. Dixie looked up at him imploringly. Vandra stared at him angrily. Toxique looked at the floor and wrung his hands, not able to look up for fear of meeting his father's eyes. But only one cadet would not look up, refused to meet his eyes . . .

'Les,' Danny said, 'come up here, please.' At the sound of his friend's name Toxique emitted a low moan and rolled his eyes. Vandra grasped his hand in an attempt to comfort him. Les got to his feet and walked forward slowly until he stood alone in front of the dreadful tribunal of the Ring of Five.

'Tell us what you know,' Danny said. He could see Les hesitate.

'Don't lie, Les,' Danny said. 'If you don't tell the truth, I'll call Toxique up here and get it anyway.'

Toxique moaned even louder. Vandra put her arm around him and his father turned his head to give his son a bleak look.

'Les?' Danny said.

'I . . . I saw Devoy,' Les said. 'Me and Toxique. He was in . . . the torture room.'

'Tell them,' Brunholm said. 'Don't hold anything back, Knutt.'

'What was he doing?' Danny asked.

'He was . . . he was polishing things. He was oiling the iron maiden.' There was a shocked silence as if people had not really believed the accusation before.

Longford's voice rang out.

'You may pass sentence, I think, Danny. No time like the present.' Danny turned to Longford and met his eyes. The whole room could all but see the depth of malice and cold calculation that flowed between the two members of the Ring. In that moment Danny was the Fifth, all that Longford had wished him to be. He turned back to Devoy and those near to him flinched at the dark power that showed in his face. Toxique senior flexed his fingers. He knew exactly what Devoy had done and why he had done it, but that did not matter now. He held the power of life and death, and Devoy, looking into his eyes, knew how capable he was of exercising it.

Suddenly Vandra got to her feet. She took Danny's

ring from her finger, her eyes accusing, and threw it at his feet. Danny picked it up and then spoke.

'Master Devoy, by your own admission and on the evidence of others you have transgressed against the Twelfth Regulation, for which there is only one sentence . . .'

'Excuse me . . .' A weary, civilised voice spoke out. 'Excuse me?'

The Unknown Spy had sat unnoticed at the foot of the dais throughout the proceedings. Now he was looking up at Danny, a thoughtful expression on his face.

'You're Steff and Grace's boy, aren't you? I wondered what had happened to you after all these years. They covered it up, you know. They didn't want people to know.'

Danny stood like a statue, staring at the Unknown Spy, who looked back up at him.

'Didn't make you out to be a wrong 'un. Grace had her moments, of course, but when she was with Steff she was different. That was what upset them, you know. Didn't think it was possible, and didn't think it was desirable either. Steff wouldn't have liked you involved with this Ring business. Wouldn't have liked it at all.'

Turmoil raged in Danny. Time stopped still. He could still feel the presence of the Ring in his thoughts, but there was another presence, something that was his own, a person that had parents called Steff and Grace. With a great wrench he freed his mind. A calm descended over him, a calm in which he saw everything with absolute clarity. He turned to Devoy.

'You restored the torture instruments, didn't you?'

Devoy nodded, his eyes fixed on Danny.

'But you didn't do it to torture anyone,' Danny went on. 'Far from it. You did it to save a cadet. You knew that Toxique had not assassinated anyone as was required by his family law. You hoped to save him by pretending that he had developed a talent for torture, a talent that Wilsons was nurturing. You were going to show his father round the chamber and pretend that Toxique was torturing people in it. Then you could say, "You can be proud of your son now. He has a profession, even though it is not as an assassin." Isn't that right, Master Devoy?'

Devoy nodded slowly. His face, as always, was a mask. 'It would have been seen as an honourable profession for a Toxique,' he said. 'Not as honourable as an assassin, of course, but it would have sufficed to avert the wrath of his father.'

'What is this?' Longford's voice cut across the silence in the room like a whiplash. 'Is he, or is he not, involved in the maintenance of a torture room? His reasons for doing so are irrelevant. Danny, instruct Toxique. Finish this now!'

Danny shook his head. The other members of the Ring were on their feet now, anger on their faces.

From the hall, Dixie, looking bewildered, spoke out. 'What's going on here?'

'It was all a sham from the start,' Danny said, 'a scheme of Master Devoy's. Once he had renovated the torture room, he saw the possibility of using it for another purpose. He had himself accused of torture and imprisoned.'

'Why?' It was Spitfire's turn to look bewildered.

'Because he knew there were traitors in Wilsons. Information had been escaping. With the Treaty Stone broken, it was imperative that these traitors be exposed. Brunholm was in on it, of course. He allowed Ness to replace Blackpitts. He invited the Ring to take over Wilsons, knowing that the traitors would come out into the open. As they have done. Exshaw and Hotspur are the real traitors. The others, like Smyck, are merely foolish.'

Danny had never liked Brunholm, but he had to admire the way he'd pretended to be a traitor to Wilsons. He nodded to the man, who stood and bowed curtly. Nurse Flanagan eyed him coldly.

'An elegant strategy, Master Devoy,' Longford

said with a smile, 'and it almost came off – would have, if I had not had the foresight to bring a large force of Seraphim with me.' All eyes in the ballroom turned to the Seraphim, roosting like vultures outside.

'However, as I say, it almost succeeded, but unfortunately for you it didn't. You have your traitors, but I still have Wilsons. Any resistance will of course be met with the sternest reprisal. Danny, I will deal with you later. You have disappointed me twice. You are obviously not the true Fifth. Never mind. You are not the first mongrel that history has thrown up. There will be more. But I cannot have you alive, Danny, trying to disrupt my schemes. You have interfered for the last time. Ness!'

A long knife appeared in the Cherb leader's hand. A flick of his wrist and it flew through the air, its deadly point aimed straight at Danny's heart. The ballroom was frozen. Danny could see the knife coming towards him, as though in slow motion, cleaving the air, knowing that he could not avoid it.

'No!' The Unknown Spy, once more forgotten at the foot of the dais, flung himself forward. The knife buried itself with a terrible thud in his chest.

Danny's hand went into his coat. The knife of Implacable Intention was at the ready before the Unknown Spy had fallen, with a low moan, to the floor. Devoy ran to his side. Danny aimed the knife at Longford.

'You know this knife never misses its intended target,' he said in a low, dangerous voice. 'Do not make me kill you. Les!' Les ran up from the ballroom. Danny handed him the knife.

'Keep it aimed at Longford. If any of them move, just throw it.'

'I know what to do,' 'Les said. 'I gave you the knife, remember?'

Danny quickly knelt beside the Unknown Spy.

'Vandra!' he called, but the Physick was already there. Her gentle hands probed the wound.

'There is nothing I can do,' she said softly, after a few seconds. 'The knife has penetrated the heart, and I am a healer, not a surgeon.'

Danny looked into the man's face. The Unknown Spy's breathing was shallow and ragged. He beckoned Danny close.

'Your father . . . your father asked me to look after you if something . . . if something happened to him. Didn't do a very good job, did I? Forgot everything, you see. Didn't realise when I saw your eyes the first time. Talking to Devoy in the cell . . . it all started to come back . . .'

'You did everything that you could, and more,' Devoy said, kneeling down beside the man.

'Maybe,' the Unknown Spy said. 'It's getting dark in here.'

'The light hasn't changed,' Danny started to say, then stopped, realising that the man was slipping away. 'Please,' Danny said, 'if you could only tell me . . .'

'I would tell Steff's boy everything if I could. It was terrible what they did to him. He told me he had discovered how to conquer all. "Pass it on to my boy," he said, "if something happens to me. Make sure he knows."'

'Knows what?' Danny cried. But a fleeting smile crossed the Unknown Spy's face as though he had seen a familiar face just over Danny's shoulder. He turned his head to one side.

'He's gone,' Devoy said gently.

Danny bowed his head. He had been so close.

'I'm sorry, Danny,' Vandra said. Every eye in the room was turned towards the little group around the Unknown Spy. Everyone, including Les, and Rufus Ness, had seen that he was distracted. Moving so quickly that his feet barely touched the floor, the Cherb circled behind Les. There was a cry of pain and Les fell to the ground clutching his arm. Ness picked up the knife of Implacable Intention.

'Thank you, Rufus,' Longford said. 'This is a most touching scene. The Fifth and the Master of Wilsons kneeling before the corpse of a raggedy old spy who can't remember his own name. Conal, I fear we will have to teach Wilsons a lesson. In your honour, Danny, I will theme the attack around the number five. Have the Seraphim slay every fifth pupil, every fifth Messenger, and it wouldn't be fair to leave the staff out, would it, so we'll have to kill every fifth one of those as well.'

Conal lifted a chair and threw it through one of the great windows. When the sound of glass falling to the floor had stopped he launched himself from the edge of the dais and flew with great slow wingbeats out through the gaping hole.

Longford turned to Danny. 'So you are Steff Pilkington's pup, are you? I should have guessed. He was a meddling fool, and he appears to have passed it on. I wonder who the mother was? Grace . . . Grace . . . let me think . . . of course . . . now I know!' He started to laugh. His laughter grew and went on and on. From outside came a great rush of wings as the Seraphim rose triumphantly into the air. Some of the younger cadets cried out in fear as the dreadful creatures drew swords. Danny lifted his eyes from the body of the Unknown Spy. Tears were streaming down his face. Longford's mocking laughter echoed round the room. Dixie saw what was in Danny's eyes.

'Danny, no!' she cried, but it was too late. There was a roaring sound as though a terrible wind stirred in the ballroom, then with a crash all the windows blew out. The Seraphim's triumph turned to trepidation then to outright panic. A gale laden with broken glass from the shattered windows broke upon them and blew them like leaves before it. With cries and shrieks they were driven across the sky, their wings useless against the wind summoned by Danny. His face expressionless, he watched as they grew small in the sky and then were gone, the only sign of their presence a few feathers floating gently to the ground. Danny turned to the four members of the Ring, but they had fled. A car engine started in the distance and wheels spun on gravel. The Ring had made good their escape. The stunned silence in the ballroom stretched on, then, as if at a signal, everyone began to talk at once.

26

TREACHERY AND LOYALTY

Danny sat alone in the summerhouse. In his hand he held the ring given him by the dead, the intertwined S and G.

'Put it on,' a voice said. He looked up to see the detective McGuinness standing in the doorway. 'They're in a right state up at Wilsons,' he said. 'Seraphim feathers everywhere. Hotspur and Exshaw fled with Longford and the rest of the Ring. Brunholm is delighted with his part. That is a great power you have, Danny. Use it wisely.'

'This coat,' Danny said softly, touching the battered old trenchcoat, 'belonged to my dad, then? Steff Pilkington. Is he dead?'

'I believe so, Danny. I would not hold out any hope for your mother and father. But I knew Steff. He was a great spy.'

'Not great enough to keep himself alive.'

'It is part of the work, Danny. Danger always follows you. And if you are good at what you do, it will catch up with you at the end. That is the fate of the great spy, if they do not turn to evil. Your father knew that.'

'He abandoned me,' Danny said. 'And my mother left me.'

'I'm not sure if you're right about that. I didn't know your mother, but Steff was not a man to abandon anyone,' McGuinness said.

'I know I am,' Danny said, 'and right now, at this moment I feel like walking to Tarnstone and taking a ferry across to join the Ring of Five – if they'll still have me. At least then I'll belong to something.'

'You will – belong to them, I mean. Owned, heart and soul. Corrupted by the Ring.'

'I'm all on my own. At least I wouldn't be alone there.'

'You're not alone here. You have friends. One of them needs you now and you're not there.'

'How could they need me? What did Longford call me? A mongrel!'

'Even a mongrel still has a bark,' McGuinness said, looking at Danny coldly, 'if he chooses to use it. Do as you will, Danny. I have work to do.'

The detective left without a backward glance. Danny sat alone in the dim summerhouse, turning the ring over and over in his hands.

*

355

Toxique waited in the hallway, his suitcase packed, Valant watching him from behind his desk but not daring to intervene. Toxique's father had been closeted with Devoy for over an hour, and Valant didn't need a Beetle of Transmission to know what was going on. Toxique had failed as an assassin. The Treaty might have been shattered, the Ring were no doubt gathering strength and planning incursions into the Upper World, but the code of the Toxiques held firm. Valant shook his head. It had always been so. He heard footsteps approaching – light, measured footsteps. Toxique raised his head and Valant saw that his eyes were dull and hopeless.

Mr Toxique strode into the hallway. He looked down at his son. There was no anger in his gaze, only sorrow.

'Let us be gone from this place,' he said. Toxique got to his feet.

'Stop!' a girl's voice cried from the doorway. Dixie stood there, shoulder to shoulder with Les. The knife of Implacable Intention was in her hand, pointed towards Mr Toxique.

'All you have to do is say the word, Toxique,' Dixie said.

'I can't,' Toxique said. 'He is my father. Put the knife away, Dixie. I have to go home with him.'

'You can't,' Les said despairingly.

'I must,' Toxique said.

'Not until my investigations are complete.' A new voice had spoken. It was McGuinness.

'What is this?' Toxique's father demanded.

'This young man is wanted for questioning in relation to the murder of the Unknown Spy's wife,' McGuinness said. 'He isn't going anywhere.'

'Murder?' Toxique's father's eyes glittered. 'Indeed, it would be a wonderful thing, but I hardly think that . . .'

'What do you not think?' Brunholm said, striding into the room. 'That our leading detective is a liar?'

'I do not accuse any man of lying,' Toxique senior said, 'but I demand corroboration.'

'Danny can corroborate,' Brunholm said smoothly. 'Can't you, Danny?'

All eyes turned to the front door. Danny stood there, his eyes moving from one to the other. The impulse to betray struggled with loyalty to his friend.

'How can I believe Caulfield?' Mr Toxique said. 'He has betrayed before.'

'No,' Danny said, 'you are right. You cannot trust me. I cannot corroborate the story.'

'I don't believe it,' Toxique cried. 'The Gift of

Anticipation told me that you would back me. It's never been wrong before!'

Danny shrugged, but McGuinness could see that his eyes were glittering.

'Come on, boy,' Mr Toxique said. Toxique got to his feet and, without a glance at Danny, followed his father out of the door.

'Danny!' Dixie cried, but he merely looked at her without expression, turned and slipped away. Dixie went to the door. The door of the long black car stood open, the engine running. Toxique put his case in the back and started to climb in. Just as his father got into the front seat there was the sound of running feet. It was Vicky, the siren.

'I heard you were going,' she said. 'I just wanted to give you this back.'

She handed Toxique a knife. A long thin blade with a jet-black handle.

'Where did you get that?' McGuinness gasped. 'It was in my evidence locker.'

'You're in a school for spies, Mr McGuinnesss,' Dixie said.

'It's the knife that killed the Unknown Spy's Wife,' McGuinness said, 'but the chain of custody is broken now. It's been handled by someone else. It's useless as evidence.'

'There you go,' Vicky said, handing the weapon to

Toxique. 'I know it's yours.'

Toxique took it.

'The crime is unsolvable now,' McGuinness said angrily.

'Unsolvable?' Toxique senior looked at his son with new eyes. 'Did you, son? Did you really commit your first assassination?'

Dixie held her breath. Toxique was too nervous to be a good liar, but he managed a half-smile. 'A Toxique never admits to an assassination, even under torture,' he said, 'but I'm glad to have my knife back. Thank you, Vicky.'

A grim smile creased Mr Toxique's face.

'Perhaps I have been hasty,' he said. 'Devoy seems to have taught you something after all. You may stay at Wilsons. And allow me to offer you my hand.'

Awkwardly the father and son shook hands. In her delight, Dixie disappeared and reappeared three times in rapid succession.

High above them, Danny and Master Devoy looked down on the scene from the library window.

'You set that up, of course,' Devoy said.

'It was no good my corroborating. A Toxique never gets caught. That would be worse than not carrying out an assassination at all. And Vicky owed me a favour.'

'Where did you get the knife?'

'Les stole it for me. He doesn't thieve much now, but he's still very good at it. He's gone with Vandra to see Daisy. She's come round a little. I wonder who did kill the Unknown Spy's wife.'

'It was Ness. He was afraid that she would reveal the Sibling Strategy and you would be forewarned about the girl – Lily – before you went to Morne.'

'The Sibling Strategy,' Danny repeated. 'Pretending to be my sister.'

'We are only at the start of a long and deadly conflict. There will be other treacheries.'

There was silence. The fire flickered in the grate. A raven in the rafters stretched its wings and settled them again, its sharp little eyes alert. Devoy looked down. Danny had the ring on his finger, the intertwined S and G.

'There are other rings in the world, Danny,' he said, 'not just the Ring of Five. There are rings that mean loyalty, friendship, devotion, love, people bound to each other. Will you stay with us, Danny? Your mother and father were bound to this place.'

Danny bowed his head. Faces swam in his vision. Stone, Pearl, the girl who had claimed to be his sister . . . He went to the window. Vandra looked up, as if she had sensed him in the night, and her eyes met his for a moment.

'You have the potential to be a great spy, Danny,' Devoy said, 'perhaps the very greatest.'

'Or to be the greatest traitor in the history of spying,' Danny said.

'That too,' Devoy said.

Danny looked down at his friend outside, then turned away from the window. He found himself looking into the Mirror of Limited Reflection. His eyes had changed; the brown and the blue were shrewd and knowing now. Treachery and loyalty were there in equal measure, and there was no telling which would win. Behind him the fire crackled again and the raven shifted in the rafters. Danny knew that Devoy was at his shoulder, but only his own face was visible in the strange mirror, a boy's face floating alone in the darkness.

Read BOOK ONE in
THE **RING** OF **FIVE**
— TRILOGY —

BOOK THREE
coming **March 2012**